KIM FLEET

HOLY BLOOD

AN EDEN GREY MYSTERY

The
Mystery
Press

For Kelly

First published 2017

The Mystery Press is an imprint of The History Press
The Mill, Brimscombe Port
Stroud, Gloucestershire, GL5 2QG
www.thehistorypress.co.uk

© Kim Fleet, 2017

British Library Cataloguing in Publication Data.
A catalogue record for this book is available from the British Library.

ISBN 978 0 7509 7996 2

Typesetting and origination by The History Press
Printed and bound by CPI Group (UK) Ltd, Croydon, CR0 4YY

Praise for

Paternoster: An Eden Grey Mystery

'A vibrant voice from the dark heart of the past'
Alison Bruce, author of the DC Goodhew novels

'This is a very cleverly constructed novel, interweaving two
different stories from two different timeframes. The attention
to detail and background research is clearly evident. Every
character has a depth that the author has painstakingly crafted.
Can't wait for the next one'
5-star Amazon review

'I couldn't put this book down!'
5-star Amazon review

'Thoroughly enjoyable read'
5-star Amazon review

'This is an exciting and very well-written crime thriller, hopefully
the first in a long series'
5-star Amazon review

PROLOGUE

LONDON

Monday, 5 January 2015

15:00 hours

It was Vasily's idea to keep score. Twelve months ago he had crossed the salesroom, hand extended, to commiserate with him for missing out on a twelfth-century reliquary containing the fingernail of Saint Catherine. Lost by a mere fifty thousand pounds.

'Well played, my friend,' Vasily said, beaming. His face was smooth and round with the flat planes and high cheekbones of his Mongol ancestors. 'But not quite as well played as me, ha!'

'Congratulations,' Luker said, stiffly.

'You know, these past two years I have bid against you, and you have bid against me, and I've been keeping tally. Five four to me, I think.'

Luker had conceded this was possibly the case. Vasily clapped him on the shoulder. 'You don't have the passion to win. That's your trouble.'

That was exactly what his elder brother had reiterated only a few days ago, when Luker had asked again to be more involved in the family business. 'You simply don't have the passion, Jonathan, not where it counts.'

An Also Ran, that was him. The second son, his whole life spent in his brother's shadow from school days to the family firm. No place for him there: his brother and father had it all sorted between them, both of them smug with their allotted roles in life. All he had was his collection – the finest in the world, if it wasn't for Vasily. But he wasn't going to come second today; today he was going to win.

He glanced across the salesroom as everyone took their seats. The air clotted with *parfum* and the confidence of the wealthy. They were a small clique, he and his fellow collectors, a band that met a few times a year to haggle over the relics of a long-gone past. Vasily wasn't in his usual place. He normally occupied a discrete yet prominent seat to the side, advertising his modesty, but today it was empty. Luker's heart beat a little faster. Without Vasily, he had a chance to scoop this one, bring the score to five all. But without Vasily bidding against him, the victory would be hollow indeed.

The auctioneer ascended the podium. Only one item for sale today: a golden tower studded with rubies and sapphires, encased in an elevated glass box. Luker was one of a select few who'd been invited to view it privately before the sale.

'Beautiful,' he'd breathed, his eyes roving over the golden cherubs that clung to the tower. At the pinnacle was a tiny window of rock crystal, and behind it was a sliver of fabric that brought tears to his eyes. A fragment of the Virgin's cloak, the cloth a faint blue tint like a scrap of sky. He had to have it.

'Good morning, ladies and gentlemen.' The auctioneer called the room to order and an excited hush fell. 'Today we offer for sale a thirteenth-century reliquary in gold, sapphire and ruby, previously in the collection of Catherine the Great. And I can open the bidding at one hundred thousand pounds.'

Luker didn't flicker. Let the dabblers play with the opening bids; his moment would come. He kept one ear on the bidding as it crept up through the tens of thousands, anticipating the sweet taste of victory when the auctioneer declared the reliquary was his. He already had a special place for it in his collection – a recess in the far wall shielded by a curtain so the light wouldn't fade that precious holy cloth. And there it would live, this portal of purity in a sullied world, surrounded by the icons and reliquaries he'd bought and treasured over the years.

'Two hundred and forty thousand pounds. Do I hear two hundred and fifty?'

A hiatus as everyone recognised the bidding was about to move into new territory. Luker rode the wave of anticipation for a moment, then caught the auctioneer's eye and gave his signal, a half-smile and a lift of one eyebrow, so insouciant it was like flicking lint from a cuff.

'New bidder, thank you, two hundred and fifty thousand pounds.' The auctioneer let the new bid sink in before calling on someone to raise it. No one stirred. Luker widened his field of vision to study the people around him. Their dropped shoulders and careful examination of the auction house catalogue betrayed them. Outbid. His heart beat a little faster. The reliquary was within his grasp. Hold on, hold on, he told himself, the auctioneer will raise the gavel soon.

'Two hundred and fifty thousand pounds,' the auctioneer said, glancing about the room. 'Are we all done, ladies and gentlemen? No more bids? If so, I give you once ...'

The door at the back of the room opened and footsteps came up the centre aisle. The gavel hung in mid-air and the auctioneer paused to smile at the intruder. Luker didn't dare turn round.

'We're at two hundred and fifty thousand pounds,' the auctioneer said. 'Do you wish to bid?'

'Three hundred thousand pounds,' Vasily announced.

'Thank you. Three hundred thousand pounds. Do I see three fifty?' The auctioneer looked directly at him and Luker slumped in his seat. It was too much. With a tiny shake of his head he was out of the game, and could only sit in mute misery as the auctioneer called fair warning, brought down the gavel, and congratulated Vasily.

'I thought I would be too late,' Vasily said as he approached Luker, his perpetual smile in place.

'You should have organised a telephone bid,' Luker said.

'Where's the fun in that? Now, what is the score? Six four to me, I think.'

'Yes, it's about that,' Luker said. A headache was starting to crush his temples and his vision was blurring at the edges. 'Well bid. Nice touch of drama.'

'Don't be a sore loser, ha!' Vasily said, squeezing his arm in an overly robust grip. 'Too much for you, eh? Your family needs to make more jelly babies so you have more pocket money, eh?'

'Liquorice,' Luker said, aware he sounded ridiculous and pompous at the same time. 'My family makes liquorice, not jelly babies.'

'Sweeties, ha? And to me, this is sweet. I take this home to Russia, where it belongs.'

'I don't believe the Virgin Mary ever visited Russia,' Luker said. 'If it belongs anywhere, it belongs in the Holy Land.'

Vasily shrugged. 'You fought a good fight, my friend, but I win again!'

As Vasily strolled away to receive the congratulations of everyone in the salesroom, Luker seethed with hatred. Sometimes he wanted to murder Vasily.

CHAPTER
ONE

Sunday, 26 April 2015

12:32 hours

'This is your idea of a hot date?' Eden asked, as the car pulled to a standstill with a swish of gravel.

'Beautiful, isn't it? The light on that Cotswold stone,' Aidan said. He squeezed her hand. 'Happy anniversary.'

'Anniversary?'

'A year today.'

'I thought that was a couple of weeks ago.' She frowned. 'Yes, it was. A year since we got talking in the pub.'

'I didn't mean *that* anniversary.'

'Then which …?' She grinned as the tips of his ears turned pink. 'Oh, *that* anniversary.' She peeked through the windscreen. 'And what sort of celebration does a girl get these days for putting up with you for a year?'

'Hailes Abbey.' Aidan was already out of the car and in full lecture mode. 'One of the greatest pilgrimage sites in Britain. More popular than Walsingham. It was on the main pilgrimage route to Canterbury, and Santiago …' He ducked his head back into the car. 'Are you getting out?'

'Sure. Just waiting for you to shut up for a moment.'

'Come on.'

'Can I have an ice cream?'

'Only if you're a good girl and listen to me droning on about history for a while.'

'Deal.'

She stepped out into a puddle and her new boots were soaked instantly. Mud seeped up the hems of her trousers, a wet tide that clung to the backs of her calves. When Aidan told her he was taking her on a date, she'd immediately thought it would be a Sunday roast at a country pub. The sort of place with old dogs and old men in the bar, and yuppies and kids called Sebastian and Jacinta in the restaurant. And that, after stuffing themselves with roast beef and Yorkshire puddings, they'd claim not to have room for anything else, then wade their way through the dessert menu. She hadn't antici-pated a visit to a ruined monastery a few miles from Cheltenham.

She zipped up her jacket and slung her bag crossways over her chest and glanced up at the ruins. It was beautiful here, though, with bright spring sunshine warming the old stones and an orange-tip butterfly flitting past. Recent rain had freshened the air. She sucked in a deep breath and let the peace settle over her. The shoes would clean and the trousers would wash, and from the look on Aidan's face, this place was special to him.

Smuggling her hand into the crook of his elbow, she said, 'Tell me about Hailes Abbey, then.'

'It housed one of the great relics of the Catholic Church: blood from Christ on the Cross.'

'I've heard about the relics. Weren't there enough bits of the True Cross to re-forest the Amazon?'

'It brought in pilgrims, though. Thousands of them.'

They went into the shop and bought tickets then walked down to the Abbey ruins. A group of four had set up a wicket at the crossing point in the church. Further off, a boy trailed behind his family, bouncing an action figure over the ruins and wailing, 'But it's boring!'

Eden glanced at Aidan's face and saw the clench of his jaw. She squeezed his arm. 'Where did they keep the relic?'

All that was left of the church was stones marking the outline, but as Aidan described it to her, it came alive. The press of pilgrims, weary and excited after days of travelling. The smell of the sick and the dying, hustling to get a glimpse of the Holy Blood, believing it would cure them.

'They would come up to this point,' Aidan said, stopping at a pile of stones. 'Then the priests would drop a curtain and reveal the Holy Blood. It was in a round phial made from some sort of semi-precious stone. They'd display it for a few moments, then hide it again.'

'What happened to it?'

'Taken away and destroyed during the Dissolution of the Monasteries.'

'How do you know so much about Hailes?' Eden asked.

'We did a project at work with the Abbey a few years back. Had to come here every day for about a month.'

'You jammy thing,' Eden said, as the sun touched the arches lining the cloister and painted them amber. 'I get a damp one-room office and you get this.'

A shout went up from across the cloister. A boy of about twelve hurtled across the grass, brandishing the action figure, the younger boy in hot pursuit.

'Liam! Give it back!' shouted a blonde woman at the end of her tether.

'Liam! We won't tell you again!' bellowed the father.

Liam ignored them, ran up to a metal barrier guarding a drainage ditch, turned to check the younger boy was keeping up, waited until he was a hand-snatch away, then dropped the toy over the edge. The young lad ran up to him and started kicking him on the shins.

'Oh dear, Action Man's gone in the ditch,' Aidan said.

'You don't have to look so pleased about it.'

'Well, this is a holy place.'

'Yeah, you can tell that by the way Henry VIII smashed it up.'

They were turning away when a scream cut the air. Eden whipped around, her senses taut. Blondie and Harassed Dad ran up to the drainage ditch.

'He's fallen in!' the mum shrieked.

'I told you to wait!' the dad shouted. 'I said I'd get it!'

Eden sprinted to the barrier and peered into a sheer twelve-foot drop. Wet stone lined the gully, pocked with ferns and moss. The boy lay at the bottom, shrieking.

'It's OK,' Eden cried. 'We're going to get you out. Are you hurt?'

A scream in reply.

The mother stood up on the barrier and leaned over as far as she could. 'Oh my God! Dylan, can you hear me?'

'I think he might be hurt,' Eden said.

She sized up the parents. The mother was in a maxi dress down to her ankles and a gnat's fart away from full-blown hysteria; the dad was puffing from just the short sprint across the grass. Neither of them was in a fit state to tackle that drop.

'I'll go down there and check him over,' she said. 'You said his name's Dylan?'

She unwound her handbag and handed it to Aidan.

'You be careful,' he said.

'Always,' she said, levering herself up onto the barrier and swinging over one leg, then the other, sending up a prayer of thanks to the inventor of spandex. She stepped along the ledge and slowly lowered herself into the gully. When her arms were at full stretch, her fingertips clawing into the top of the stone, she let go, landing at the bottom with a skid.

It was tight down there, barely space for her to move. When she turned, her elbows scraped the sides. She inched along to the boy.

'It's OK,' she said, hand outstretched as though pacifying an animal. 'I'm here to help you.'

He huddled against the side of the gully, trembling. No sign of blood. Not clutching his arm close to his body. No obviously broken bones. She puffed a sigh of relief. Getting him out with a fracture would have been tricky.

'Where are you hurt?' she said, hunkering down beside him. Pupils large. Maybe a concussion.

The boy shook his head. 'There!' He pointed to the slurry further down the gully.

Eden looked and took a step back, smothering a cry. Her heel hit the stone wall and she stumbled. There was a concerned 'Ooh' from above. She glanced up and saw Aidan's face peering back at her, creased with concern.

She fought to breathe slowly, her heart banging with shock.

She tipped back her head to call to Dylan's parents. Their faces crowding over the barrier seemed a long way away.

'If I push, can you pull him up?' she called.

She helped Dylan to his feet and checked him for fractures. He seemed to be in one piece. 'Let's get you out of here. Come this way, it's not so steep on this bit.'

They inched further down the gully, and Eden scoured the stone walls for a toehold. Cupping her hands, she told Dylan, 'Step into my hands and I'll boost you up. Grab that bit sticking out there, and put your foot there. I'll help you. Ready?'

He nodded, put his right foot in her cupped hands and she hoisted him up, guiding his feet to toeholds and ready to catch him if he slipped. He scrambled up, his shoes scrabbling for purchase. Arms reached over the barrier, grabbed his hands, and hauled him to safety. Cries of 'thank you' and maternal sobs of relief floated back down to her.

Eden crept back down the gully to where Dylan had fallen. Squatting, she peered again into the sludge. Two eye sockets glared back at her, and a jawbone grinned out of the mud.

She stood and shouted back up to the surface. 'Aidan, go and fetch someone from the visitor centre and tell them to call the police.'

'Police?' he said. 'Why?'

She stared again into the mire.

'There's a skeleton down here,' she said.

CHAPTER
TWO

Monday, 27 April 2015

08:52 hours

'You caught many scumbags lately, Eden?' Tony asked, brandishing a squeezy bottle of tomato sauce over her bacon bap. His black hair hung in a rat's tail from under his white cap.

'No, but I found a skeleton yesterday.'

His hand poised mid-air. 'What? Really?'

'Really.'

Tony puffed out his cheeks. 'I dunno, Eden, your life.' He went back to the bap. 'A good squidge or just a bit?'

'I'm surprised you have to ask, Tony,' she said, arching one eyebrow.

'A good squidge it is.' He drowned it in red sauce. 'A skeleton, huh? Another murder?'

'Not this time.' She slid a five pound note across the counter and picked up her coffee cup.

Tony folded his arms. 'You stay out of trouble. If you can.'

'Laters,' Eden said, hooking the edge of the door with her foot. Her scars prickled and she galloped along the metal walkway to her office, anxious to get inside so she could give them a good scratch. Mementoes of a time when her life was much more exciting. Too exciting, she thought, seeing again the flash of the knife, feeling the cuts across her arms and legs, suffocating on her own blood in the back of a van.

She shook herself. It was all over long ago. She was a new person now, with a new identity and a new life. It was over.

Her office door stuck and needed a kick to get it open. Coffee slopped over her hands. She plonked the bacon bap and cup on her desk and switched on the electric heater. The stink of burning dust competed with the reek of damp. Oh, the joys of working for yourself. She cast Aidan a thought. Today he would be at Hailes Abbey, excavating the skeleton she'd found, out in the sunshine all day, lucky sod. And what did she have? This year's tax return.

She powered up her laptop and opened up her accounts spreadsheet, then accessed her online bank account. The figures made depressing reading, curdling the last mouthful of bacon bap with guilt. She really couldn't afford it; considering her threadbare client list, she should be husbanding her resources.

But that was about to change, she prayed, as later that day she had a meeting with a firm of solicitors, hoping to get referrals for investigative work. It would be mostly tracking down debtors so papers could be served, but it could be a steady stream of income. For a moment she recalled her old life, working undercover. Monday mornings were spent rehashing the weekend's triumphs and soaking up intelligence on what was about to go down that week. The drug shipments coming in, the hand-over of guns and ammunition, the lorries crammed with human cargo.

If she got the gig with the solicitor, she'd be checking the electoral register, asking neighbours nosy questions, and lurking about ready to serve papers on someone whose life was spiralling out of control. Grunt work, small time, and the pay-off was slim. Still, work was work, and looking at this dismal tax return, paid work was something she desperately needed, and fast.

09:08 hours

'Alright, everyone, settle down,' Aidan cut into the chatter that swelled in the staffroom at the Cheltenham Cultural Heritage Unit.

Andy, Mandy and Trev were in the middle of their usual Monday morning catch-up on the events of the weekend. Mandy was ostensibly making a cup of tea, but her gaze kept darting to Andy, the youngest member of the team, as he entertained Trev with details of his Saturday night. A night of high romance from the way Trev was giggling and repeating, 'The dirty bitch!'

There was no way Aidan could compete with that unless he used the magic formula. Raising his voice, he called, 'Who wants to dig up a skeleton today?'

The noise faded and they all turned towards him. Pavlov's dogs, Aidan thought. For a moment he wondered what it would be like to have a normal job with normal people.

'A dead un?' Trev said. 'Where?'

'Right, sit down everyone, because this isn't going to be a simple dig.'

They assembled round the table. Trev plonked a plastic tub in the middle and peeled off the lid. 'My missus made these. Ginger nuts.'

'What's the story?' Mandy asked, biting into a ginger nut and dropping crumbs down her sweater. The team competed to wear the most hideous jumpers they could find, and today Mandy won with a lime and scarlet striped monstrosity.

'A skeleton has come to light at Hailes Abbey. It's a non-traditional burial by the looks of it, so we need to retrieve the bones and work out how they got there.'

'Where is it?' Andy asked. He was not long out of university and sported an eyebrow piercing and blond quiff.

'That's the problem,' Aidan said. 'It's at the bottom of the drainage channel that fed the fishponds and latrines.'

'Lovely,' Trev said, rubbing his hands together. 'There could be all sorts down there.'

'The problem is it's very deep and very narrow.' Aidan looked pointedly at Trev's paunch. 'We're going to need hard hats, and possibly harness and ropes to get down there.' He groaned silently at the thought, his stomach already jerking at the prospect.

Mandy and Trev exchanged looks.

'I haven't had ropes and harness training,' Andy said, his mouth pulling down at the corners.

'I've got a special project for you,' Aidan said. As Andy bemoaned the injustice of this, he added, 'There's a nice box of pottery shards for you to rebuild into a Roman amphora. I've told the director at Chedworth Villa that you're the best in the business with a tube of super glue.'

'Cool!' Andy perked up no end at the prospect of the jigsaw ahead. That would keep him quiet for days, if not weeks.

'Mandy, you OK to go on the harness?'

'Sure,' she said. 'But can I go home and get some old clothes first?'

Aidan stared at her ripped, faded jeans and hideous jumper. 'Course,' he said.

By ten o'clock they were ready to leave. The equipment was piled in the back of the van, and Trev, Mandy and Aidan squashed into the front seats. Trev was at the wheel, and as he reversed out of the Unit's car park, he rammed a tape into the van's ancient tape player. The *Grease* megamix filled the cab.

'I love this one!' Mandy exclaimed. Being squished between Aidan and Trev didn't stop her from dancing along to the music.

'Go greased lightning!' Trev bellowed, a semi-quaver behind.

Aidan sighed. This was not good. He had the prospect of

dangling on the end of a rope and crawling around in an enclosed space all day, and to top it off he had Trev and Mandy's mobile disco to endure.

'Summer loving happened so fast!' Mandy screeched, only slightly in tune.

Trev yanked up the volume. 'Not joining in with the wella-wellas, Aidan?'

Aidan rested his head against the side window, a headache punching at his temples. Only another nine miles to go.

They parked the van in the Abbey car park and trudged across the grass to the drainage ditch. At this time on a Monday morning the Abbey was quiet, just an old couple listening to audio headsets and eating ice creams on a bench in the cloister.

'It's down there,' Aidan said, standing on the metal barrier and peering into the drainage ditch.

The barrier shuddered as Trev hauled himself up. 'Where?'

'In the mud at the bottom. Cranium and mandible.'

'Christ, who spotted that? I can barely make it out.'

'Eden. We were here yesterday and a kid fell down there. When she went to get him out, she found the skull.'

Trev clapped him on the shoulder. 'Have you ever thought of taking her on a normal date? I hear there's this thing called the cinema that girls like these days.'

Aidan shoved his hands in his pockets. 'I'll go and tell them we're here. You two bring the equipment out of the van.'

'How are we going to fix the harness?' Mandy said. 'That fence isn't secure.'

He rattled the barrier. Bugger, she was right. That meant they'd have to use ladders, his second least-favourite thing after ropes and harness. For a moment he cursed Eden: trust her to trip over a dead body on what was supposed to be a romantic date.

By the time he came back from the visitor centre, Mandy and Trev had lugged the toolboxes, crates, ladder and ropes out of the van and were setting up stall next to the drainage ditch.

'We're ready to go,' Mandy said. The ladder was in place at a steep angle, its feet mired in muck.

'Who wants to go first?' Aidan asked. Mandy blinked at him. 'OK, OK.' He grabbed a hard hat and rammed it on his head. Sucking in a deep breath, he climbed up onto the metal barrier, swung his leg over and inched along to the ladder. It wobbled as he stepped onto it and he grabbed at the barrier, head swimming. 'Bloody hell!'

'It'll be fine once you're down there,' Trev called.

'You can hold the ladder steady for me,' Mandy added.

Slowly he made his way down, his feet hitting the bottom with a squelch. The ditch was tight; very tight. Crushing down panic, he shouted up to Mandy, 'I've got the ladder, you can come down.'

She slid down the ladder like a bricklayer, unconcerned by either the height or the enclosed space. They were now very close, dancing round each other in an effort to avoid accidentally touching one another.

Aidan splashed down the ditch to the skull. Taking a trowel out of his pocket, he gently scraped away the mud around it, loosening it until he could slip his fingers underneath and lift it out.

Mandy was armed with a box lined with bubble wrap. 'There you go, Yorick,' she said, as she swaddled the cranium.

'Here's the mandible,' Aidan said, levering it out of the mud and sliding it into the box next to the skull.

'Any other bones?'

'Nothing obvious.' He pointed to the end of the ditch. 'My guess is that the skeleton's been washed down here. There could be bits all over the place. You start digging down there, I'll dig this bit.'

They worked for two hours, unearthing finger bones, a few ribs, and a tibia. Mandy boxed them all up and climbed to the surface to hand them to Trev for cleaning and cataloguing. Trev's singing as he scrubbed the bones in a bowl of water drifted down to them, and they shared a smile as the repertoire morphed from 'I've Got a Brand New Combine Harvester' to 'Unchained Melody'.

'Do you do requests?' Aidan called up, when Trev tried and failed to hit one note in three.

Trev's head appeared above. 'What?'

'Can we have some proper music, please?' Aidan said. 'A nice bit of Chopin. Or some Beethoven.'

'Nah. I can do you the Spice Girls?'

Brilliant. So far they'd recovered only half a skeleton and they'd covered the whole of the exposed part of the ditch. After fifteen feet it plunged into a narrow tunnel running underneath the Abbey, black as hell and exhaling a dank, earthy smell. Water dripped off the stone roof and streaked the sides with mould.

Chances were there were more bones in there, hidden in the slurry like sausages in toad-in-the-hole. He'd have to go in, see if he could unearth them. And that meant squeezing into a space the width of his shoulders and crawling along in the dark with only a head-torch to light the way. His heartbeat was suddenly very loud. He turned to speak to Mandy and order her into the tunnel instead of him. Her eyes met his. Trev's caterwauling floated down to them. If he chickened out, even worse, made a woman go instead of him, he'd never live it down. He might – just – persuade Mandy to take pity on him, but Trev? Never.

'I'm going to check out this tunnel,' he said to Mandy. His voice was unnaturally high.

'Alright,' she said, unconcerned.

Slowly he dropped to his knees and inched into the tunnel. His hard hat bumped the roof. He crouched lower, the torch beam shooting over the rocks and making eerie shadows, a sinister puppet show. No bones helpfully lay on the surface. Gulping, he set about excavating the sludge.

Almost immediately he found the other tibia and a few stray teeth. He crawled deeper into the tunnel and dug over the next few inches. Nothing. Shuffling forwards again, he knelt on a stone. Pain shot into his kneecap. He grabbed the stone and hurled it out of the tunnel. Another few inches and there was a nest of ribs.

He was almost in the middle of the tunnel now. A small arch of light about twenty feet ahead of him: daylight, freedom, fresh air. He focussed on it as he crept along the tunnel, digging and scraping. Nearly there.

Just as he was about to edge out and take a break, his trowel hit something hard. Gently he scraped back the mud and felt it over with his fingertips. Something smooth and round. He eased the point of the trowel underneath and levered it out. Scuffling backwards, he emerged from the tunnel and looked at the object in his hand.

It was a bottle, about twelve inches high. He rubbed away the mud with his thumb and held it up to the light to see it better. It glowed deep claret. The long neck was sealed with a tall silver stopper in an intricate design of swirls and leaves. For a moment, he was unable to think, unable to move, barely able to breathe.

'Jesus Christ.'

15:21 hours

Eden walked the short distance from her office to her appointment. Rodney Road was home to language schools, estate agents and a Swedish restaurant, and had a pleasing mix of architectural styles: a squat former chapel in plain Victorian brick, a modernist block in battleship grey, and a line of Regency buildings in mellow Cotswold stone. The offices of Slater, Slater and Hughes were housed in one of these: a tall, narrow building, its windows caged by fluted ironwork. Eden took a moment to admire it, chiding herself for a pang of envy.

She pushed at a wide, glossy door and entered a hallway with a marble floor and a floating staircase. Reception was through a door on the left. A woman in her late fifties, sporting lilac hair with cream streaks like a raspberry ripple, greeted her with a smile.

'I've got an appointment with Mr Hughes,' Eden said. 'Eden Grey.'

'Take a seat, he's just finishing up with his last client,' the woman said.

Eden selected a green button-back leather chair and browsed through a brochure on pensions.

She didn't have to wait long. Footsteps clattered outside, and a strong male voice called, 'I'll be in touch,' then the door opened and Simon Hughes came in.

He was a dapper man in his sixties, in the solicitor's uniform of pinstripe suit and sober tie. His socks, just peeking above well-shod feet – handmade Italian leather by the looks of it – were startling emerald green.

'Miss Grey?' He held out his hand. 'Simon Hughes. I'll be with you in a moment.' He handed a cardboard file to the woman behind the desk. 'Gwen, can you get these notes typed up soon as and email them to the other side? We're on a deadline with this one, I'm afraid.'

Gwen didn't seem perturbed by the rush. She coolly took the folder and said, 'Of course.'

'Come this way, Miss Grey. Or is it alright to call you Eden?'

'Eden is fine.'

'Can you bring up two cups of coffee, Gwen? When you're ready.' As he led the way upstairs, he turned to Eden. 'Gwen, my secretary, makes the best coffee in the world. I'm terrified she's going to get a better offer elsewhere.'

'Has she been with you long?'

'Only a few months, but already indispensable.'

Simon showed her into a large room on the first floor. Windows stretched from the ornamental ceiling to the eau de Nil carpet. At the far end of the room was a large mahogany desk freighted with files and legal briefs tied with ribbon.

Simon waved her to a chair, and took a seat opposite. 'Lovely to meet you, Eden, and I'm very interested in your proposition. We do have a couple of private investigators we work with, but it's always good to have some new blood. Can you tell me a bit more about your work?'

She outlined her private eye career so far, its emphasis on insurance cheats, dodgy spouses and missing schoolgirls. 'I've also done quite a lot of corporate intelligence work,' she added. 'Getting insights into industry movers and shakers, assessing their likely stances on future projects, delving into company records and looking for sweet points.'

'Interesting.' Simon uncapped a fountain pen and jotted notes in the worst handwriting she'd ever seen. 'And what about surveillance work? Any experience of that?'

'Oh yes. Lots.' Hours in a sweaty car watching a doorway until the mark came out; one officer following on foot, another ready to take over; a constant change and exchange of hunters so the target never knew he was being followed. Not until the final moments, anyway, the flash of the cuffs, the scuffle, and the reciting of his rights. She licked her lips. 'I've done it as part of the insurance scam work.'

And when tracking down human traffickers, drug runners, and pornographers. The sort of people who make the world dark and miserable and full of pain. Oh yes, she could do surveillance.

'You're not bothered that it can mean long hours and it's quite boring?'

Twelve hours straight watching a warehouse. The only thing to see was a metal roller shutter, not even some amusing graffiti to keep her entertained. And at the end of it, it seemed the inform-ant had got the wrong bloody warehouse. Now *that* was boring.

Eden smiled. 'I'm quite used to it.'

'Right.' Simon snapped the notebook closed. 'I'll keep your details on file, and when something comes in, I'll give you a bell. How about that?'

'Sounds perfect. Thank you.'

As they stood, Simon added an afterthought, 'It'll probably be something quite dull, you know.' He shrugged. 'Still, all in a day's work, eh?'

As she headed back to her office, her phone rang.

'Hi, it's me.'

'Hi Aidan, what you up to?'

'Want to come and see what you've started?'

'How do you mean?'

'We've dug up that skeleton you found.' His voice was breathless. 'Fancy a trip to Hailes Abbey? We got more than we bargained for.'

17:14 hours

Eden was surprised to find cars lining the lane to the Abbey and an outside broadcast van occupying the car park. She left her car on the grass by the village church, then headed into the Abbey precincts.

Aidan was standing in front of the crossing point, a camera pointing at him and a fluffy boom mike hovering over his head. A reporter in a scarlet jacket glanced at her notebook then asked him another question.

'Who found the skeleton?' the reporter asked.

'Actually it was my girlfriend, Eden, who found it.' He caught sight of her and beckoned her over. 'There she is.'

The camera swung round to her. She turned her face away. 'I don't really want to be filmed …' she started.

'You found the skeleton?' the reporter said, undeterred. 'Tell me how that happened.'

'Well, a child fell into the drainage gully and I went to get him out, and there was a skull down there.'

'You rescued a child? That's very brave of you.'

'Not really.' She tried to edge away. 'That's enough now, I don't want to …'

'And what's your name?' the reporter asked.

'It's not relevant …' she began.

'Eden Grey,' Aidan said at the same time.

'Thank you, Dr Fox and Eden Grey,' the reporter said, then addressed the camera full on. 'This is BBC Midlands Today, at Hailes Abbey.'

As soon as the first reporter started to walk away, another scurried over. 'Dr Fox! Dr Fox, ITV News here. Tell me about the skeleton. How long has it been there?'

'What's going on?' Eden asked, but Aidan had already launched into his answer.

'We're not sure how old the skeleton is at present. We'll only know that once we've done more tests,' Aidan said. 'At the moment our job is to painstakingly remove, clean and examine these bones to form as detailed a picture of the individual as possible.'

Seeing Trev looming nearby, Eden went over, holding up her hands in a 'what the hell?' gesture.

Trev crushed her in a bear hug. 'Eden, you're a star! Aidan says you're the one who got us this stiff.'

'And obviously we'll treat these remains with the utmost sensitivity and respect,' Aidan concluded.

The reporter took a step forwards. 'You're the Director of the Cheltenham Cultural Heritage Unit. Are the remains going to be taken to Cheltenham or will they stay at Hailes Abbey?'

'That's undecided at the moment,' Aidan said. 'Bearing in mind the significance of today's find, it's likely that they'll go to an undisclosed location for testing and analysis.'

The interview finished and he caught up with Eden.

'Come with me,' he said, taking her hand and leading her through a throng of reporters and TV technicians to the visitors' centre. Word had got around that Eden was the one who'd found the skeleton, and she pushed away cameras and microphones, repeating, 'I don't want to be interviewed, thank you.'

Inside, Aidan took her through the shop to a small staffroom, and then into a store room, packed with archaeological find boxes on metal shelves. She caught the labels on some of the boxes: *chancel tiles; C14th pottery; statues.* The skeleton was laid out on a trestle table in the middle of the room.

'Why the circus?' Eden asked. 'Just for a skeleton?'

Aidan's eyes burned. 'It's not the skeleton. When we excavated we ... I ... found something else.'

'And?'

He wriggled his fingers into a pair of white cotton gloves and gently raised the lid of a cardboard finds box. Reaching inside, he brought out a round, reddish bottle with a long neck. 'This.'

'A perfume bottle?' she hazarded. 'Is it glass?'

'It'll have to be tested, but it might be garnet or beryl.' His voice was hoarse. 'You don't know what it is, do you?'

Eden shrugged. 'Just a pretty bottle.'

'No.' He pointed to a copy of an etching pinned to the wall. The characters depicted wore mediaeval clothes and processed with a canopy, under which was a man holding a cushion bearing a round bottle with a long neck sealed with a tall silver stopper. 'See the resemblance?' His gaze shifted back to the bottle. 'It's the Holy Blood of Hailes.'

CHAPTER
THREE

Newgate, September 1571

The straw piled against the far wall of the cell heaved and rustled. Counting the rats made a change from cracking fleas or betting on which drop of water would slide down the wall first. A cough racked the air. The beggar in the corner across the cell was dying, spewing his lungs up in an arc of blood.

'Shut up and die quietly, you bastard!' Lazarus shouted.

Silence for a moment. Maybe he had died, as ordered. Then the retching started again.

He'd die in here, too, no doubt. Everyone has to die sometime, somewhere, may as well be here. In his own country, at least. He thought back over his last few brushes with death. The bare-knuckle fight with a madman outside a tavern in Cadiz. The doxy in Calais who'd stabbed him for his coins. And then there were the paid for deaths, the sword and stiletto and gunpowder deaths and the gold coins in his breeches to take the taste away.

He splayed his fingers on his thighs. Three missing, cut off at the knuckle on his left hand. The price he paid for doing another man's dirty business.

Hawking up a gob of phlegm, he spat it onto the floor near the rat. 'Dinner time,' he said.

He stared at the rat; the rat stared at him. It was waiting for him to die. He could smell the wound on his leg festering. A few more days in here and it would poison him altogether, and then the rat would enter his mouth and guzzle its way into his stomach and back out of his throat. He'd seen it before. Men dead in ditches and the rats swimming out of their silent screaming mouths.

He crawled over the stone floor towards the rat. It held his stare, never flinched. It thought it was quick. He knew he was quicker, snatching up the rat with practised speed.

'Now who's going to eat who?' he asked.

Footsteps in the corridor outside. They halted at his door. An eye appeared at the grille. 'Prisoner, stand back!' a voice ordered.

A key scraped in the lock and a boot kicked the door open. The swollen wood grated against the floor.

'Out!' the warder said. He caught sight of the rat in his hand. 'Leave your friend.'

Lazarus held the rat by the neck between his fingers and yanked its tail hard. The neck bones snapped. He tossed the rat at the warder. 'A token of my gratitude,' he said, as he walked out of the cell.

The warder jabbed his staff in his back all the way down the corridor, up two flights of stone steps lined with spitting sconces, and into a set of apartments hung with tapestries and with freshly strewn herbs on the floor. He crushed lavender and rosemary underfoot, releasing a long-forgotten scent of summer as he was marched through the antechamber and into a small withdrawing room. A fire burned in the grate. Apple logs, from the scent. Heavy draperies shrouded the windows and doorways. No draughts to rattle old bones here. In the centre of the room was a plain oak table with two oak chairs set opposite each other.

'Mind your tongue,' the warder said, giving him a final kick in the arse, then left him.

He peered round, senses taut. He wasn't alone. Not that he could hear a man's breath or smell his skin, but he knew there was another here, hiding in the shadows.

He didn't speak. To speak first showed weakness. He waited, enjoying the stroke of the fire on his legs. How long it had been since he was warm. Months, he reckoned, since they'd hauled him out of that whore's bed, clamped on the irons and dragged him here. That was the last time heat had warmed his flesh, with the woman's hot thighs wrapped round his.

A figure revealed itself. A good few inches taller than him, whip-like, sinuous. A hint of plush velvet, a thick padded doublet. A flat pale face with dark almond eyes and a pointed black beard, expertly trimmed.

'You're the man they call Lazarus?' the figure asked.

'Who wants to know?'

The blow stunned him. A leather-clad smack right across his chops, snapping back his head. He rubbed his chin and reset his head on his neck.

'You are Lazarus?'

'Yes, they call me that.'

'You have a real name, too, I take it?'

'Matthew Sweet is what my parents decided in their mercy to call me.' He jutted his chin, waiting for the next blow. It didn't come.

The stranger flapped a document at him. 'You are here because you injured a man in a fight.'

When Lazarus didn't answer, the man continued, as if reading from the document. 'You were brawling with a man named White. You tried to throttle him with your bare hands.'

They both glanced at Lazarus's hands, at the stumps where his fingers used to dwell.

'And you bit off his ear.'

'Aye. I did.' White's foul breath in his face as he squeezed his neck; Lazarus's hands jabbing at White's neck in return as he fought him off. Faces so close they were like lovers. White's ear in his mouth. His teeth gnashing through skin and gristle; the bloody gob of it in his mouth.

The stranger looked again at the paper. 'And you ate it.'

Lazarus shook his head. 'If that's what they say then they're lying. I did the decent thing and spat it into the fire.'

The mangled lump in the flames, hissing, then extinguished.

Pointed-beard looked him over for a long time, then folded the document and slid it inside his jacket. 'Someone has a job for you, Lazarus,' he said.

'Who?'

'My Lord Cecil.'

Lazarus laughed. 'Cecil, my arse. Just hang me if you're minded to.'

'We might well, Lazarus, but first, there's something we need you to do.'

'Oh?' Lazarus said. So that was the size of it. They never did their own killing, these men. Not when murder was cheap and easily had. 'Who and when?'

'Patience, patience.' The stranger pointed to one of the oak chairs. 'Sit. I'll tell you our dilemma.'

Lazarus sat where he commanded a view of the whole room. He kept the fire behind him, knowing it threw his face into shadows and made him unreadable. The stranger saw his calculations and laughed.

'I see we have chosen well,' he said. 'You know your craft.'

'I should do, after all these years.'

The man took the seat opposite him. 'I am Robert Sidney. I work for Lord Cecil.'

'Never heard of you.'

'Good. Our work is not to be broadcast like peas in a field,' Sidney said. He tugged off his leather gloves, one then the other, and laid them, fingers touching, on the table. 'Our Sovereign Lady the Queen has a number of ungrateful subjects who are causing her great sorrow.'

Lazarus studied the stumps of his fingers. 'So?'

'There are some who doubt Her Majesty's right to reign. There are some who plot to replace her with the Queen of Scots.' Sidney steepled his fingers and rested his chin on them. 'There are many heretics, foolishly blinded by an erroneous faith, who would assist in this treason.'

'You want me to hunt down and kill every Catholic in the country?' Lazarus said.

'No, just one in particular.' Sidney leaned back in his chair. 'He lives in Gloucestershire. You were born there, hm? It's your home.'

'Born, yes, but I have had no home since I took to the road to make my living.' From slaughtering cattle to slaughtering men. Not so different. The butcher had found him dipping his finger in a pool of blood and licking it when he was five years old and orphaned by the sweats. And there were times when he killed a man, felt the judder of the knife as it met bone, and his hand was slicked with blood. These times, too, he licked his palms clean.

Sidney was still talking. 'There is a priest, living outside Winchcombe. You know it?'

His heart stilled for a beat. 'I have heard of it.'

'His name is Brother John. Our intelligencers tell us he is plotting.'

'You want me to bring him in?'

'No,' Sidney smiled. 'I want you to make him disappear.'

CHAPTER
FOUR

Wednesday, 6 May 2015

10:15 hours

'Do take a seat.' The doctor didn't look at him, but studied the computer screen and clicked the mouse a few times. 'There we are. Scan results. Let me see.' There was an extended pause. 'Right.'

The doctor swivelled round in his seat to face him, his hands pressed together between his knees. 'I'm not going to sugar the pill, Mr Luker, it's not good news.'

The headache he'd had for weeks now punched harder at his temples. He nodded for the doctor to continue.

'It's a brain tumour, I'm afraid, and it's not in a very helpful place.' The doctor waved a pen over the image on the computer screen: the white outline of Luker's skull, inside it a jumbled, scribbled porridge. The doctor was talking, an esoteric language of tests and areas of the brain and procedures that meant nothing to Luker. All he could do was stare at the picture of his brain and hear the word 'tumour' echoing over and over again.

Eventually the doctor shut up and asked, 'Any questions?'

'What next?' was all Luker could manage.

'We'll operate, and hopefully we'll get all of it out, but I won't lie, it's a tricky business and we might have to leave some of the tumour there.'

'What's ...' His lips stuck to his teeth, he had to run his dry tongue over them and attempt the question again before the words came out whole. 'What's the prognosis?'

The doctor rubbed his eyes. 'It's not good, to be frank with you. But try to keep positive.'

'Is that all you can say?' Anger flared and he sat on his fists to stop himself punching the computer screen. 'Is this the best you can do?'

'It's how it is, unfortunately,' the doctor said. 'I'm a doctor, Mr Luker, not God.'

There was peace to be had, held in their sexy heavy-lidded gazes. Saints and Madonnas, all-knowing, surrounded him. He dragged his chair to the centre of the room and collapsed into it, his tired mind fixing on old prayers and invocations. He would find solace here, in this room filled with religious icons who had heard and answered the prayers of the faithful for centuries. Yet today their succour eluded him: mere painted boards tarted with gold leaf.

The reliquaries, too, mocked him with their incompetence. Scraps and leavings of little-known saints. No real power, not for this. Not for a tumour munching its way through his brain. How could a few strands of hair or a fingernail paring effect his rising from the dead?

He needed a miracle.

Tuesday, 15 September 2015

11:00 hours

'It is lovely, eh?' Vasily's voice boomed behind him. Luker spun around, reluctantly dragging his eyes away from the reliquary.

'Shame it's not titty milk.' Vasily made a face. 'Only tears. Still.' And he shrugged.

It was the shrug that did it. Power surged through Luker. This time, it would be his. Damn Vasily, he didn't appreciate the true worth of reliquaries, just collected them like a schoolboy scavenges birds' eggs. Not like him: he knew and understood and loved the relics. And believed them, too. This one, containing the precious tears of the Virgin Mary, would be his. He needed it.

Vasily took his usual place at the side of the saleroom, his numbered paddle on his lap. Luker sat diagonally opposite and slightly behind so he could observe him without being observed. His heart banged against his ribs and he took some steadying breaths.

The auctioneer ascended the podium and the room fell silent. Bidding opened at two hundred thousand pounds. Luker blinked. He hadn't anticipated it being so hot so quickly. He sat tight as the bidding rose, a trickle of cold sweat fingering between his shoulder blades.

'Three hundred and fifty thousand pounds.' The bidding was slowing. The early bidders had put down their paddles and were shaking their heads with regret.

'Three sixty,' Vasily called.

'Three seventy.' Luker was in the game.

Vasily waved his paddle like a fan and the auctioneer called, 'Three hundred and eighty. Do I hear three hundred and ninety?'

Luker caught the auctioneer's eye and raised his eyebrow a fraction.

'Three hundred and ninety. Thank you. Do I hear four hundred thousand?'

This was getting very hot indeed. His breath was shallow and his palms slick. He had to have this. Not the gold, not the jewels, not the exquisite craftsmanship, but the holy relic it contained. He would pay this amount if it was in an old sauce bottle. It was his only chance.

'Do I hear four hundred thousand?'

No one moved a muscle. Just a few more seconds and it would be his. The auctioneer glanced at Vasily, who gave an almost imperceptible shake of his head. Luker clenched his fists so tight his nails dug into his palms. Almost over.

'At three hundred and ninety thousand pounds then, ladies and gentlemen, if you're all done. Going once, going twice.' The auctioneer raised the gavel, his eyes sweeping the room.

'Five hundred thousand pounds.'

A gasp shuddered round the room.

'Five hundred thousand pounds I'm bid, thank you, sir. Any further bids?' He caught Luker's eye and he shook his head. Half a million pounds. Far too much for him. He stared at Vasily's back, wishing he would drop down dead.

'At five hundred thousand pounds, then.' The gavel came down. 'Sold to you, sir, well done.'

Applause rippled through the saleroom followed by a gust of astonished laughter at Vasily's daring. He stood and bowed to left and right, his round, smooth face beaming, then came over to Luker.

'No hard feelings, eh?'

'Actually, I really wanted that one,' Luker blurted out. He fingered his scalp where the hair was just growing back.

Vasily studied him for a moment. 'My friend, you try to play with a straight bat, that's your trouble.' He dug his smartphone from his pocket and flicked his finger over the screen. 'See this?

Bought it two months ago. Finger bone of Mary Magdalene. Beautiful, ha?'

Luker squinted at the photograph on Vasily's phone of a golden reliquary studded with sapphires and pearls. It was truly exquisite. His mind chased the details. Surely he'd know if a Magdalene relic went up for sale? 'But I haven't seen any sale details for that,' he said.

Vasily tipped back his head and laughed. 'No, my friend, you wouldn't.'

'So where did you buy it? Is there a new auction house specialising in relics?'

Vasily lowered his voice. 'Who says I bought it cleanly?'

It was a moment before Luker caught on. 'You bought this illegally?'

Vasily shrugged and stowed his phone back in his pocket. 'Everything in this world is available,' he said, 'for a price.'

CHAPTER
FIVE

Monday, 26 October 2015

14:43 hours

'I'm afraid our client is running a little late,' Simon Hughes said, as he ushered Eden into his office.

'That's fine,' she said, taking a seat in a leather chair that was so slippery she had to plant both feet on the floor to stop herself sliding off. 'You can fill me in on the background before he gets here.'

Simon pinched the bridge of his nose. 'It's all quite delicate,' he started.

Eden raised an eyebrow. 'Are we talking official secrets delicate?'

'No, no, nothing like that. More … *celebrity* … delicate.'

'Tell me more.'

'You may or may not have heard of Lewis Jordan,' Simon said. 'He's a TV producer. An independent.'

'Didn't he do that exposé of suicide cults?'

'Yes. Won an award for it, if I remember rightly.' He brushed an invisible speck of fluff from his knee. His trousers hitched up a fraction, flashing his socks. Today's were a vibrant turquoise colour. 'Lewis Jordan's coming to Cheltenham to make a documentary. Unfortunately, he's been getting a number of unpleasant letters and is worried.'

'Poison pen letters?'

'Quite so. I need you to find out who's sending them so they can be stopped.'

'Why hasn't he got someone on it before?' Eden asked. 'No offence, Simon, but why choose a Cheltenham firm of solicitors to handle this, not one of the big London sets?'

Simon gazed out of the window and didn't answer immediately. Eventually he said, 'He has a previous connection with Cheltenham.'

Before Eden could comment, there was a commotion on the stairs outside, and a voice boomed, 'Is he up here, Gwen? I'll go straight in, eh? Blimey, this place has gone upmarket since last time.'

And Gwen's voice, irritated, saying, 'Wait a moment, I'll let him know you're here. He's got someone in there.'

Too late. The door bounced back on its hinges and a tall, dark man erupted into the room. Gwen pushed past him, her face twisted.

'Sorry, Mr Hughes, I said you were in conference but he …'

Simon silenced her with a wave of his hand. 'It's quite alright, Gwen. Perhaps a tray of coffee?'

'Peppermint tea for me, if you have it.' The man flashed a set of expensive dental work. Veneers or implants, slightly too large, Eden thought.

He advanced on them, pumped Simon's hand, then turned the full force of his personality on Eden. 'Lewis Jordan,' he said.

Eden sized him up. Late thirties, maybe early forties. Botox injections from the droop of that eyebrow. Curly hair cropped close to his scalp; toffee-coloured skin, very smooth and toned. Expensive, spicy aftershave, too liberally applied. A black cashmere overcoat slung over his shoulders like a gangster. His eyes were dark and deep-set, the lashes webbed with mucus.

'Eden Grey,' she said, determined her grip would match his. 'Mr Hughes asked me to be here. I'm a private detective.'

'My own private eye. Now I know I've arrived!' Lewis announced, throwing himself into a chair. 'Now Eden, let me tell you what the deal is.'

Eden slid a notebook out of her bag and hunted down a pen.

'I'm here to make a documentary,' Lewis said. 'You remember a few months ago there was a big fuss about that skeleton at Hailes Abbey?'

Eden hid a smile. 'I remember.'

'When they dug it up, they found something amazing.' Lewis lowered his voice and bent in close to tell her in an awed tone, 'The Holy Blood of Hailes. You've heard of it?'

'Yes, in fact my boyfriend …'

'So what I'm going to do is investigate this blood. It's going to be CSI Hailes Abbey, you get me?'

'Hm-mm.'

'Money no object. I've sweet-talked the studio into stumping up.' He winked at Simon. 'So it's going to have the full forensic works. And I'll be there filming the whole way.'

Gwen rattled in with a tray of coffee and Lewis's peppermint tea in a chipped china beaker. She dumped it beside him with a curt, 'That's yours,' then poured and creamed coffee for Eden and Simon with as much graciousness as if she was understudy for the Queen.

No one spoke while she was in the room. As soon as the door closed behind her, Lewis Jordan continued, 'The trouble is, Eden, I've been getting these letters. Nasty, y'know what I mean?'

'When did they start?'

'A few weeks ago.'

'You've taken them to the police?'

Lewis huffed. 'Plod. Like I'd speak to them.' A look she couldn't interpret passed between him and Simon.

'Do you have the letters on you?' Eden asked.

Lewis fossicked about in the inside pocket of his coat and extracted a large envelope. He tossed it over and Eden pulled out a sheaf of papers.

You don't deserve to live

I'll tell the world what you are

Keep looking over your shoulder, sick boy

One word from me and your life is over

Each message was printed onto a single sheet of ordinary, cheap A4 paper, the sort found in a million offices and homes throughout the country.

'Have you still got the envelopes?' Eden asked.

'Only one.'

It was a plain white A4 envelope, available from a high street stationers. Self-adhesive flap so no DNA there. The stamp was for a large letter, probably bought as part of a strip of self-adhesive stamps, but it might be worth checking for saliva, just in case the letter writer was careless, or confident. No postmark, only a biro scratch through the stamp.

'Anything else? Phone calls? Text messages? Any threats on social media?' Eden asked.

'Nothing like that,' Lewis said, 'but some flowers came for me a few days ago. I wasn't at home – my cleaner took them in. She thought it was a hoax and chucked them in the bin. I only found them when I took the garbage out.'

'What sort of flowers?'

'A wreath. All dried up and dead.'

'Any message on it?'

'A card saying "This is what you deserve".'

'Nasty,' Eden said. 'Do you still have the wreath and the card?'

'No, I'd emptied the garbage on them before I realised.' Lewis grinned. 'Didn't want to keep them covered with bacon fat and tea leaves.'

'Shame,' she said, 'we could have traced the florist from the card.'

'What do you think, Eden?' Simon asked. 'Can you do some digging?'

'I'll certainly see what I can find out.' She addressed Lewis. 'Are you worried about your personal safety?'

Lewis dug a handkerchief from his pocket and rubbed at his eyes. 'I can't believe someone hates me that much. Me! I've never done anyone any harm.'

'I can give you some advice on how to protect yourself,' Eden said.

Lewis shook his head. 'No one would hurt me, but yeah, between us, these letters have shook me up.'

Eden folded the letters back into the envelope. 'I'll keep hold of these and see what I can find out. I need you to write out a list of everyone – *everyone* – who might be even the slightest bit niggled with you. OK?'

'Sure, if you think it'll help. It won't take long. 'Scuse me a minute.' He pulled a small bottle out of his pocket and in a practised movement, tipped back his head and put a drop in one eye, then the other. He sat back up, blinking. 'Right, Eden, we've got work to do. I've got a very interesting meeting to get to and a skeleton to look at. Wanna come?'

Eden glanced across at Simon, who shrugged and said, 'Let me know if you need anything. Nice to see you again, Lewis.'

As they left, Lewis poked his head into reception and called, 'Great to see you again, Gwennie. Looking lovely, girlfriend.'

Eden couldn't see her reaction, but she heard a foot connecting at high speed with a metal bin and a muttered comment that sounded suspiciously like, 'Drop dead.'

As they walked down the High Street, Lewis told her more about the documentary. 'I rang the people at the Cheltenham Cultural Heritage Unit – they're the guys who dug it up. They sound like a right bunch, going to be perfect on camera. I'm thinking tweedy professor, a bit eccentric: audiences love that.'

Eden, lengthening her stride to match his, doubted that Aidan would see it that way. Lewis was right: this would be a very interesting meeting.

The Cheltenham Cultural Heritage Unit was only a stone's throw from Cheltenham Minster, the town's remaining mediaeval church. They cut through the churchyard with its chest tombs and squirrels, sandwich wrappers and beer bottles, to a Georgian townhouse opposite the museum. The forecourt was filled with cars: Aidan's elderly but gleaming black Audi rubbed shoulders with three cars of dubious heritage: rusting, multi-coloured, and ancient.

Lewis pressed the bell and Trev opened the door.

'Eden! Can't get enough of me, eh?'

'I'm only human, Trev,' she said, squeezing past. 'Trev, this is Lewis Jordan.'

'The film guy who's going to make us all famous. Great to meet you.' Trev crushed Lewis's hand. 'The gang's this way.'

Trev led them down to the basement and into a room filled with metal shelves crammed with cardboard boxes of archaeological finds. The skeleton was in a side room, laid out on a gurney.

Aidan glanced up as they came in. He was dressed in a sharp, slim-fitting black suit, grey shirt and impeccable tie. Clear skin, clean fingernails, not a wisp of nose or ear hair. Eden sneaked a glance at Lewis, amused to see the disappointment on his face. So much for the tweedy professor.

'Dr Aidan Fox,' said Aidan, shaking hands. 'I'm the director of the Cultural Heritage Unit. I see you've already met Trev.

And these are Mandy and Andy, both archaeologists.' He paused and peered past Lewis to Eden. 'What are you doing here?'

'I'm working with Lewis,' she said.

'Besides, she did find the skeleton,' Trev interrupted. 'Only fair she should be in the film.'

Lewis rounded on her. '*You* found the skeleton?'

Eden shook her head. 'It's not important.' She caught him appraising her. 'And I don't want to be in any film.'

Lewis seemed bewildered by the thought that anyone would eschew the chance to be famous. He recovered quickly, though, and advanced on the gurney bearing the skeleton.

'So this is our guy,' he breathed. 'Where's the rest of him?'

'The skeleton was disarticulated,' Aidan said, 'and spread over a large area. We excavated what we could, but it's not unusual for some of the bones to be missing.'

'So there might be bits of him out there somewhere?'

'Very likely,' Aidan said. 'Finding them is another matter.'

'What can you tell me about it?' Lewis said.

'The skeleton is male, and at least a couple of centuries old.' Aidan gave a wolfish smile. 'The police were pleased to hear that. Meant they could cross it off their homicide figures.' He continued, 'Fully grown but no signs of arthritis or bone deterioration that you expect in old age, so I'd guess between twenty-five and forty-five years old.'

'And what about the blood?'

'Blood?' Aidan frowned at the dry skeleton.

'You know. The Holy Blood. The thing you found with him,' Lewis said.

'We don't know for definite that it was with him,' Aidan said, crossing his arms. 'And the Holy Blood of Hailes was destroyed during the Dissolution of the Monasteries.'

Lewis flapped his hands. 'Whatever. Where is it?'

Aidan nodded at Mandy, who selected a box from a shelf and opened it. In a nest of bubble wrap lay the crimson bottle with the silver stopper. She handed a pair of white cotton gloves to Lewis. He put them on and picked up the bottle, holding it up to the light.

To her astonishment, Eden detected the glint of tears in his eyes as he gazed at the bottle.

'The Holy Blood of Hailes,' Lewis whispered. 'The Holy Blood of Hailes.'

'We don't know that,' Aidan began. 'It's probably a replica that was used to …'

Lewis butted in, 'We'll get it tested. DNA, carbon dating, the works.'

Trev whistled. 'Cost a bit.'

'Money's no object. Not for this.' Again that gleam in his eye. Lewis laid the bottle back in its box as gently as if it were a newborn infant. 'I've arranged for an expert to come down and look at this skeleton.'

Eden saw Aidan bristle, and recognised the slight to his professional dignity. He was a bones man; he knew what he was doing, and the suggestion that Lewis dismissed his judgement and skills hurt him. From the corner of her eye she saw Mandy and Trev draw themselves up. They felt the snub, too.

Lewis, blind to the fact he was offending everyone in the room, continued, 'She couldn't get here today. She's pretty important, done a lot of war crimes trials in the past.'

Aidan let out a groan.

'But she's agreed to come down tomorrow and have a look at the skeleton, take samples and get it analysed for us.' Lewis grinned round at everyone. 'She'll tell us what's what.'

Aidan caught Eden's eye as Lewis rattled on. 'She's called Dr Lisa Greene. Very clever from what I've heard. You'll love her.'

As a parting shot, Lewis added, 'And I'll have a cameraman with me tomorrow, so if you could all look the part,' a pointed glare at Aidan's immaculate suit, 'I'd appreciate it.'

Lewis was staying at the Imperial Hotel: a neoclassical building guarded by a line of pillars, standing at the top of the Promenade and commanding a view down the whole street. Opposite was a gun carriage left over from the Crimean War, commemorating a battle that had long since fallen from collective memory.

'I used to swing on that,' Lewis commented as they passed, and negotiated their way through the revolving door into the hotel.

As they entered the lobby, a slender woman in a short organza skirt, thick tights and Doc Martens bobbed out of the coffee lounge brandishing an iPad. In her late twenties, she had matte black hair cut in an Eton crop, the merest suggestion of pale blonde roots glinting along her parting.

'Lewis! There you are!' she announced. 'I've emailed the press releases but *Grazia* wants to send round a photographer, and BBC Midlands Today is coming to interview you in …' she tipped her wrist to read her watch. It was a heavy, man's watch on a broad silver band, '… ten minutes.'

'Who's this?' Eden asked.

'Xanthe Fleming, my private assistant,' Lewis said. He slipped his arm round Xanthe's waist and pulled her to him. She wriggled free of his grasp by elbowing him in the ribs and rattled through a hectic interview schedule that would occupy him for the rest of the afternoon and well into the evening.

Upper crust girls' boarding school, Eden decided, and a couple of pints of blue blood. Probably appeared in *Country Life* as deb of the month before hoofing off to a redbrick university to study fine art.

Time to take control.

'Can I speak to you both for a moment?' Eden said. 'We need to get some things clear.'

'Sorry, which publication are you?' Xanthe said, consulting the iPad.

'I'm Eden Grey, I'm a private detective.'

Lewis frowned. 'What's up?'

Eden steered them into the coffee lounge and to the far end where they couldn't be overheard by the girl on the reception desk.

'I think it would be better if you kept a low profile,' Eden said. 'Announcing to the world exactly where you are and what you're doing isn't a good idea.'

'I can't vanish off of social media,' Lewis said. 'Everyone will think I'm in rehab.'

'You've been getting hate mail,' Eden reminded him. 'And you're paying me to advise you. Let me tell you – the best way to protect yourself is to be invisible.'

Xanthe tutted. 'But I've sent out the press releases now and had a lot of interest. Everyone wants to know about the new documentary. This holy relic thing is trending. Or it will be soon.'

'Can you pull the press releases?'

'No,' Xanthe said. 'They'd never publish anything I sent them ever again. It could take months to rebuild Lewis's profile!'

Eden doubted that. 'OK, but don't send any more. Radio silence from now on, right?'

Xanthe cocked an eyebrow at Lewis, waiting for his cue.

'You really think this is necessary, Eden?'

'You were worried enough to hire me, what do you think?' she said.

Lewis nodded at Xanthe. 'Keep it quiet for a while. We'll do the big splash when the documentary's ready.'

Two men, one brandishing a camera, bashed through the revolving door.

'That'll be Midlands Today!' Xanthe squealed, springing up to greet them.

While Xanthe fussed over the cameraman and reporter, Lewis turned to Eden. 'Find out who's sending those letters,' he said. 'To be honest, Eden, they're freaking me out.'

Eden went home and spent an hour on the Internet researching Lewis Jordan. A search engine brought back thousands of hits, many from gossip magazines and celebrity kiss-and-tell exposes. A string of beautiful pouting girlfriends. All blonde, she noted. Lewis definitely had a type he favoured, but there were also a number of encounters when he'd strayed from the blueprint and picked up a girl in a bar, in a club, at a TV party and made the mistake of being photographed smuggling her into his flat. And then there were the pap snaps – Lewis leering and drunk as he went into or came out of a lap-dancing club. For a serious documentary maker, he lived like a premier footballer.

When it came to people who could have a grudge against Lewis, there was no shortage of contenders. One article interviewed an aggrieved ex-wife of one of Lewis's friends. Not only had Lewis groped her in the kitchen at a dinner party, but she swore that he'd corrupted her husband.

'He was a kind, loving husband who adored spending time at home with me and the children,' she averred. 'Then Lewis appeared on the scene and suddenly he was out late every night. Sometimes he didn't come home at all, just came rolling in next morning, reeking of drink. I found receipts in his pockets for strip clubs and peep shows. That's not my husband. It was Lewis who took him to these places. When I found cocaine in his things, I threatened to leave him. He just laughed in my face. I took the children and fled.'

Lewis was an all-round bad boy, leading others astray if this article was to be believed. It wasn't the only one that claimed Lewis's high living had swept others along in the current. Other disaffected wives and girlfriends happily spilled the details to the gossip mags. Prostitutes, drugs, gambling; men of high morals and family values inveigled into debt and sleaze.

'We had to sell our home to clear his debts,' one loyal yet furious wife admitted.

Were any of these wronged wives resentful enough to send poison pen letters and a wreath of dead flowers, Eden wondered. She tipped the letters onto the table. With what she suspected was a rare moment of perspicacity, Lewis had labelled the back of each one with the date it was received and the address it was sent to.

'You don't deserve to live' was sent to Lewis's flat, and received on 17 September. A week later he received 'I'll tell the world what you are', also at his home address. The next letter was sent to a studio address and was received on 3 October. It read, 'Keep looking over your shoulder, sick boy'.

She went back to the gossip sites and created a timeline of Lewis's misdemeanours, hunting for a pattern between offending the wives and a poison pen letter appearing. Nothing obvious, and some of these sensation stories related to events over two years before. Why start sending the letters now, when the marriages were either dead or the couple had made up and moved on?

Eden rubbed her eyes, stretched, and went over to the TV. It chuntered away in the background while she re-examined the letters. The writer could handle punctuation, she noted, half-admiring the meticulous placing of the comma in 'Keep looking over your shoulder, sick boy'.

The sound of Lewis's voice brought her head up sharply.

'It's going to be CSI Hailes Abbey,' he was saying, his face filling her TV screen. 'I held that relic this afternoon. Held it my own hands.' He brought his hands into shot, demonstrating their ordinariness. The note of wonder was back in his voice and his eyes gleamed the way they'd done when he beheld the Holy Blood relic. 'I had the Holy Blood of Hailes in my hands,' Lewis said again. 'The Blood of Christ, in my hands, and I tell you, it made me feel immortal.'

CHAPTER

SIX

Monday, 26 October 2015

13:21 hours

'Hello, you're through to personal banking, this is Susie speaking. How can I help you today?'

'Good afternoon, I'd like to withdraw some cash, please.'

'Of course. If you just pop into your local branch, they'd be delighted to help you with that.'

'You don't understand. I want to withdraw rather a large amount of cash.'

'Right.' Susie twizzled her finger beside her ear to demonstrate to the girl opposite her in the call centre that she'd got a right nutter here.

'And I want to collect it tomorrow afternoon. Can you arrange for it to be ready for me?'

'If I can just take some details.' She held her fingers stiffly as she clattered them over the keys: her shellacked nails were too long for typing and she disliked the jar of her nails on the keyboard. She waited while the customer's details came on screen and swallowed an exclamation of surprise. Maybe not a nutter: the account was bursting with money. Adopting a more respectful tone, Susie asked, 'How much cash do you wish to withdraw?'

'Two hundred thousand pounds.'

CHAPTER
SEVEN

Tuesday, 27 October 2015

07:01 hours

A paper swan was on the pillow next to her when she awoke. Eden rolled over, one arm slung over her eyes to blot out the glare of the bedroom light. Aidan was up and dressed, and sitting on the end of her bed.

'Morning, sleepyhead,' he said.

'What time is it?' she mumbled.

'Seven.'

'God.' She struggled to sit up. 'You're up early.'

'Got to get home and changed. Early start today. I want to make sure everything's ready before her ladyship arrives.'

Of course. Lisa Greene, the expert on bones that Lewis had drafted in from Oxford; Aidan's ex-girlfriend.

'Don't take any notice of Lewis,' she said. 'He doesn't know what makes a good archaeologist, or even good research. He just wants some eye candy for his documentary.'

Aidan snorted and she squeezed his hand.

'So what's today's offering?' she said, picking up the swan. 'That's pretty good.'

'If you pull its tail, it bobs its head,' Aidan said, demonstrating.

She'd bought him a book of papers and origami instructions for their anniversary. 'First year is paper,' she'd said, knowing that the precise lines and geometric shapes would please his mind. He sought regular patterns, counted objects over and over, and even now was drawing an outline round the pattern on her duvet, trying to make it fit into a symmetrical shape. He'd thrown himself into the origami. Every time he saw her now he presented her with a new folded design.

'You remind me of a swan,' he said. 'Calm on the surface and frantic paddling underneath.'

'True.' She thumped the pillow and positioned it more comfortably behind her head.

'Want some coffee?'

'Lovely.'

He disappeared into the kitchen and she heard him clattering about. Probably rearranging her mugs so the handles all pointed the same way, she thought, fondly. He returned with a tray of coffee and a plate of toast.

'You're not bad, for a boyfriend,' she said.

'Look, I don't want you to worry about Lisa,' he began. 'I know last time I saw her she was ...' he hesitated, searching for words.

'A bit of a bitch?' Eden supplied.

Aidan winced. 'I wouldn't put it quite like that.'

Eden sipped her coffee. It popped her eyes open; Aidan always made rocket fuel. 'I know Lisa's sort,' she said, twining her fingers in his. 'It'll be alright.'

'See you later?'

'Sure.'

She reached for her dressing gown slung on the bedpost and shrugged it on, then followed him to the door to let him out of her flat. He kissed her and slid his hand around her waist, the heat pressing through the thin silk robe.

'See you at the coalface,' she said, and locked the door after him, securing the deadbolt and fastening the chain.

Her flat was in an Art Deco block of brown and cream brick, and had a balcony. She unlocked the door to the balcony and stepped out, hopping from foot to foot as the chill seeped into her bare feet. Sipping her coffee, she looked out over rooftops to the spire of a church, now converted to a restaurant, and to the hills beyond. The air was cool and delicious, playing delightfully on her skin. It and the socking coffee revived her tired mind and set her brain spinning for the day. Just as she was negotiating her way through the slurry at the bottom of the cup, the phone rang.

'I hope that's not Lewis,' Eden muttered to herself. He hadn't struck her as an early riser. She picked up the phone. 'Hello?'

'Hello, Jackie,' said a smooth voice.

She froze.

'I know you're there, Jackie. Or Eden, as you call yourself now.'

Hammond. The gang leader who'd found out she was an undercover officer. In her mind she saw his face close to hers, the deadly calm with which he slit her across each arm, each thigh, and then stuck the knife in her stomach. Not to kill her, not right then, just to hurt her enough so she couldn't escape from the much slower death he had planned.

'What do you want?' she hissed, clenching her teeth together to stop herself heaving with fear.

'I saw you on television,' Hammond said, his voice a sensuous drawl. 'Just can't keep out of trouble, can you?'

She couldn't reply.

'Just thought I'd ring and let you know I haven't forgotten you, Jackie,' Hammond said. 'That's all.'

And he hung up.

She replaced the receiver, her hands shaking. Since testifying against Hammond she'd created a new identity, left London and made a fresh life in Cheltenham. Her parents, her friends, her ex-husband had all been told that she'd died, and in truth her old self had died. It had been too dangerous for her to remain. But now Hammond had seen her on TV. Who else had seen her? Who else knew that she was alive and where to find her?

09:42 hours

'You ready for today, Eden?' Lewis said.

When she arrived at his hotel he was still in the dining room having breakfast, so she joined him at the table and took a cup of coffee. Xanthe was also there, making notes on her iPad.

'Sure,' Eden said, her mind still churning over Hammond's phone call. His voice reminded her of all she had lost, and her chest ached with grief. Her parents had been told she was dead. They had a grave to visit and talk to, though who was in it was moot – a John Doe down and out, or strange fruit harvested from the Thames. At least they had closure; for her there was constant fretting whether they were coping, whether they had swum through sorrow and were at the other side, hoping they were, and yet resentful at the same time that she could be forgotten. When her parents lost her, she also lost them, and every day she grieved.

'The crew's coming from London,' Lewis said. 'They'll film the whole thing, then we'll go to Hailes and do some mood shots, get some actors playing monks and pilgrims. It'll be awesome.'

'Lovely,' Eden said. Put it all to one side, she told herself, deal with it later. With an effort, she smiled at Lewis, poured herself more coffee, and snaffled a banana and a croissant. Just as she was biting into it, the receptionist came over.

'Mr Jordan?' she asked. 'This was delivered for you.'

She handed over a large white envelope. Everyone stared at it.

'Thanks,' Lewis said, eventually.

'Want me to take a look?' Eden said, wiping her fingers on a linen napkin. She dug a pair of latex gloves out of her backpack and snapped them on. 'In case there are fingerprints,' she explained, as Xanthe goggled at her.

The envelope was addressed to Lewis Jordan c/o the Imperial Hotel. The address label was handwritten in capitals in black biro, and the stamp was blurred with a London postmark. Eden slid a butter knife under the flap of the envelope and slit it open. Inside was a single sheet of ordinary A4 paper. The message was printed at the top of the sheet and read:

You should be ashamed of yourself. You don't deserve to live.

10:06 hours

There was an electric blue Mazda MX5 parked outside the Cheltenham Cultural Heritage Unit when they arrived. While they waited for someone to let them in, another vehicle arrived: a people carrier with three people squashed into the front seats. They tumbled out and unloaded case after case of equipment.

'Here's the crew,' Lewis cried, high fiving the two men. They were both in jeans, T-shirts and padded navy gilets. The third person was a woman, mid-twenties, with long glossy brown hair caught in a high ponytail so tight her cheekbones squeaked.

'Who's she?' the woman demanded, eyeballing Eden.

'My detective,' Lewis said. 'This is Eden. Eden, this is Jocasta.'

Jocasta? What sort of name was that to lumber a child with, Eden thought. She made to shake hands with the girl, but was frozen by the stare she received. Jocasta raked her up and down, taking in Eden's black slim-fitting jeans, electric blue leather jacket, and backpack.

'Jocasta's my researcher,' Lewis explained. 'Aren't you, Jo-Jo?'

Jocasta shot him a murderous look and Xanthe looked up from her iPad, frowning.

The door opened and Mandy said, 'Oh!' when she saw how many people stood outside.

'Hey, Mands,' Lewis said, pushing past her. 'I've got the whole crew here today. Ready to make TV history, babe?'

Mandy flushed and pressed herself to the wall to let everyone squeeze past: Xanthe, whose eyes remained glued to her iPad; Jocasta with a disdainful swing of her ponytail; the two technical guys with cameras and boom mikes and cables; and finally Eden.

'Jocasta, Xanthe, these are the archaeologists,' Lewis introduced the team.

'Xanthe and Jocasta?' Trev echoed. 'Funny names you Londoners have. I'm Trev, short for Marmaduke, and Mandy is short for Anastasia. Andy, here, however ...'

'Yes, thank you, Trev,' Aidan cut in, with a despairing look at Eden that made her want to giggle. 'I think we get the message.' He turned to Jocasta. 'Don't mind Trev, he's from Bristol.'

'Morning, Mandy,' Eden said, with a smile. 'It's going to be quite a day.'

Her phone rang while they were setting up the equipment. Silver umbrellas, boom mikes, lapel mikes, light readings. Lewis had a laptop open and was running through the filming schedule he'd written, who was to be on camera, panning and establishing shots, back lighting and wild sound. The amount of faffing that was required before any filming could start made her head spin, and when her mobile rang she answered automatically without registering the incoming number.

'Eden Grey,' she said.

'Eden, it's me, Miranda.' Miranda Tyson, her old boss from her undercover days. A fierce, outspoken woman who took no bullshit in a macho world.

'Miranda?' Eden dropped her voice and scuttled out of the room, searching for a quiet place. The staff kitchen was empty. She dashed inside and closed the door, snapping on the air vent above the sink to drown out her conversation and foil any eavesdroppers. Aidan's team were a notoriously nosy lot. 'What's happened?'

Miranda calling was never good news. She wasn't supposed to know Eden: she was from her previous life, the life that was dead and buried, the life before Eden Grey was created.

'It's not good,' Miranda said.

'It never is. Hammond?'

'You got it, sweetie.'

'He called me this morning, said he'd seen me on TV.'

'He's been moved to another prison,' Miranda said. 'They had him in maximum security for a while but he's kept his nose clean, the sneaky bastard, so they downgraded him.'

Eden blew out her cheeks. 'Figures. I was on TV months ago. It was odd he mentioned it.'

'Evidently saving it up until he could get to a phone.'

'What can I do?'

'Just watch your back, sweetie,' Miranda said. There was a click on the line and Eden imagined her lighting a cigarette, the flash of the huge tiger's eye ring Miranda always wore. A deep exhalation and a rattly cough. 'He's a vicious bastard.'

Eden's scars prickled. 'You don't have to tell me.'

Another sharp inhale and puff that ended with a cough. Miranda had been a dedicated smoker since she was fourteen and it sounded like it was catching up with her. 'Just keep your eyes peeled, hey.'

Eden was unable to speak. She felt as though she'd swallowed a stone.

'And Eden?' Miranda said. 'I'm sorry.'

Lisa Greene had elected to dress in full green surgical scrubs to examine the skeleton. With her petite figure and red-blonde hair in a pixie, she cut a dashing and self-important figure next to Trev in his saggy jeans and Metallica T-shirt, and Mandy in her stripy jumper. Aidan felt a right chump, preparing for TV fame by wearing a tailored midnight blue suit and a pale lavender tie.

He flicked Eden a smile as she came back into the room. She smiled back, a moment of complicity: she understood how much he hated this sort of fuss. For a second he was grateful for Lisa's presence there. She might be muscling in on his territory, but she was also going to draw the fire of the filming.

'That's me ready,' Lisa told him, smoothing down the scrubs in case he'd failed to notice her attire.

Before he could reply, Lewis shouldered himself forwards and was pressing Lisa's hand. 'I'm so pleased you agreed to star in my documentary,' he said, raising her hand to his lips.

Lisa pinked and fluttered her eyelashes. So much for professionalism.

'What beautiful skin,' Lewis continued. 'We'll make sure you're lit properly.' He turned to bark instructions to the technical guys and they hustled about with cables and silver light reflectors. Aidan wondered how long it would take to return his basement to normal after this circus. 'It'll take a while to get set up,' Lewis said. 'How about you check over this skeleton, then we'll film you giving your conclusions?'

'Sounds good to me.' Lisa went to the dispenser on the wall and pulled out two latex gloves. She snapped them on with relish, then turned to Aidan and ordered, 'I'll dictate and you make a note. We'll confer as we go. Alright?'

'Yes, miss,' Aidan said. Lisa always was a bossy boots.

After two hours scrutinising the skeleton, Lisa was ready to make a preliminary conclusion, and the technical guys were happy with the lighting and sound quality in the basement. The camera was set up, a boom mike hovered overhead, and Lewis called for an initial take. Lisa scuttled out of the room and returned a few minutes later wearing fresh lipstick. She also bore a whiff of cigarette smoke overlaid with a squirt of musky perfume. It was not welcome in this enclosed space.

'Ready,' Lisa said, her eyes bright.

'OK, Lisa, what can you tell us about this skeleton?' Lewis prompted.

Lisa looked straight into the camera. 'It's the skeleton of a male, full grown but not yet showing signs of age-related degenerative diseases like arthritis. I'd estimate an age of between twenty-five and forty-five. There's considerable wear on the teeth, so I'd put the age at the further end of that.'

'That's wonderful!' Lewis said. 'Now, let's do that again, and you pick up the bones and teeth and show us what you're talking about. OK? And ... action.'

Lisa rattled through it again, picking up the bones as directed. Then Lewis asked her to do it again, this time explaining it all to Trev, who with his stubbly chin and beer belly, fitted Lewis's template of an eccentric archaeologist. Trev bounced forwards, anxious to share the moment of fame. Aidan leaned against the wall at the back, completely side-lined in his own lab. Everything Lisa was saying was exactly what he'd told Lewis yesterday. Seemed you needed lipstick to be convincing these days.

Lisa continued. 'There are a number of healed wounds on the skeleton. Here, on the shoulder, and here, on the leg. I'd say these were caused by knives, but the injury on the shoulder is much more serious and was probably caused by an axe. The wounds have healed, though; you can see where new bone has grown. The wounds on the leg took some time to heal, and you can see from the pocking that an abscess formed.' She gazed into the camera. 'That would have been extremely painful.

'What's interesting is that three of his fingers are missing from his left hand. Some of the bones are missing from the skeleton, but that's to be expected with a skeleton that's been scattered – you often don't get all the bones.' She paused and pointed to the left hand. 'But here, there are cut marks in the bones, indicating that these fingers were amputated, perhaps because they were damaged or diseased. Another possibility, looking at the other injuries on the bones, is that the fingers were cut off in a fight.'

'How can you tell that?' Trev asked, on cue.

'For each amputation, there's more than one cut mark on the bone,' Lisa said, with relish. 'That's not unusual. There was no anaesthetic in the past so he would have been held down for the operation, and he probably wriggled about a bit.'

'What else can you tell, Lisa?' Trev asked.

'The muscle attachments are deep, suggesting a well-built man, strong and muscular,' Lisa said. 'The right shoulder and arm muscles were larger than the left, so he was right handed. I'd say that these muscles were developed through hard physical work. Normally I'd say he might have been a blacksmith or a farm labourer, but coupled with the knife and axe wounds, and the amputated fingers, I'd guess that he was a soldier. It's his sword arm that's highly developed and strong.'

'Wow!' Lewis's eyes shone. 'And how did he die? Can you tell that?'

Lisa's lips quirked. 'You don't have to be Sherlock Holmes to work out how he died.' She held up the skull and turned it round to show the back. There was a deep depression in it. 'Head injury to the back of the skull. You can see that the skull is indented here and there's a fracture radiating from it.'

'He fell and hit the back of his head?' Lewis prompted.

'No, it looks to me like it was caused by a blunt instrument.' Lisa stared at the skull for a long moment for maximum effect before she pronounced, 'Someone bashed his head in.'

The lights were piercing, drilling straight through his skull. That and Lisa primping and pouting at the camera, and it wasn't long before his head was throbbing. Aidan slid down the cool wall and rested his head against it, seeking relief. None to be found.

'You alright?' Eden whispered, beside him.

He pinched the bridge of his nose. 'Headache.'

'Want some painkillers?'

He nodded. She rummaged in a side pocket of her bag and produced a foil strip and a bottle of water. He took them gratefully and gulped down a couple of paracetamol.

'Keep them,' she said, as he handed back the tablets. 'You might need more later.'

She knew him so well, had witnessed dozens of his headaches and more than a couple of migraines in their time together. She gave him a sympathetic smile and took a slug of water herself. He puffed out his cheeks and watched the pantomime play out.

So much for being director of the Cultural Heritage Unit: he was completely redundant here. Even Trev was getting more of the action that he was. Trev, with his orotund Bristol accent and yokel appearance. He'd already addressed Lisa as 'my lover' twice on camera. He wondered if Lewis Jordan would keep that in.

And Lisa was loving every minute. Being the centre of attention, that's where Lisa was happiest. He remembered that year they were together as postgraduates in Cambridge. How he crawled with jealousy the whole time, watching Lisa flirting and ensnaring a troupe of worshippers. Now she was making a big deal of taking samples from the bones and teeth for isotopic analysis. That pert little grin as she wielded the drill and caught the bone shavings and tooth dust. He sighed again and reminded himself that Lewis's mob was paying for all this analysis. Without it, they would have quietly boxed up the skeleton and filed it on a shelf to await burial.

By three o'clock in the afternoon, they'd finished with the skeleton. Lewis called for the Holy Blood to be brought out and it was Mandy's turn in the spotlight. She'd put on a new jumper this morning: pale blue and grey stripes, with a floral blouse peeking out at the collar and cuffs. No makeup, she addressed the camera bare-faced.

This time, the initiate who had to be told about the object under examination was Lewis Jordan himself. Lewis prepared for his moment by extracting a bottle of eye drops from his jacket and placing drops in each eye in one smooth movement. He blinked a few times and checked his appearance in his phone, then took his place beside Mandy at the table and wriggled his fingers into a pair of white cotton handling gloves.

Trev brought out the box containing the artefact and placed it reverently in front of them. Lewis peered into the box and grinned. 'You know, Mandy, some people would pay a lot of money for a relic like this.' His grin widened. 'And I mean a *lot* of money.'

Aidan knew that Mandy had spent the past months since they excavated the skeleton mugging up on Hailes and the Holy Blood, so he was annoyed on her behalf when she drew out the phial and Lewis's opening question, clotted with emotion was, 'So this is part of the Holy Grail?'

Mandy faltered. 'Er, this looks like the drawings we have of the relic known as the Holy Blood. It was brought to Hailes Abbey in the thirteenth century, and …'

'So if this contains the blood of Christ, it's linked to the Holy Grail, which gave people eternal life?' Lewis persisted, taking the phial out of Mandy's hands and holding it close to his face to gaze at it.

Mandy shot a look at Aidan, her face flaming. He pushed himself forwards from the wall. Eden's tablets had barely taken the edge off his headache.

'Can we stop filming for a moment, please?' Aidan said, planting his fists on the table. 'What's this about, Lewis? No one's said anything about the Holy Grail. And in fact, all we can say about this find is that it *seems* to resemble the Holy Blood relic.'

Lewis's eyes gleamed. 'But if we can link this to the Holy Grail, and King Arthur and Glastonbury, how much more powerful it would be.'

He heard Lisa smother a laugh with a cough.

'I'm sorry to disappoint you, Lewis,' he said, 'but we're scientists, here. We don't go in for a lot of mumbo-jumbo, even if it does make for exciting TV. We're here to examine the *facts*.'

Mandy mouthed a silent thank you and he gave her a small smile of solidarity.

'So, Lewis,' Aidan continued, 'how do you want to do this section? I suggest we let Mandy tell Trev all about the relic. She's done a lot of research.'

'What about Glastonbury, and the Holy Grail?' Lewis asked.

Jocasta, the researcher, interrupted. 'I've got a druid on standby to talk about that, Lewis,' she said. 'He's a pencil for Friday.'

'Good girl, Jo-Jo!' All was well in Lewis-land again, and he agreed to let Mandy and Trev discuss the archaeology in their own way.

'Forget about the camera,' Aidan told them. 'Just pretend it's a normal day at work and you're discussing a find. Just talk about it the way you usually would. OK?'

'Thanks, Aidan,' Mandy said.

'Deep breath, Mandy,' he said. 'Look at Trev and tell him what your research has revealed.'

Trev clapped Mandy on the shoulder. 'Alright, Mands, let's you and me have our moment of fame.'

Aidan returned to his post by the wall and watched the filming. Trev and Mandy started out self-consciously, but soon got into the swing of it, batting questions back and forth, drawing out the facts about mediaeval pilgrimage and beliefs about relics.

'The Holy Blood was removed from Hailes during the Dissolution of the Monasteries,' Mandy said. 'It was taken to London, where it was examined and declared a trick. It was duck's blood coloured with saffron in the bottle. The abbot himself admitted that the blood was a fake – regularly topped up with animal blood and simply there for the pilgrims who paid to see it.'

'And what happened to the Holy Blood?' Trev asked.

'It was destroyed,' Mandy said, 'thrown into the fires at Smithfield.'

'So what do we have here?'

'A good question, Trev. It looks like the images we have of the Holy Blood. We need to test the silver in the stopper to find out how old it is. If I hold this up to the light, you can see there's a sediment in the bottle. That could simply be mud from where it's lain buried for centuries, but until we test it, we don't know for sure.'

'What could that sediment be?'

'Medicine, an infused oil, or perfume,' said Mandy. 'Until we test it, we won't know. This is pure speculation.'

Lewis clapped his hands. 'And cut! Great job, Mandy and Trev, and leads us nicely into the next bit: testing the contents of that bottle. And for that, we need the doc.'

Aidan jerked forwards, but it wasn't him that Lewis meant. He wanted Lisa. Again. She sprang to attention, nodding eagerly as Lewis gave his instructions.

'We'll film you taking a sample from that bottle for analysis,' Lewis said. 'Just like we did with the isotope thing. Your hands, nice and steady, really professional. You do this every day of your life.'

'I do, pretty much,' Lisa said.

'Great stuff.' Lewis put his arm around her shoulders and squeezed. 'You look fabulous on camera.'

'Thanks, Lewis.'

The cameras crept forwards and the lights intensified as Lisa took up position with the phial, a narrow scalpel and a test tube. Carefully she unstoppered the bottle, peered inside, and slowly inserted the scalpel. All the air seemed to be sucked out of the room, and Aidan heard his heart banging. They could be making history right now, testing a genuine relic from the Middle Ages. The thought frightened him, as childhood admonitions about faith and not questioning God's will jostled with his training as a scientist.

Lisa evidently had no such misgivings, scratching at the sediment then removing a few scrapings and dropping them into the test tube. She sealed it, wrote out the label and gazed into the camera. A collective sigh rippled across the room.

'Done,' she said. 'We'll send this off to the lab for analysis and see what they come up with.'

Lewis clapped his hands. 'That's enough for today, peeps. We'll check the footage tonight and reshoot tomorrow. Back here at eight o'clock.'

'In the morning?' Trev said, a horrified look on his face.

Lewis took Lisa's hand in his and kissed it. 'You were magnificent,' he said. 'You look fantastic on camera. Born to it.'

'Maybe we could talk later?' she said, flashing her eyes.

'Looking forward to it already.' Lewis dropped her hand and snapped his fingers at Jocasta. She trotted over. 'Jo-Jo,' Lewis said, 'take my laptop for me, there's a good girl. I'm off to see a special lady.'

The room was loud with bustle as the technical guys wound cables and packed up cameras, Mandy and Trev excitedly rehashed their TV fame, and Xanthe and Jocasta ran through the next day's schedule. Eden gathered up her bag and jacket and mouthed 'See you later' to him, before hurrying out after Lewis. Aidan escaped to his office, glad to leave the circus behind and have a few minutes' peace. He'd only just got there when there was a tap on the door, and before he could answer, Lisa swanned in. She was wearing a black sheath dress that showed off her petite figure, cream and black kitten heels, and had a cream jacket slung over her shoulder. Quite a transformation from the green scrubs she'd sported all day.

'So, where are you taking me?' she asked, leaning against the doorframe in a seductive pose.

'You're going back to Oxford, aren't you?'

'Hardly!' she snorted. 'I'm not battling my way down the A40 only to come back at the crack of dawn tomorrow.'

'Where are you staying then?'

'Lewis has paid for a hotel room for me. I need my beauty sleep.'

'Right.'

'You're supposed to disagree and say, "Lisa, a hundred years of sleep couldn't make you more beautiful than you are".'

'Right.'

She sighed. 'So come on, let's go for dinner.'

'It's too early.'

'OK, drinks and then dinner. And then who knows, dancing until dawn.'

'I thought you said you needed your beauty sleep,' he said. 'Besides, you're seeing our esteemed producer, aren't you?'

'Jealous?' she asked.

'Hardly.'

'So come on then!' she said, exasperated. 'Two old friends can go for dinner, can't they?'

He knew she wouldn't give up until she got her way. With a sigh, he switched off his computer and unhooked his coat from the back of the door. 'I'll just check that Mandy and Trev are OK to finish up here.'

When he returned, Lisa had her jacket on and was waiting by the open front door. They set off on foot towards the High Street, past Marks & Spencer and the Regent Arcade to where the shops became smaller, huddled together.

'You still like Thai food?' Aidan asked.

'Yes, love it.'

'There's a pub here that does a good Thai curry.'

'Oh.' Her face fell. 'Not a Thai restaurant?'

'It's very good.'

When they pushed through the swing door into the pub, he was pleased to see it was full of university students making the most of the early bird curry special. He'd calculated right. They found a table squashed in the middle of the pub, surrounded by braying undergraduates, and ordered at the bar.

'You still seeing whatshername?' Lisa asked, taking a sip of white wine.

'Eden? Yes.' Aidan had a glass of lime and soda. The headache was still pounding and alcohol was never a cure.

Lisa gave a tinkling laugh that didn't fool him for a minute. He knew that laugh – it presaged cunning and spite and was fuelled by Lisa's wholehearted conviction that whatever she wanted, she would get.

'Eden and Aidan. Aidan and Eden,' Lisa chanted, her head cocked on one side. 'Sweet. Like having names that rhyme.'

'Yes, it's lovely, isn't it,' he said, determined not to be goaded. There was a flyer on the table, advertising a student production of *Measure for Measure*. He took it and started folding it, making the edges sharp with his thumbnail, the straight lines and angles soothing his mind.

Lisa didn't answer, just studied him over the rim of her wine glass. 'You thought any more about my proposition?' she asked.

His stomach lurched. Not this again. Months ago, suddenly working together on a couple of skeletons that had been found during an excavation, Lisa had told him she wanted a baby. At thirty-five, with neither husband nor boyfriend, she'd chosen him to be the father.

'Time is ticking on, Aidan,' Lisa said. 'And you haven't even had the decency to give me an answer.'

He sat back in his chair and folded his arms. 'That's because it's preposterous,' he said, suddenly losing his temper. 'I don't see you for what, ten years? And then you show up and ask – no, *demand* – that I father a child with you. I mean, for God's sake, Lisa.'

'I haven't got time to fanny around with romance, Aidan,' she snapped.

'Why me?' he said. 'There must be a dozen men in Oxford who'd happily knock you up.'

His voice had grown too loud, and there was a sudden silence as the noise in the pub dropped away. He lowered his voice and hissed, 'You could have a one night stand with anyone you liked and be pregnant by breakfast.'

She twisted her lip. 'Are you jealous?'

'Of course I'm not jealous. We're not together any more, Lisa. Remember?'

She glanced down at her hands. A tear escaped and slid down her cheek. Pure crocodile. She didn't bother to brush it away. In a small voice she said, 'I want the best for my child. And to be honest, Aidan, I think I made a mistake. I think *we* made a mistake, splitting up.'

'Jesus, Lisa,' he breathed. 'We went out when we were post-grads. It was over ten years ago. A lot of things have changed.'

'I know.' She looked at him fiercely. 'I've changed. I've real-ised I shouldn't have let you go.'

Another tear. His hands slid across the table and held hers. She locked her fingers in his, and two more tears fell.

His mobile rang. Releasing her hands, he hunted around in his coat pocket and found his phone. 'Hello?'

It was Trev, his voice squeaking as he panted out the problem.

'Stay there, Trev, I'm on my way back. I'll be about five minutes. Wait there for me.'

He ended the call and stood. 'I've got to go,' he said. 'There's a problem at work.'

'What about our meals?'

'You have them. You're eating for two. I've got to go.'

Lisa pulled on her jacket. 'What is it?'

Aidan ran his hand through his hair, shocked by what Trev had told him. 'The Holy Blood of Hailes. It's missing.'

CHAPTER
EIGHT

Wednesday, 28 October 2015

09:57 hours

Eden glanced at her watch. Still no sign of Lewis. So much for the demand for an early start. Mind you, from the sounds she'd heard coming from his room the evening before, he might well be recovering and in need of a lie in. Idly, she wondered who his lover had been. Xanthe, or Jocasta, or someone else entirely? From the gossip magazines, Lewis had no shortage of women willing to jump into bed with him.

She'd gone to see him around half-six, but finding him out, had popped back around eight, concerned by the poison pen letter he'd received. When she'd opened it and read out the message, 'You should be ashamed of yourself. You don't deserve to live', Lewis had turned a porridgy colour and all his usual swagger left him like a retributive wind sweeping through a Biblical land. Lewis was rattled.

There was no chance to talk to him alone, not with Xanthe's regular bulletins from Twitter, Jocasta always hovering at his elbow and the technical guys in everyone's way, so Eden had returned to the hotel hoping to ask Lewis again who hated him enough to send those threatening letters.

She'd made her way along the corridor to his room and lifted her hand to knock, then hesitated. A woman's laugh came from inside the room, answered by a sexy purr from Lewis. If he was getting it on with a new bird, she didn't want to blurt in with her libido-crushing questions about anonymous letters. It could wait until the morning. So, she'd turned around and gone home, thinking she'd catch Lewis during an early breakfast before filming. But the night of passion must've taken it out of him, because there was no sign of Lewis and the crew was getting antsy.

'We haven't finished looking through yesterday's footage,' one moaned. 'Until we do that, we don't know what we need to reshoot today. Could mean an extra day filming, and that's going to knock out the whole schedule.'

Xanthe materialised, her fingers dancing over the iPad. 'Lewis having breakfast in his room?' she asked.

'No one knows,' Jocasta said. 'I went up and knocked over an hour ago and there was no reply.'

'I'll get him,' Eden said, idly wondering if last night's chick was into kinky tricks and had left Lewis trussed to the bedpost. Try keeping that out of the gossip mags.

She trotted up the stairs to Lewis's room and knocked. No reply. Empty breakfast trays lay outside the bedroom doors along the corridor. There was nothing outside Lewis's door, not even a newspaper. She rapped again. 'Lewis! Lewis, it's Eden. It's getting late and everyone's eager to get to work.'

No response.

'Lewis? Lewis, are you OK?'

She pressed her ear to the door. No sound. She tried the handle. The door was locked. Eden glanced up and down the corridor. No sign of a chambermaid or anyone delivering breakfast in bed. No sound of a linen trolley rattling along the corridor, either.

She hunted in her bag for her purse and slid out her library card and flexed it. Nice and bendy. She slotted the card into the gap between the door and the frame then, tugging the door sharply towards her, flexed the card over the strike plate and the door swung open.

As she stepped inside something crinkled underfoot. She bent and retrieved an envelope from the floor. She folded the envelope and put it in her bag.

'Lewis? It's Eden.'

The room was in darkness, heavy drapes shrouding the windows.

'Lewis? Time to wake up.'

She stepped over to the windows and stumbled, falling heavily on the floor. When she yanked open the curtains and let in some light, she saw what had tripped her. Lewis, lying face down on the carpet, a huge wound in the back of his head, his body haloed in red.

Eden rushed to turn him over. The sight that met her sent her staggering back in shock, a scream escaping from her throat.

Lewis's eyes were burnt out. Two holes gaped in his face, the flesh puckered and raw. His lips hung open and inside his mouth was black: tongue, teeth, lips. There was a black stain on the carpet where he'd lain.

Choking, Eden ran to the door and shouted, 'Help! Someone help!' into the corridor.

A chambermaid in a blue uniform appeared, a frown between her eyes. 'What's the matter?' she asked.

'Get an ambulance,' Eden said. 'The man in room 204 has collapsed. No, don't go in, just get help quickly. Go!'

The girl scurried away and Eden returned to the room. Pressing her fingers into Lewis's neck, she checked for a pulse. Nothing. She sat back on her heels, fighting panic. Remembering her training, she checked again for a pulse. Too easy to miss it when you're in a state. Too easy not to keep your fingers in place for long enough to detect life. Her skin crawling, she counted a full minute. Nothing.

Already there were footsteps and loud voices in the corridor outside. She didn't have long. The police would be called soon and she'd be muscled out of the picture. Lewis was her client. He'd called her in to protect him and look what a fucking shambles she'd made of that. Soon there'd be plod all over the room. This was her chance to get ahead of the game.

She met the startled hotel manager at the open doorway.

'Mr Jordan has been attacked,' Eden told him in a low voice, standing aside just enough so he could register the horrific state of Lewis's face. The manager blanched and looked as though he was going to be sick. 'We need an ambulance and the police straight away. And don't let anyone else come in this room – it's a crime scene.'

'Who are you?' stammered the hotel manager.

Eden took out her identification. 'Eden Grey, private detective. I was hired by Mr Jordan. Now go and get an ambulance and the police.'

The hotel manager hurried away. Here was her chance. Starting at the doorway, Eden scanned the room while she drew latex gloves out of her bag and slipped them on. The room was neat and tidy, the drawers firmly shut, the wardrobe doors closed. A heavy lamp with a stone base stood on the chest of drawers, its plug and flex coiled on the carpet. The bed hadn't been slept in, though there was an indentation in the duvet where someone had sat on it. Lewis himself was in a bathrobe tied tightly at the waist, his long brown legs sticking out and his bare feet looking strangely vulnerable. Steeling herself, Eden bent to his face, gently wafting the air towards her nose. The smell caught in the back of her throat, making her gag.

She lifted his arms and legs, noting the stiffness in the elbows and knees, and breathed hard through her mouth for a moment, fighting the urge to vomit. Clamping her lips tightly shut, she bent and touched the bloodstain on the carpet and raised her gloved fingers to her eyes. The blood was sticky; when she rubbed her fingers and thumb together it formed stringy webs of blood. Bloody marks tracked across the carpet. Shuddering, she jerked a tissue out of her pocket and wiped her fingers.

In the bathroom, Lewis's bottle of eye drops lay uncapped on the floor. She stepped over it and checked out the contents of Lewis's washbag: condoms, aftershave, men's grooming products in black and grey bottles. The bathroom held two hotel bath sheets, one neatly folded on the metal rack above the bath. She sniffed: biscuits. The scent of an industrial tumble dryer. The second was in a heap on the floor, still damp. The bin held only a soggy teabag, an empty liquorice packet, and a tissue smeared with red lipstick.

A commotion out in the corridor startled her. She snapped off the latex gloves and shoved them in her bag. As she went to the door, her eye caught something on the bedside table. Eden stared at it, her mind whirring. How could that be here, in this room where Lewis Jordan had met a violent death? Without thinking, she scooped it up and put it in her pocket.

It was an origami swan.

CHAPTER
NINE

Winchcombe, September 1571

They gave him a horse for his journey. A broken-backed nag that plodded slower than he could walk and kicked up mud so his leggings were coated and thick with mire. Still, a horse was a horse. No wading through the lanes on his own two legs. Old injuries pained him, the wound in his leg tormented him, and he was glad these mornings to clamber aboard his mare and let her set the pace.

He kept to the back lanes. His face was the sort to threaten children with. Say your prayers or Lazarus will visit you in your dreams. Do as you're told or Lazarus will come for you. Safer to stay out of sight so no one could remark on the scarred stranger who passed through. The country was watchful; uncertain and afraid.

Sidney had bid him farewell when they released him from Newgate.

'Lord Cecil thanks you for this service,' Sidney had said, a sly leer on his face. As Lazarus hauled himself into the saddle and gathered the reins into one fist, he'd added, 'And he says if you fail in your mission, don't bother to come back. You won't rise from the dead again, Lazarus.'

With that he'd slapped the nag's rump and guffawed as she skittered and slid over the cobbles. Lazarus swore an oath under his breath and brought the mare under control. When he'd found Brother John, he'd come back and slit Sidney's throat for him.

Lazarus. The name haunted him. It had been his since he was five years old. The only living thing in a house slaughtered by the sweats; his father and mother dead, jaws gaping, side by side in the feather bed; his brothers and sisters in a stiff line on the truckle bed, and him in the middle, squashed between the baby and his older brother, alive.

The midwife who found him crossed herself. 'Sweet mother of Jesus, the child's alive.' She'd plucked him out of the nest of bodies and cooed to him. 'Been there a while, my poppet, from the looks of you.'

She'd handed him over to the woman who'd broken into the house with her, both of them alerted by neighbours reporting there'd been no sound from the house these past days, and set about laying out seven corpses.

'Looks like he died hisself and rose again from the dead,' she said, often, to any who would listen, and to a good many who wouldn't. 'A regular Lazarus he is.'

So Lazarus he was. Through fights that weren't his own, battles he was paid to win, and other people's enemies he was contracted to kill. Death had breathed its foul breath in his face on many occasions, and each time he'd been pulled back from purgatory to live and kill another day.

Only Theresa had known him truly, Lazarus thought, as he wrapped his cloak about him and settled to sleep in a pile of leaves after a long day trudging the byways. Her face floated in front of his eyes as sleep captured him. Theresa, with her long oiled hair and slick slender body. There was a time when he thought of staying forever in the circle of her arms. Her and the child. They were everything to him.

That night he dreamed of her. Her dark eyes luminous, flashing in the night as she rose above him, twirling her hips and driving him wild with lust.

'Matthew,' she whispered. 'Matthew, the child cannot stay here.'

In the dream he turned his head and saw the child, little Mariam, crouched in a corner. The same dark eyes as her mother, the same smooth olive skin. She caught him staring at her and smiled a gap-toothed smile that twisted his heart.

'Dadda,' she said, and suddenly he was awake, drenched with sweat and shivering with cold.

A pink dawn was staining the horizon and the morning star pierced the dark dome overhead. He dragged himself up, his hips groaning and his scars aching, and went in search of the horse. Pissing against a tree, he saw the dark shape of the nag, a blacker shadow in the gloom and he whistled softly to her. She clopped towards him, dragging her hobble. He pressed his face into her warm flank, snuffing up the warmth of her, for a second overcome with gratitude for another living thing to share his hell.

'Come on, old girl,' he said. 'Let's find this troublesome priest.'

He entered the town early, seeking only to fill his saddlebags with bread and ale, then leave to take up his journey again. To his surprise, though the baker's fire was hot and the scent of pies seasoned the air, there was no sign of the baker apart from a tray of puddings left to cool on a windowsill. Lazarus scuffed around outside the shop until shouting drew his attention away. Shielding his face from gawpers with his hood, he sought out the cause of the commotion.

A crowd was gathering in a nearby street, the number swelling with each minute. Heads poked from upstairs windows to watch and cat-call as a nightshirted family was prodded from their beds and out into the chill morning air.

'Search it again,' shouted a man with a black beard and a thick head set on muscular shoulders.

The crowd bayed as four men brandishing pikes marched into the house.

'There is nothing to find!' cried the father of the family, his face white. 'I swear we have done nothing wrong.'

'That's not what we've been told,' Blackbeard growled.

The upstairs windows were flung open and a mattress hauled out. It landed with a whump below, and two more men with pikes stabbed it until the stuffing swirled in a cloud down the street. Another followed, and another. All were ripped to shreds.

'What's happening here?' Lazarus asked a matronly woman who stood with her arms tucked under her breasts.

'Papists,' she spat, barely looking at him. 'They came seven nights ago and searched and found nothing. Now they're back.'

And meant to find something, judging by the sounds coming from within. Floorboards being prised up, stairs dismantled, furniture broken to sticks. A trunk was hefted out of the window and broke open, spilling its innards into the dust. Blackbeard swooped, holding up a rosary and a crucifix. The crowd jeered.

'What have we here?' he demanded, pushing his face close to the father of the family. The man's mouth worked silently.

'Treason!' Blackbeard cried. He tossed the rosary on the ground and stamped on it. The wife clutched her husband, trembling like a sapling.

Blackbeard took a flint from his jacket and built a pyre of the trunk, the mattresses and the broken furniture that flew from the window. Lighting the straw, he bellowed, 'Death to the enemies of the Queen,' and the crowd echoed him.

The fire took hold quickly and smoke clotted the air.

One of the pikemen hurtled out of the house and handed a tile to Blackbeard.

'What is this?' he said, advancing on the family.

'It is but a tile,' the wife said. Blackbeard raised his fist as if to strike her, but at that moment the youngest child piped up, 'Father Renaldo brought it.'

The crowd fell silent at the words as foreboding shivered through them. Lazarus drew back. This was treason indeed. One thing not to go to church and pay the fine, another to hear a Catholic Mass within your home. The family – father, mother, three children – were dead, betrayed by their heresy.

'And where is this Father Renaldo?' asked Blackbeard.

The mother shook her head violently. 'You cannot listen to a child, sir. A stupid boy he is, too.'

'Where is Father Renaldo?'

The woman shrank back. 'He is not here, I swear.'

'We'll find him.' Blackbeard shouted to the men inside the house. They appeared, shaking their heads and empty handed. 'Burn it,' he said.

Grabbing sticks from the fire in the street, the men thundered back inside the house. Within minutes, smoke poured from the windows and flames licked at the walls. The men retreated outside and stood, leaning on their pikes and waiting. After what seemed an interminable time, a young man dashed from the house and collapsed, coughing his lungs up, his skin blackened. The men dragged him up by his arms and hauled him over to the family.

'Who is this?'

The father sank to his knees with a moan. 'Please,' was all he was able to say.

'Been hiding seven days and nights,' the woman next to Lazarus commented. 'Starving, no doubt. Serve him right.'

The young priest was in a bad way. His legs gave out beneath him every time he was hauled to his feet and his eyes stared wildly about him.

'Father Renaldo?' Blackbeard addressed him. A whimper in reply. Blackbeard grabbed his chin, his fingers digging into his flesh. 'You are a priest?'

He let him go only to smack him across the face. The priest's head snapped back and hung loose on his neck.

'Tie them,' Blackbeard ordered, and the men jumped to work, binding the waists of everyone in the family and joining them in a ragged, barefoot chain. The priest was fettered with iron, though it was clear to Lazarus the man had no strength to blow his nose never mind escape, and was loaded head first over the back of a horse, his rump in the air.

The crowd jeered as the men took up position each side of the family and marched them down the street. Blackbeard mounted his horse and grabbed the reins of the animal that carried the priest, jerking it into a trot to jolt the priest's bones every step of the way.

Out of the corner of his eye, Lazarus caught sight of a figure escaping through the crowd: a rat-faced boy with a fluffy chin.

'Who is he?' Lazarus asked the woman, pointing out the lad.

'He worked for the family, was their apprentice,' she said. 'Was turned out three months ago for stealing. Lucky not to hang.' She sniffed. 'It was most likely him who told them where to find the priest.' She hitched up her skirts, the morning's entertainment over. 'Least he will have coin to keep him a few weeks more.'

The crowd ebbed away with a sense of righteousness well played. Lazarus returned to his horse and set out along the road, his appetite evaporated. He would buy provisions at the next town, when the stink of smoke and treachery was gone from his throat. On his way out of the town, he passed the band of men and their prisoners. The priest was muttering prayers to the horse's stomach; the father was near collapse and had to be prodded upright every few paces. Lazarus swivelled his eyes away from the procession and kicked his horse on to a canter, escaping the high road as soon as he could.

From then on he kept out of the towns, scuttling into hamlets only long enough to buy provisions, and dodging back to obscurity again. When he approached Winchcombe, the sight of the green Cotswold hills ignited memories in his heart. Taken to live in the butcher's family, learning how to slit a pig and catch the blood; mincing flesh into puddings; the iron salt tang that hung over the house and shop. Was this home, he wondered, as the old horse slogged down the main street. No one now to recognise him or even remember the orphan child the butcher took in.

The horse's lungs were leather, cracked and wheezing. Lazarus fingered the coins in the bag at his waist. A night in an inn. A warm stall and good feed for the mare; a pallet and blanket for him; and a plate of meat and bread. He turned the horse's head towards the inn and swung painfully out of the saddle.

'Brush her down and give her food and water,' he ordered the stable lad who scuttled out to greet him. The boy blanched at the sight of him and grabbed the reins, yanking the horse away.

Lazarus tugged off his leather gloves and stumped into the inn. 'A bed for the night, food, and ale,' he demanded.

The innkeeper looked him up and down, wiping his hands over the front of his apron. 'We've not welcomed you before, stranger,' he said.

'Nay,' said Lazarus.

'You travelling through?'

'Aye.' Lazarus coughed. 'Thought to see the old Abbey on my way.'

The innkeeper shook his head. 'Not much left of it now. Though it's risen again in many houses.'

Lazarus recalled the stone dwellings lining the main street. Stone pilfered from the destroyed Abbey. And why not? No point it lying smashed and mossy on the ground. He remembered the Abbey from his childhood, its imposing towers and the bustle of activity. All gone.

'And the other Abbey, Hailes, is gone too?' Lazarus asked.

'A long time ago,' the innkeeper agreed. He took a leather beaker from a shelf and filled it with beer from a barrel. It frothed and spattered onto the floor.

'It was a place of healing,' Lazarus said. He fingered the scar down his face with his left hand, revealing the stumps where his fingers had been.

'There is physic to be had there, for those in need,' the innkeeper said, sliding the beaker of ale over to Lazarus.

Lazarus threw some coins down on the table. 'A warm, dry bed is what my tired bones need tonight,' he said.

His bed was in a dormitory: a long room that ran the length of the inn. The beds lay in two lines facing each other, low to the ground. Lazarus's hips screamed as he lowered himself onto his pallet. Though there was space for twelve people in the room, to his relief he only had four bedfellows: two young men who snored like the devil, and a couple who claimed to be husband and wife, though from their endearments and soft glances they had not yet met before a priest. They occupied the furthest corner of the room and squirmed beneath the blankets all night.

Lazarus took the pallet opposite the door. Old instincts: his escape was ready should he need it. He fell asleep almost the moment he lay down and covered himself with the blanket. He woke in the deep part of the night to snoring and lovers' murmuring. A flea bit his neck. His scratched it and slept again. When he woke, it was dawn.

He rose and folded the blanket onto the pallet, and trudged downstairs, startling the innkeeper who was still in his nightshirt.

'You're an early riser, my friend,' he said.

'An old habit,' Lazarus said. 'Bread, beef, ale, when you're ready.'

The look he gave the innkeeper sent him scurrying to his chamber for clothes, and he reappeared shortly after and set about preparing Lazarus's breakfast.

'There is physic to be had in Hailes?' he asked, grinding on a tough bit of beef. 'My horse needs a poultice. She's nearer to glue than horseflesh.'

'They say he can cure animals as well as man,' the innkeeper said. 'He?'

'An old monk. He worked in the infirmary at the Abbey, and stayed there to minister to the sick after the place was pulled down.'

'Where might I find him?' Lazarus gulped a mouthful of beer. 'Maybe he can cure my aching bones as well as my horse.'

'He has a cottage in the old Abbey grounds. Go to the village of Hailes and ask for Brother John. They'll tell you where to find him.'

'Brother John?'

'Aye. He works miracles, so they say.'

Hailes village was a cluster of wattle-and-daub cottages around a central flattened circle of earth. Beyond lay the ruins of the Abbey: a skeleton of jagged stones and empty windows raising its fists to the sky. Lazarus dismounted when he saw scraps of smoke rising from the cottages, and led the wheezing nag into the village. There was an inn at the edge of the village: a timber-framed house that was as crooked as his horse's back.

A girl sat outside the inn, shelling peas into a bowl clamped between her knees. Her eyes narrowed as Lazarus approached.

'Can a thirsty man get ale and bread here, mistress?' Lazarus asked.

She glanced at his scars then scurried into the inn. Lazarus's paw was in the bowl and the sweet peas in his mouth before she'd reached the inn door. A pea popped on his tongue. How long since he'd tasted them. All those years in the Holy Land, with fruits and dried meat, and he'd yearned for a freshly shelled pea.

Theresa had never understood when he told her about his homeland. She'd gazed at him with her large, dark eyes full of merriment, and traced her plump fingers down his chest to his groin.

'Tell me about the English girls,' she'd whispered, her hot breath alive in his ear.

'They couldn't hold a candle to any I've seen here,' he'd said, his hands in her hair as her mouth moved down his body.

He rubbed his eyes to wipe away the memory of Theresa. A long time ago now. A long time since he'd left her dead body sprawled on the bed, mouth gaping and bloody where her teeth had gnashed against her lips.

The girl reappeared with a hunk of bread and a beaker of ale. He tossed her a coin and took up a place in the shade in the ley of the inn. The ale was sour and the bread hard. It had been baked two days ago and the mice had had their turn before him, judging by its nibbled edges. He tore off a corner with his teeth, softening it with the ale and swilling it round his mouth several turns before swallowing.

The girl watched him from the stool.

'Don't be afraid, mistress,' he called. 'I know I am the stuff of nightmares, but I am just a poor sick man.'

'You travelling through?'

'I have been told to find physic here,' he said.

The girl nodded. 'He's at the Abbey.' She stared at the stumps of his fingers and the scars on his face. 'Though whether he can help you, I cannot say.'

The ale and bread didn't refresh him, but he left the horse with a bucket of water and a nosebag, and walked to the Abbey. The gatehouse was gone, the stones pulled down and the lead carted away. There was little left of the Abbey church either, the windows empty eye sockets and the altar exposed.

Sheep grazed amongst the ruins. They lifted their heads and stared as he walked past. One side of the Abbey was laid out in a garden. Lavender, lady's mantle, sage, rosemary, sorrel. Apple trees spread their branches against a wall, soaking up the sun. Kneeling beside a clump of feverfew was a man in long dark robes. As Lazarus's shadow fell over him, he turned.

'Good day, my friend,' he said.

He was an old man, in his sixties by the look of him, and his skin was burned to the colour of acorns by the sun. A large nose dominated his thin face, but the main feature was a pair of bulging blue eyes.

He struggled to his feet with difficulty and took up a walking stick and propped it under his arm. 'You have come far, my friend,' he said. It wasn't a question.

'A goodish way,' Lazarus agreed.

'And have seen many troubles.'

Unthinking, Lazarus fingered the scar down his face. 'True enough, as any can see.'

The blue eyes pierced his for a long moment. 'And your soul has known much sorrow.'

Lazarus laughed. 'I long ago stopped worrying about that.'

The eyes never left his face. 'Perhaps you should.' The old man steadied himself on his walking stick. 'I can help you,' he said. 'I cannot make your fingers grow back, but I can ease those pains in your hips that trouble you at night. And I can ease the nightmares that will not go away.'

He turned and walked to the far end of the garden, and set about snipping twigs of rosemary and stripping the leaves.

'Who are you?' Lazarus called.

The old man turned. 'I am Brother John.' He held Lazarus's gaze for a long, silent moment before he said, 'Do you not know me, Sweet Matthew? I knew you at once. You've come home, I see.'

Winchcombe, March 1536

The pig, its insides plundered, hung from a hook in the killing shed. A stench of singed bristle choked the air. The blood was still warm as it poured into the bowl.

'Take that to the kitchen, boy,' Samuel, the butcher, ordered.

Matthew took up the bowl and a little of the blood slopped onto his hand.

'Don't you spill a drop, boy.'

Head down, concentrating on the blood sloshing from side to side, Matthew inched across the yard towards the open kitchen door.

'Don't take all day about it!' The roar behind him made him jump. The bowl jerked and fell from his hands, landing with a smash on the cobbles, and the blood spread in a scarlet river.

Two heavy footsteps behind him. Matthew cowered and scrabbled for the broken pieces of pottery. A hand grabbed a fistful of his hair, wrenching him to his feet. His scalp was on fire.

'You stupid bastard!' Samuel shouted, his face so close that spittle landed on Matthew's lips. 'You'll pay for that.'

He let go of his hair, but only so he could land a punch on the side of Matthew's head. His neck snapped back and for a moment pinpricks of light danced in front of him. As his head righted itself, a punch landed on the other side. This one felled him, and he sprawled in the spilt blood.

'Get up, you bastard!' Samuel shouted, his bulk heaving.

Matthew curled into a ball, his arms wrapped round his head. Dimity would be out soon, he prayed. She always stopped Samuel before he went too far.

'Get up!' A kick in his ribs. 'So you're a coward as well as a useless boy!' Another kick.

Matthew dug his fingernails into the cobbles and dragged himself along a few inches closer to Dimity in the kitchen. She must've heard the racket by now.

He tried calling, 'Dimity! Dimity!'

'She won't help you,' Samuel said, stamping on his arm. 'She knows better than to cross me.' He swung back his foot and slugged Matthew straight in the face.

All was black, he didn't know how long for, but when he could see again, he made out Dimity hugging the kitchen door, crying. A bruise circled her eye.

'Dimity!' he tried to cry, but the word came out as a froth of blood and spit.

'Get up,' Samuel said. 'Get up I tell you.'

Matthew saw the foot swing back again, and flinched, his arms around his head, waiting for the blow.

'Stop!'

Matthew peeked out and knew he was dead already. A tall man in white robes stood over him, the sun behind his head casting a halo over his fair hair.

'What are you doing to this child?' the angel of death asked.

'He's a useless piece of shit.'

The angel of death crouched down next to Matthew and asked gently, 'Are you hurt, child?'

Matthew attempted a nod, and winced with pain.

The angel stood. 'You have hurt this child before now.' He directed a glance at Dimity, cowering by the kitchen door, who gave a barely perceptible nod.

'Five years we've had him,' Samuel said. 'Fed him and warmed him at our fire, and this is how he repays us?'

'I'm sure he didn't mean it.'

'And all the other times? He didn't mean those, neither?'

The angel of death regarded Samuel for a long moment. 'I will take the boy,' he said.

'What?'

'He can be useful to me.' He bent to Matthew and asked, 'Can you stand?'

He helped Matthew to his feet, and putting one arm about him, started to lead him out of the yard.

'Now hang on a moment!' Samuel called, running after them. 'That's my boy. You can't just take my boy.'

The angel fixed him with a look from piercing blue eyes. 'He is not your boy, he is an orphan who your wife, in her pity, took in. He has been troublesome to you, but he can be useful to me. I relieve you of your responsibility.'

And with that he turned and led Matthew away, through the town, and out along the dusty road to the Abbey.

'Am I dead?' Matthew asked.

The angel laughed. 'No, you're not dead, and once I treat those cuts you'll be good as new.'

'Then who are you?'

'I am Brother John,' the angel said. 'Infirmarian at Hailes Abbey.' Matthew looked at him properly: a large nose in a long, bony face; a young man's face. Brother John was not yet thirty. 'And what do they call you, child?'

'I am Matthew Sweet,' Matthew answered. 'But some call me Lazarus, on account of how I survived the sweats when the others didn't.'

The blue eyes appraised him for a moment. 'Matthew Sweet. Sweet Matthew. Very well.'

He took Matthew into the infirmary, where he stripped him off and tutted at the blue and green mottling his body: a map of the beatings Samuel had dispensed.

'I feared you had been hurt more,' Brother John said, 'seeing all the blood on your clothes.'

'It's pig blood,' Matthew said. 'I dropped the bowl.'

To his astonishment, Brother John tipped back his head and laughed. 'Thank God for that,' he said.

Matthew laughed in return, then fingered his cut lips. 'Ow.'

'You're made of strong stuff, Sweet Matthew,' Brother John said, as he painted ointment onto the cuts from that day's kicking. 'How old are you?'

'Ten, Brother John.'

'Old enough to work and young enough to learn. How would you like to be my apprentice, in the infirmary?'

Matthew looked around at the bottles and jars, the spices and herbs hanging up to dry, and at the soft features of this man, and nodded.

Brother John brought him a sour-tasting potion in a leather beaker and tucked him up in clean linen in a corner of the infirmary dormitory. He shared the room with an ageing monk who muttered to himself in the far corner. Though the windows were too high up on the wall to see out, a defiant March sunshine painted the boards with warm stripes. Matthew fell asleep to the chimes of the Abbey bell calling the brothers to prayer.

When he awoke, Brother John's cool hand was on his forehead.

'You've slept well, my friend,' the monk said. 'Almost a whole day and a night. Are you hungry?'

He was, and he grabbed at the bowl of mutton broth and barley that Brother John handed to him, tipping it to his lips.

'Steady! There is plenty.'

'I thought monks didn't eat,' he said, through slurps of broth.

'We fast, as good men do, but that does not apply to you.'

'Why?'

'Because you are a lay brother, not a monk,' Brother John said. 'The lay brothers' lodgings are on the other side of the Abbey. Warm, too, and you can chatter all you want. I'll take you there once you are well again.'

Matthew glanced around at the long room. 'Can't I stay here? With you?'

Brother John sucked in a breath and thought for a moment. 'Brother Abbot will not like it, but then he is seldom here. And if he discovers you, we will tell him you're my servant in the infirmary and I need you close at hand at all times.' He smiled. 'How does that please you?'

'Very much,' Matthew said. He finished the broth and slid his finger around the bowl, scooping up the remains of the thick, greasy soup.

'You must rest again today,' Brother John said. 'But tomorrow I think you will be mended enough to start your lessons.'

'Lessons?' He didn't like the sound of that.

'Aye, boy, I'll teach you all I know.'

And he did. Each morning, the two went to Brother John's garden, where he grew the herbs and plants he used in his ointments and syrups. With infinite patience, he explained how to tend each plant, and what effect each one had on the body.

'This will strengthen the heart of a man whose blood is sluggish,' he told Matthew one day, as the foxglove spikes unfurled. 'But don't ever give it to a man in good health, for it may kill him.'

'Kill him?'

'All things are good, in the right measure,' Brother John said. 'But in the wrong measure, they may harm a man or send him to his death.'

The afternoons were spent mixing medicines and pounding roots into plasters so the infirmary was always well stocked should any come to the door seeking relief. At night, once the great bolt was shot across the Abbey gates, and the monks settled to their devotions, Brother John and Matthew dwelled before the infirmary fire, a Bible open between them, and Brother John taught him how to read.

One evening, almost a month after he'd arrived at the Abbey, while he was spelling out the Sermon on the Mount by the wayward flame of a small fire, Matthew was struck with a deep and shocking emotion. His words faltered and his heart stammered in his chest.

'Matthew? You do not know the word?'

'I do know it, Brother, it's just ...' he shook his head and continued with the reading, but late that night, when the darkness closed around him in his bed in the infirmary, he picked the emotion raw again and at last was able to name it. Contentment. For the first time in his life he was safe.

He turned onto his side and mumbled a prayer of thanks to the God he'd just begun to know, and was asleep before he could reach amen.

CHAPTER
TEN

Wednesday, 28 October 2015

10:58 hours

'I'm Eden Grey,' Eden told the police inspector. 'I'm a private investigator.'

Detective Inspector Ritter's eyes narrowed. His suit hadn't encountered an iron for a long time and creases ran like tramlines across his jacket and trousers. With his greasy blond hair and tired skin, he looked as sharp as a felt hat. 'I see,' he said. 'And what was your relationship to Mr Jordan?'

They were in an empty hotel room at the end of the corridor. Ritter commandeered the desk and chair by the window, the dull light throwing the lines round his eyes into sharp relief. There was nowhere for Eden to sit, so she perched on the ridged box meant for suitcases.

'He'd hired me to investigate some poison pen letters he'd received,' said Eden, cringing inside as she said it. Fat lot of use she'd been and now her client lay stiffening and bloody on the floor of his hotel bedroom.

'What sort of poison pen letters?' Ritter scrubbed his biro on his notebook, trying to make the ink flow. When he got no joy with that, he tried swirling it on the back of his hand. It wasn't his day. Eden silently removed a pen from her bag and handed it over.

'Pretty non-specific threats,' she said. 'You don't deserve to live. Better watch out. That kind of thing.'

'And he didn't think to report these to the police, to have them investigated properly?' Ritter said. He gave a sarky emphasis to 'properly'.

'No.'

'And why might that be?'

'Who can say?' Eden said, airily. *Don't upset the local plod*, that was the rule when she was undercover. They might be thick as shit but antagonise them and they can be an awkward bunch of sods. And they stick together.

'So you were investigating these letters?' Again, a mordant weight to 'you'.

'Yes.'

'And how far had you got?'

'No shortage of suspects,' Eden said, with a stab of relish at the dismay on his face.

Ritter grubbed in his pocket for a packet of nicotine gum. He unwrapped three pieces and folded them into his mouth.

'The door was open when you got here?'

Eden swallowed. This was going to be tricky. 'No, it was locked. I broke in using a library card.'

Ritter stared at her, his mouth champing at the gum, making a wet, smacking noise. 'You broke into a room where a man had been murdered?'

'I didn't know he'd been murdered,' Eden said. 'And to be honest, at this moment in time neither do you. There's no official cause of death yet, is there?'

Ritter glared. 'I need your contact details so I can interview you formally. You'll have to come to the station for that.'

She opened her mouth to object. Unless she was arrested, she was under no obligation to help the police nor to attend the police station, but one look at the expression on Ritter's face and she closed her mouth again. Seemed the nicotine gum wasn't helping his mood; she didn't want to push him into an arrest. Not when she wanted a head start on the investigation.

'Did you touch anything?' Ritter asked.

'No,' she said, looking away then making eye contact. Nothing like a hard stare to get a copper's hackles up. It was a great way to overcompensate on the 'I am totally innocent' look.

Ritter snapped his notebook shut. She wasn't fooled. As she headed to the door, the final question came, as she knew it would.

'One last thing, when did you last see Lewis Jordan alive?'

'Just before six o'clock yesterday evening,' Eden said. 'After he'd finished filming for the day.'

It was almost the truth. She had seen him last at that time, but she'd heard him two hours later.

'Is that all?' she asked.

'For now,' Ritter said.

'You can keep the pen,' she said, and scarpered.

She peeped into Lewis's hotel room as she went back down the corridor. The room buzzed with white-suited figures and a camera flashed. Eden hurried past to the top of the stairs. Glancing back, she saw Ritter watching her from the end of the corridor. She started down the stairs, waited at the bend, then crept back up again. Ritter had gone.

She hurried down the corridor to a door marked 'Staff Only'. The door was unlocked. Slipping inside, she found a chambermaid's trolley and shelves of towels, cleaning products and bottles of shampoo. She loaded extra towels onto the trolley, unhooked an overall and slipped it on. There was a cotton cap in the pocket. She pasted down her hair with her palms and tugged on the cap, then opened the door and trundled out with the trolley.

At room 203, she tapped on the door and waited.

'Housekeeping!' she called, and the door opened. 'Morning,' she said, grabbing an armful of towels and going into the room.

'Morning,' said a middle-aged man in grey trousers and a pale blue shirt. A laptop was propped open in a moat of papers on the table.

'Fresh towels for you,' she said, bustling into the bathroom. 'Hope you weren't disturbed last night.'

'Why?'

She cocked her head towards the wall. 'Man in the room next to you – had a big fight. People complained. The manager had to go up!'

'I was out until two this morning,' he said, yawning. 'And when I got in I hit that pillow and was dead to the world.'

'You didn't hear the fight?'

He rubbed his eyes. 'Nothing.'

'That's good.' Eden grabbed the dirty towels in the bathroom. 'Have a nice day.'

She shoved the towels onto the trolley and rattled past Lewis's room to room 205. The door opened almost immediately to her knock.

'More tea, coffee, sugar?' she said.

'That'd be great, honey.' An American accent, the owner a barrel-chested bear of a man in his late sixties. A well-upholstered woman with blue hair sat by the window, a set of maps spread before her.

'Hope you weren't disturbed last night,' Eden said. 'There was a problem in the room next door.'

'Irwin, I told you I heard something!' the woman exclaimed.

'He woke you up?'

'No, it was only about ten, but I was trying to settle down and it was very inconvenient.'

'I'm so sorry to hear that,' Eden said. She fetched a selection of miniatures from the trolley. 'Can I offer you these to say sorry you were inconvenienced?'

'Well now, that's very kind,' the woman said.

'What were they fighting about?' Eden asked casually, rubbing a duster over the chest of drawers.

'I couldn't hear clearly,' the woman said, 'but it was something about money. And then there was a thump and it all went quiet.'

'How awful for you,' Eden said.

'That's right,' the woman squinted at the embroidered name on Eden's overall, 'Rose. I'm a very light sleeper and the slightest thing wakes me.'

'I didn't hear a thing,' Irwin announced. 'Slept like a log until Myrna woke me at midnight.'

'I heard a scream!' Myrna exclaimed.

'A scream?' Eden made her mouth into a round O. 'You must've been very frightened.'

'I was! I'd just gotten to sleep and then there was a scream and a door slammed. Just after midnight it was because I had to get up then and fix me a drink to get off to sleep again.'

'I'm so sorry,' Eden said, and fetched a few more miniatures from the trolley.

'Gee, thanks, Rose,' Irwin said, following her to the door and pressing a twenty pound note into her hand. She slipped it into the pocket in the overall, and her fingers brushed against something cold and metallic. She drew it out: a pass key to every room in the hotel.

'Have a nice day!' Eden called, and went back to her trolley. She parked it back in the stores room and returned her overall to its hook. Ruffling her hair into its usual style, she slunk from the room and escaped down the stairs.

The hotel car park was to the side of the hotel: a rectangle of tarmac too small for the Bentleys and Mercedes crammed in there. At one end was a cluster of industrial waste bins, colour-coded in red, yellow and brown. A single CCTV camera, positioned above the side door into the hotel, surveyed the car park.

Eden stood underneath the camera and assessed the range of the CCTV, identifying a blind spot just where a sleek BMW was parked. Skirting the range of the camera, she hurried over to the BMW, planted her hands on the door, and rocked it. Within seconds, its lights were flashing and an alarm sounded.

She groped about on the ground until her fingers closed around a half-brick. Steeling herself, she laid her hand flat and smashed the brick down. Clutching her hand to her chest, she ran round the hotel to the main entrance.

'There are some kids chucking rocks at the cars in the car park,' she told the receptionist, breathlessly. 'Better get Security.'

The receptionist jabbed a button on the phone and within seconds a bald-headed man joined them.

'I'm Security,' he said. 'What happened?'

'Kids throwing stuff at the cars in the car park,' Eden said. She held out her hand. 'I yelled at them and they threw a brick at me. Look!'

'Ooh, that's nasty,' the receptionist said.

'Right, I'll see what the little buggers are up to,' said Security, hitching up his trousers and sauntering out to the car park, evidently hoping the little buggers would be long on their way by the time he got there.

'Can I use your Ladies?' Eden said, waving her injury. 'I think this needs cleaning up.'

'Course you can.' The receptionist pointed the way.

As soon as she was out of sight, Eden ducked down a side corridor and sprinted to the security office. The door stood wide open. Some security, Eden thought. Inside was the messiest desk she'd ever seen, piled with old coffee cups and teetering piles of paper. A single screen flashed images from a number of different CCTV cameras. In the top right-hand corner, Security ambled round the corner to accost the rock-throwing little buggers. Eden watched him stand with his back to the hotel, hands on his hips and shaking his head.

On a shelf behind the desk was a pile of DVD cases. She pulled out the case from the bottom and the one on the very top. Opening the top case, she found a DVD marked with the previous day's date. She slipped it from the case and slid it into her bag, replacing it with the DVD from the bottom of the pile. Quickly she shoved the two cases back in place. As she was about to leave, she caught sight of a clipboard hanging from a peg on the wall. The staff roster. She tugged the top sheet free, folded it, and hid it in her bag, then made her way to the bathrooms.

Her hand was swelling and purple, and the skin was grazed but not cut. She ran it under the cold water tap for a while, feeling her finger ends tingle. It looked much worse than it was. Maybe she could kill two birds with one stone? Or at least with one half-brick.

The bar was empty of customers, the barman faffing about with the optics.

'What can I get you?' he asked, when she came in. She caught the staccato rattle of consonants. Eastern European, she guessed. He had oiled blue-black hair like a gangster: his comb had left ridge and furrow marks through it.

'Actually, some ice, please.' Eden held up her hand. 'Though if you can do a coffee, that would be nice, too.'

'Coming up. You been in the wars?'

Eden pulled a face. 'I saw some kids throwing stuff at the cars outside, and when I shouted at them, they chucked a brick at me. Caught my hand.'

The barman bent over her injured hand, tutting. 'Lucky it didn't catch your head.'

'I know. Don't know what I was thinking of, shouting at them like that. You hear about kids carrying knives these days, but I just didn't like what they were doing.'

'On the house,' the barman said, setting a cup of coffee down on a white and gold paper coaster in front of her. 'Ice coming up.'

There was a yellow Marie Curie Cancer Care collecting tin at the end of the bar. Eden fished out the twenty pound note Irwin had given her and stuffed it into the collecting tin. A memory came out of hiding as she did so: a colleague from the old days was diagnosed with breast cancer and asked the team to sponsor her to get her head shaved before chemo. A number of them also got shaved in solidarity, and for weeks they chuntered about prickly scalps because it was easier to talk about that than ask how the chemo was going. Eden's boss, Miranda, had offered to shave her head, too, but in the end she was testifying in court and so simply paid a donation to Marie Curie.

'I don't want anyone to think I'm chickening out,' she'd said, pushing a hundred pounds in twenties into the collecting tin. How she missed the camaraderie, Eden thought.

'There you go.' The barman plonked down a plastic bag filled with ice. Eden flinched as she pressed it on her swollen fingers.

'Thank you,' she said. She held her right hand out. 'I'm Eden.'

He briefly pressed her fingers. 'Gabor.'

'You're a long way from home, Gabor. Where are you from? Poland?'

'Hungary,' he said. 'You know it?'

'I do, actually. Budapest is beautiful.'

He beamed at her. 'That is my home city.'

'You worked here long?'

'About seven months. You a guest in the hotel?'

'No. I'm working for Lewis Jordan, the TV producer.'

'The flash guy?'

'That's him.'

Gabor whistled. 'Wouldn't mind being him for a day – all those pretty girls he got round him.'

'Yeah, he's popular with the chicks, alright,' Eden said. 'Was he in the bar last night?'

'No,' Gabor said, thinking for a moment, 'but maybe he order room service.' He glanced at her. 'You need to know?'

'Yes. I'm in trouble, Gabor. I was supposed to be looking after him and he got attacked last night.'

Gabor held up a forefinger. 'I check.' He rootled around under the bar and drew out a blue hardbacked notebook. He licked his forefinger and flicked through the pages. 'Let me see. What room is he in?'

'Room 204,' Eden said, thinking Lewis was probably being slotted into the back of the mortuary van about now.

'Two glasses of whisky. Ordered at nine forty-five and taken straight up.'

'Isn't there whisky in the mini bar?'

Gabor chuckled. 'If you call that whisky. He ordered from the bar – Laphroaig. Doubles, too.'

Eden mentally reviewed Lewis's hotel room. Were there two glasses left in the room? She was sure there weren't. So where were they?

'What happens to the glasses?' she asked.

Gabor shrugged. 'Guests leave them in their rooms for chambermaid to collect. Or they put the tray back outside the door. If they don't want to be disturbed, eh.' He gave a wink.

'Were you working in the bar last night?'

'Yes. From six.'

'Was it busy?'

'No,' Gabor said. 'Friday and Saturday are busy times, but not Tuesdays.' He grabbed a glass and polished it on a cloth. 'There was a man who waited here for a long time. I think his date didn't come. He kept ringing her on his phone, was saying "I'm waiting for you!" but she never turned up.'

'How long did he wait?'

Gabor puffed out his cheeks. 'Two hours. Long time. Must've been a special lady, hey?'

'And then he went to his hotel room?'

'He wasn't a guest. I asked him for his room number but he said he wasn't staying here, just meeting someone.' Gabor chuckled. 'He came here straight from work, I think. He had a briefcase with him. Not so romantic, eh?'

'When did he leave?'

'I had my break at nine thirty. When I come back on duty, he was gone.'

Eden sipped the coffee. It was hot and rich. 'You make a good cup of coffee, Gabor.' She leaned her elbows on the bar and smiled at him. 'Tell me about Budapest.'

Twenty minutes later, her hand was numb and frozen and the swelling was receding. She left the bar and found Lewis's team huddled together in the hotel lounge. Xanthe had her arm round Jocasta, who was weeping loudly. When she caught sight of Eden, Xanthe whispered something to Jocasta, untangled herself, and ran towards her, her face white with shock.

'Eden, the police have told us all to wait here. They said Lewis is dead.' Her mouth worked. 'What's going on?'

'Lewis was attacked last night,' Eden said. 'When did you last see him?'

'You think I did it!'

'I'm just trying to piece together what happened.'

'Won't the police do that?'

'Humour me.'

Xanthe trembled as she said, 'Me and Jocasta and the technical crew came back to the hotel together after filming. We were all going out for dinner. Lewis had already gone off somewhere on his own.'

'Where did he go?'

'He didn't tell me.'

'And when did you get back last night?'

Xanthe puffed out her cheeks as she thought. 'I don't know. Pretty late for a school night.'

Eden turned as someone called her name. The hotel manager bustled towards her, his cheeks two deep purple blotches. When he shook her hand, her palm came away wet.

'Can you come into my office for a moment?' he said, and led her away.

As she took the seat offered to her, she prayed he hadn't rumbled her chambermaid impersonation and free hand with the mini bar miniatures.

'The police say Lewis Jordan was killed,' the hotel manager said. 'They think it was a robbery gone wrong.'

'Oh?'

The hotel manager pressed his fingertips together and visibly brought himself under control. 'Can I speak to you in confidence?'

'Of course.'

'I'm very worried that one of the staff might be involved.'

Eden waited for him to continue. A pulse twitched in his temple and a sheen of sweat oiled his lip.

'Over the past few months, we've had a number of thefts from the hotel.'

'What kind of thefts?'

'Items taken from guests' rooms. Mostly petty pilfering – a pair of shoes, a DVD, a bottle of perfume.'

'Anything of value? Jewellery, money, credit cards?'

He shook his head. 'Nothing like that. Because it was such minor stuff, I didn't tell the police. I thought it was more damaging to the hotel to make it public, so I compensated the guests and tried to tighten up security.'

'Anything go missing from the hotel itself?'

'The usual – sheets, towels, toiletries. There's always some, in every hotel. We've had slightly more taken than I'd expect, but not enough to worry. It was the thefts from the guests that bothered me.'

'Who do you suspect?'

'Anyone who has access to the rooms – the chambermaids, cleaners, the porter. But most of our staff have been here for years and this problem is quite recent.' He paused. 'I can't imagine anyone doing this. We like to look after our staff here.'

Eden sized him up. 'You need to tell the police,' she said. 'If they think Lewis disturbed someone stealing from him, they need to know there have been other thefts.'

'The publicity could sink the hotel.'

'And a murder won't?' she said.

Remembering the letter she'd found shoved under Lewis's door, she asked, 'What do you do with guests' mail?'

'How do you mean?'

'Do you keep it in a pigeonhole and hand it over when they come in or out, or is it taken to their rooms?'

'It should go straight up to their rooms,' the hotel manager said.

'And if they're not in?'

'We slip it under the door.'

'And what time is your post normally delivered?'

'Early. About seven o'clock,' he said.

Allowing a few minutes for the post to be sorted and summoning someone to deliver it to guests, the letter was slid under his door about seven-thirty, while Lewis lay dead in his room.

She worked her thumb under the envelope's flap and pulled out a single sheet:

You can't escape. I know where and what you are

It had a handwritten white label on it and was addressed to Lewis at the hotel. It was postmarked in Gloucestershire the day before. Was it a bluff from the murderer, sending a letter that they knew would get there after the victim was already dead? Or was Lewis's death a robbery gone wrong, after all?

There was no one waiting in Simon Hughes' offices. Gwen was in her usual place, battering away at the keyboard of a PC, her raspberry-ripple hair bouncing with the effort.

'You seemed to know Lewis Jordan when I was here on Monday,' Eden said.

Gwen harrumphed. 'Oh I know him all right. Lewis Jordan indeed!'

'What do you mean?'

Gwen stopped clattering. 'Lewis Jordan is his TV name.' Scorn sharpened her words. 'He's not Lewis Jordan. He'll always be Lee Jones.'

'Lee Jones? How did you know him?'

'Let's just say he was a regular here. Should have given him frequent flyer points.' She jabbed her finger at a chair against the wall. 'We could put a plaque on that chair, the number of times he was there, skinny little kid, a bail sheet in his hand.'

'Bail sheet?'

Gwen's eyes met hers. 'You know the type – little sod who makes everyone's life a misery. Lee Jones was the sort of kid who should have been drowned at birth.'

'Interesting. Someone killed him last night.'

Gwen's fingers stole to a crucifix hanging at her throat. 'What?'

'The police think it might be a robbery gone wrong. But you say he was in trouble a lot when he was young …'

Gwen swivelled her eyes back to her computer screen. 'I didn't say anything of the sort.'

'What sort of trouble was he in, when he was Lee Jones?'

Gwen didn't answer. She frowned at her keyboard, where her hands lay motionless.

Eden waited in silence until Simon Hughes came to collect her. She declined a cup of coffee and settled herself opposite him. Rain squalled against the window and darkened the room enough to need lights even though it was midday.

'Sorry to barge in on you like this,' Eden began, 'but I thought I should tell you that Lewis Jordan was found dead this morning. Looks like foul play, I'm afraid.'

'My God,' Simon said. 'What happened?'

'The police think he might have disturbed a burglar, but …'

'You're not sure.'

She shook her head. 'I want to investigate it myself. There's the poison pen letters for a start. I've been paid a week in advance, and I'd like to see what I can turn up in that time.'

'Most people would just take that money and leave it,' Simon said.

'I'm not most people.' She waited for a beat then asked, 'Did Lewis make a will?'

'Not with us,' Simon said. 'He might have seen a solicitor in London, of course. But as far as I'm aware, he didn't make one. It's not unusual – some people are superstitious about making a will. Think it's tempting fate.'

'So assuming he died intestate, who would inherit?'

'His next of kin.' Simon bounced his fingers against his lips. 'As far as I know, that would be his mother. I believe she's still alive.'

'What's her name?'

'Tracey Jones. I haven't heard from her for a long time, but she used to live on Princess Elizabeth Way.'

'Last time I was here, I asked why Lewis chose your firm instead of going to one in London,' Eden began. 'You said he had a previous connection.'

Simon leaned back in his chair. 'I think it was a case of better the devil you know. He'd used our firm in the past.'

'When he was Lee Jones?'

Simon looked startled. 'He told you that? I thought he wanted to hide his previous incarnation.'

Eden didn't correct him. 'So he simply used the solicitors he'd always gone to?'

'Basically.'

'Tell me about Lee Jones.'

'It's the old story, I'm afraid. No dad around, his mother an alcoholic, unable to cope with him. In and out of foster homes all his life. Shoplifting, petty theft, criminal damage.' Simon paused to think. 'He seemed to go straight for a while, had a good foster home, then he went off the rails. His foster mother threw him out and he ended up in juvenile detention.'

'What happened?'

'A burglary, I think. The usual pattern, alas. Start small and get bigger. Shoplifting turns to housebreaking, and next thing you know they've been in prison longer than they've been out. But Lewis … Lee … was different. When he was in juvenile detention he learned film-making and realised he had a knack for it. And, importantly, he loved it. So, he cleaned himself up, got some qualifications and went to college to study film. Then he reinvented himself as Lewis Jordan and forged a highly successful career as a documentary film maker.' Simon shrugged at the twisting path that life can take.

'Until someone bludgeoned him to death in a hotel room,' Eden added.

CHAPTER
ELEVEN

Wednesday, 28 October 2015

12:27 hours

Where was the bloody film crew? They'd told everyone to be ready to start filming at eight, and now it was after twelve and not a peep from them. Maybe they'd decided to shelve the archaeology altogether and go all out for druids and the search for the Holy Grail, Aidan thought, viciously stabbing an eraser with his paperknife.

He went to his office door and called to Trev, 'Get everyone in here, will you, Trev?'

Trev, Mandy and Andy trooped into his office. They all looked grey and exhausted: the stress of the evening before had left its mark. Aidan shut the door behind them.

'Lisa's outside having a ciggy,' Mandy said.

'This doesn't concern her,' Aidan said. He pulled his chair round from behind the desk so the four of them were in a circle. 'You all know we've got a problem. Last night, someone took the artefact we recovered with the skeleton.'

'The Holy Blood,' Trev said.

'We don't know that it is the Holy Blood,' Aidan said. 'But yes, that.' He took a deep breath and tried to keep his voice steady. It wasn't easy: a scream of 'What the fucking hell is going on' was threatening to erupt. 'If any of you took it as a joke, or to piss off Jordan, or because you hate me, that's fine. But please, return it now and nothing will be said.'

Three people stared at the floor.

'It's been a crazy couple of days with the film people here,' he made an attempt at levity, 'with their bonkers names and obsession with the Holy Grail, so I understand if you forgot what you were doing and took the artefact. And I promise you, there'll be no repercussions if you put it back now.'

'I didn't take it, Aidan,' Mandy said, tears in her eyes.

'Nor me,' said Trev, 'though I'd like to strangle whoever did.'

Andy shook his head. 'Not me.'

'It's more likely it was one of the film crew,' Mandy said, folding her arms tight across her chest. 'They had no respect for archaeology.'

Despite the tension pounding in his skull, Aidan smiled at this. 'Alright,' he said. 'But think back and see what you can remember from when we were packing up last night.'

Chaos is what it had been, with equipment everywhere and people tripping over cables, and blokes loading boxes into a van, and that mardy Jocasta glaring at everyone and Xanthe getting in the way and blathering about Twitter. Why the hell didn't he lock up himself last night? Why the hell did he leave Mandy and Trev to see everything was packed away and the Holy Blood stashed in the safe? Because of sodding Lisa that's why. Insisting they go out for dinner, and he was so embarrassed he'd given in.

Months it had taken to get the funding for the research into the skeleton and the artefact. Months of negotiating with the film company, agreeing a timescale, arguing about professional fees and access to the results. And finally he'd brought it all off and what happens? Someone steals the fucking Holy Blood. And now he was going to have to call the police and report it, and the whole world would know he was an incompetent twat.

He groaned aloud. This was no good. His head was banging and every muscle in his body ached as if he had the flu. He unhooked his jacket from its coat hanger and slipped it on. Despite Lewis's comments about looking the part, he'd elected to wear a dark blue suit for today's filming. Stuff Lewis. He had Trev with his horrid jumpers and hair sprouting every which way, and Mandy with her brightly coloured plaits and intensity, that should be enough beardy-weirdyness for any documentary.

'I'm going out for a moment,' Aidan said.

'What if they turn up while you're out?' Mandy asked.

'Tough.'

He clipped down the street, glad to be out of the stifling atmosphere of the Unit. Andy, Mandy and Trev were hunched and afraid; he'd barely spoken to Lisa since she'd wafted in on the dot of eight o'clock, fully made up and ready to be filmed, not wanting a rehash of the previous evening's spat. Over the past few hours she'd got progressively crankier, asking every few minutes if the TV crew had arrived until he thought he'd strangle her if she asked again.

At the corner of the street, he slowed his pace and on impulse went up to the Catholic church. A moment of hesitation, then habit propelled him inside. The smell of incense and dust, familiar in memory, cast him back to his childhood. A prickly collar and a jacket with too-long sleeves. 'You'll grow into it,' his mother had always said.

His fingers dipped into the holy water stoop before he registered what he was doing. He crossed himself, went inside, and genuflected self-consciously. The church was empty apart from a woman praying in a side chapel. He walked to the front, slipped into a pew, and gazed up at the crucified Christ above the altar.

'I'm in a horrible mess,' he muttered, half to himself. 'I've lost the Blood. I've lost your blood, though we don't know for certain it is yours yet. But it's gone, and if it doesn't turn up, it's going to be the most embarrassing moment of my career. If I have a career after this. The man who lost the Holy Blood.' His head sank onto his clasped hands. 'Help,' he said. 'Help me.'

A woman trying to defy middle age by dyeing her hair in purple stripes walked past and gave him a funny look.

'Sorry,' Aidan said, mortified. 'Just talking to … you know.' He twitched his head towards the statue of Christ.

The woman didn't answer, but hurried past him into the side chapel. The woman there greeted her, and they bent their heads together, whispering. A few words carried across the nave, 'It's done now, Rose,' and the other woman sobbing.

What am I doing here, spilling out my troubles to a bit of painted wood and plaster, Aidan thought. He kept his pleas silent from then on. The words came unbidden into his mind. Hail Mary, full of grace. Our Father, who art in heaven. I believe. He mentally recited a decade of the rosary, the cadences as familiar as the scent of home; the words as soft and comforting as a childhood blanket.

After a while, a cramp in his leg made him get up. His mind was calmer, tranquilised by ritual and the familiar patterns of words. Even his headache had receded. Maybe, just maybe, a miracle had occurred, and the Holy Blood would be back in the safe when he got back to work.

It wasn't, but Eden was waiting for him, prowling round his office with the force of a captured wildcat.

'Where've you been?' she demanded, shutting the door firmly and leaning against it.

'I went to clear my head,' he said, not wanting to admit he'd been praying in church. 'Is the film crew back? No one's done a scrap of work this morning, they've all been waiting for their moment of fame. Trev's overdosed on coffee just to stay awake.'

When she didn't reply, he said, 'Eden? What is it?'

'When did you last see Lewis Jordan?'

'Yesterday, at the filming. You know that, you were there.'

'Did you see him later that evening? Think very carefully before you answer.'

'What the hell's the matter with you?' Had she found out that he and Lisa left together? 'Lewis left about six, same time as you. What's this about?'

'So you didn't see him later? Perhaps you went to his hotel room?'

'Why should I? He wasn't even filming me for the documentary.'

Eden held his gaze. 'I found Lewis Jordan dead in his hotel room this morning. It looks like murder.'

'Jesus! What happened?'

'I don't know yet. But his corpse was not a pretty sight.'

He staggered as a thought struck him. 'Do you think I killed him?'

His voice had risen. Eden shushed him and glanced at the door. They both knew Trev and Mandy had big ears.

'I'm only asking what the police will ask you when they put together a timeline of his last hours,' she hissed. 'But I'm asking you particularly because when I found Lewis, I also found this.'

She took an origami swan out of her pocket and tossed it onto his desk.

Aidan picked up the swan and unfolded it. A flyer for a student production of *Measure for Measure*. Shit. 'Where was it?'

'Beside the bed,' Eden said. 'Is it yours?'

He swallowed, a fist closing round his heart. 'No.'

Her eyes bored into his. 'It's got the same nick in the beak that you did in the swan you made for me.'

A horrible feeling of dread swept over him and sweat prickled between his shoulder blades.

'I didn't see Lewis Jordan last night,' he said.

'And you didn't make this swan?'

His breath caught in his throat. 'No.'

CHAPTER
TWELVE

Wednesday, 28 October 2015

14:15 hours

The blocks of flats that lined Princess Elizabeth Way harked back to the golden age of the British Empire: Ceylon House, Rhodesia House, Canada House. The irony wasn't lost on Eden that the flats were built at exactly the time the last vestiges of the British Empire were claiming independence.

Tracey Jones – Lewis's mother – lived in Malaya House, a red-brick building with cream-coloured stone balconies laden with mini greenhouses, old mattresses and bicycles. It overlooked a swathe of soggy grass and two bedraggled weeping willows.

Her flat was on the third floor, up a flight of stone steps, no sign of a lift. From the state of Tracey's face, the police had already been round to break the news of Lewis Jordan's death. Her eyes were puffed up, so swollen her eyelashes stuck out like pins. Her nose was scrubbed raw, and her skin had the skimmed milk bluey hue of deep shock.

'Mrs Jones?' Eden enquired, softly.

'Miss.'

'Miss Jones. I'm Eden Grey. I was the one who found Lewis this morning. I wanted to come and see that you were OK.'

Tracey stepped aside and let her into a narrow hall with a busy carpet. She was ushered into a stifling living room with a gas fire burning at full pelt. There was a cream leather settee and chair, a widescreen TV, and another headachey carpet. A single picture was displayed in the room: a large photograph of Lewis in a dinner jacket and bow tie, brandishing an award of some sort.

Tracey Jones was a dumpy woman of about sixty with a mono-boob, a big square face and coarse blonde hair. She wore a blue jersey dress, thick purple tights and leopard-print slippers. Evidently Lewis inherited his flamboyance from her. She dropped into the armchair and waved at Eden to take the settee. A half empty glass of clear liquid stood on the floor beside her chair.

'I'm so sorry about Lewis,' Eden began. 'It must be an awful shock for you.'

Tracey reached for the glass and took a slug. 'Lee. He was always Lee to me.' Tears poured down her cheeks and she sobbed into her hands. 'He was my little boy.'

Eden went over to her and rubbed her back while she wept. 'I know you don't feel like talking right now, but Lee hired me to help him and I want to find out who did this.'

'The police said they were robbing him. Little bastards.'

'That's one line of enquiry,' Eden said. 'I'm not so sure.'

Tracey's head shot up. 'You think someone did it deliberately?'

'Maybe. Can you think of anyone who ...'

'No! No one! He was a beautiful boy. No one would ever want to hurt him.'

'OK.' Eden waited while Tracey cried, then when it seemed the fit was over, she gently offered to make her a cup of tea and went down the hallway to the kitchen.

She snooped while the kettle boiled. Half a pint of milk, a hunk of cheese and half a tin of baked beans in the fridge. A freezer stuffed with microwave meals. The sink was full of washing up: it seemed Tracey saved it all up throughout the day and did it in one go. A pot plant that had once been a geranium squatted on the windowsill, its soil crammed with cigarette butts. A stash of empty vodka bottles under the sink. An ordinary, depressing life.

Hunting for something sweet to combat shock, Eden found the biscuit tin was stuffed with bills. She flicked through them. About a dozen credit- and store-card statements, all of them with several thousand pounds outstanding, many with 'Final demand' stamped across the top. There were statements from pay-day loan companies, too, showing interest that had rapidly built to an astronomical amount. A quick calculation and she almost dropped the biscuit tin: Tracey owed almost fifty thousand pounds. She stuffed the bills back in the tin and carried two mugs of tea into the living room.

'When did you last see Lee?' she asked.

'Yesterday. He come round about six.' The thick Gloucestershire accent rolled the words into soft pellets.

'How was he?'

'Excited. He was always excited, he was that kind of boy,' Tracey said. 'But yesterday he was mega excited.'

'About the documentary?'

'Nah, something else. He wouldn't tell me what it was, he just kept on saying, "Ma, we're nearly there".'

'Nearly where?'

'I dunno. He liked to keep secrets, my Lee. Liked to surprise me.'

'What time did he leave?'

'Let me think. About seven. Maybe half past.'

Eden sipped her tea. The milk was on the turn and left a rancid taste in her mouth. She put the cup down. 'Tell me about Lee.'

'I was nineteen when I had him,' Tracey said. She dug a photo album out of a cupboard and showed Eden a picture of a fat brown baby with a wide smile. Just a few days old and already

Lewis's ready charm was discernible. 'Look at him. Lovely, isn't he? Even when he was a runny-eyed kid he was lovely.'

'What was wrong with his eyes?'

'Conjunctivitis. Soon as he got rid of one bout he had another. You won't believe how many pillow cases and towels I had to wash.'

'Was Lee close to his dad?'

'His dad never hung around long enough to see him.' She sighed. 'He knew I was pregnant, then soon as I started to show and talked about settling down together, he was off. Never heard from him again.'

'Must've been hard, bringing Lee up on your own.'

'It was. And lonely, y'know? That's when I started drinking. Something to do in the evening when the baby was asleep, and it helped me get off to sleep, too. Pretty soon I needed more and more to get me off to sleep, and when I was awake, I forgot I had a kid. He was off with his friends, out on his bike getting up to mischief, like boys do.'

'What happened?'

Tracey shrugged. 'The Social come round, said there were concerns, and they took him away.' Her voice cracked on the last word and her shoulders heaved. When she'd recovered herself, she continued, 'He came back here for a while, then I'd make a mess of it and they'd take him away again. Poor little kid, never knew where he was going to be, who he was going to be with.'

Eden remembered what Simon Hughes had told her. 'Didn't he stay with one family for a longer time, though?'

'Her! Yes, she looked after him for about a year. Bloody Godbotherer she was, always dragging him off to church and telling him to ask forgiveness or some nonsense.' Tracey blew her nose into a tissue. 'I'll say one thing for her, though, she made sure Lee saw me regular. Said it was important for him to know his family, so she organised for us to see each other. At the Social office, mostly – like you can talk to your boy in an office with all those people sitting round and listening and making notes.'

'Sounds grim,' Eden said, swamped by a wave of sympathy.

Tracey nodded. 'I used to save up things to tell him – things I'd done, what the neighbours were up to, what I'd been watching on TV y'know, so there was always something to say. And you know he never rolled his eyes or acted moody, like most teenagers would.' Tracey gave her a fierce look. 'I loved him for that, will never, never forget it to the end of my days.'

'He loved you,' Eden said.

'He did. When things went wrong for him and they sent him to Borstal, he wrote to me every week. Ma, he says, I'm making a film and it's brilliant. And then he went off to college and made more films and next thing my boy's in TV. He's somebody. But he never forgot his Ma. Come home when he could, rang me every other week. "Don't you worry about a thing, Ma," he said. "Everything's going to be fine. I'll see you right". That's what he said yesterday when he came round. "I'll see you right".'

'What did he mean by it?' Eden asked.

Tracey shrugged. 'He'd helped me out with money before. I thought he meant that.'

'He was going to give you some money?'

'He didn't say exactly, but that's what I thought.'

Eden hesitated before she asked the next question. 'Did Lee tell you whether he'd made a will?'

'A will? He didn't need a will. He was too young.' Tracey wiped her eyes. 'Besides, I'm all he's got. I knew it would come to me.'

Tracey gave her the name of Lewis's last foster family, who he'd lived with for a year. She couldn't remember the address, but thought it was somewhere in Warden Hill. Eden dashed home to run a check online, and turned up two potential addresses. Picking up the phone, she dialled the first number.

'Hello, is that Mrs Taylor? Can I just check that you're the Mrs Taylor who used to be a foster parent? No? I'm sorry, I've got the wrong number.'

No one answered the second number, but Eden was keen to get as much information as she could before Inspector Ritter twigged what she was up to and closed down her investigation. She scooped up her Cheltenham street map and headed out to Warden Hill.

The area had a backdrop of hills cloaked in cloud. The streets themselves seemed flat, hunkered in the valley; lines of low-lying houses and regimented bungalows. Rose Taylor lived in a street perpendicular to a row of shops: a small supermarket, a café, and a shop that sold disability aids. Her house was a 1950s bow-fronted semi of award-winning ugliness, iced with beige pebble-dash and with the front garden paved over with pink and cream cracked paving slabs piped with weeds.

Eden went up to the door and rang the bell. There was a handwritten sign waterproofed with Sellotape next to the bell: No cold callers, no sales persons, no junk mail, and no flyers, please.

She rang the bell again, listening for movement inside the house. Nothing. There was a side gate into a back garden, a peeling wooden affair the height of her head. It was bolted on the other side, too far down for her to reach over. As she came back up to the front door, a neighbour pulled into the next driveway.

'Hello!' Eden called. 'I'm looking for Mrs Taylor.' She went over and flashed her private investigator's ID.

'She might be at work,' the neighbour said.

'Do you know where she works?'

'One of the hotels in town.'

Something crashed in Eden's mind. 'Which one?'

The neighbour shrugged and hefted a shopping bag out of the boot. 'I don't know. One of the posh ones, I think.' She hauled the bag to her front door. 'Course, she might be out with her daughter.'

'Is it just her and her daughter living here? No Mr Taylor?'

'He died years ago.' The shopping was unloaded now and the neighbour turned away.

'Thanks for your help,' Eden said. She left her car where it was and went to the café to think. It was hours past lunch time and her stomach was complaining about the lack of service. She ordered a jacket potato and tuna mayonnaise and a mug of builder's tea, and spent a few minutes reviewing what she'd learned so far about Lewis Jordan.

Sweet Fanny Adams, that was what. Twenty-five years ago he'd been in trouble and had gone straight. His mother was a debt-ridden alcoholic and he seemed to be a devoted son. He hadn't made a will, but the only relative he had anyway was his mother. He was charming, full of himself and a one man sha-gathon, but none of this added up to enough to get him killed. Maybe the police were right: it was a robbery gone wrong. But when she searched Lewis's hotel room that morning, it hadn't seemed like a typical robbery. Nothing had been disturbed, no drawers hanging open, no furniture turned over. Perhaps they'd killed Lewis before they'd started and simply fled, but instinct told her there was more to Lewis's death than ordinary robbery. The poison pen letters, for a start. And his burnt out eyes, for another. How had that happened? It would be a tremendous coincidence for Lewis to be the victim of two separate crimes in the same day, and she didn't trust coincidence.

She paid for her lunch and returned to Rose Taylor's home. This time, a yellow light shone through the porthole in the front door.

'Rose Taylor?' Eden said, when the door was answered by a well-built woman in her sixties. 'I'm Eden Grey, I'm a private investigator. Can I ask you some questions about Lewis Jordan?'

'Who?'

'You knew him as Lee Jones.'

'What's he done now?'

'Can I come in?'

Rose waddled as she walked, throwing out her left leg to the side, and her skirt was hitched up on her hip bones so it was higher at the back than the front. The room she showed Eden into was crammed with furniture that was too large, and too copious, for the space available. Every inch of the walls was covered with photos of children: school photos and family snaps of up to fifty children.

'Are these all the children you've fostered, Mrs Taylor?' Eden asked.

'Yes, every one of them. Even if they were only here for a week.'

'Which one is Lee Jones?'

Rose shook her head. 'Not him.'

On the settee, sitting close to the fire, was a woman in her early forties. Life had evidently not been kind to her: her face was thin and drawn, with the droops and lines of someone who's suffered from long-term depression. There was an air about her, too, of hopelessness and defeat. She barely looked up as Eden came in and said hello. Eden took a seat in an armchair covered with tapestry fabric.

'Can I ask you where you work, Mrs Taylor?'

'I'm housekeeper at a hotel.'

'Which hotel? The Imperial?'

Rose blinked. 'Yes, as a matter of fact, though what it's got to do with …'

'And you fostered Lee Jones?'

'A long time ago.'

'Lee Jones, now called Lewis Jordan, was found dead this morning, in the hotel where you work,' Eden said, watching Rose carefully.

'I had heard that he'd died,' Rose said.

'When?'

'It was on the news earlier.'

'So you did know that Lee Jones was Lewis Jordan?'

Rose was flustered by this. 'Yes, they must've said on the news … or someone told me that Lee had changed his name.' She tangled her fingers in the folds of her skirt. 'I can't remember now, but I knew before.'

'Before what?'

'Before you told me.'

Eden let the silence swell, then changed tack. 'It's a bit of a coincidence, isn't it? The boy you fostered dies in the hotel where you're housekeeper?'

'I didn't kill him!'

Eden held her gaze. 'I never said he was killed,' she said. 'I told you he'd died.'

'On the news, they said he was killed.'

That might be true: she'd check when she got back home. Eden let it go for now, and pressed on. 'Were you at work on Tuesday?'

'Yes, I was on earlies. I finished at twelve-thirty.'

'Did you go back to work that day? Maybe left something behind and you went to fetch it?'

'No.'

'Why aren't you at work today?'

'I don't work Wednesdays.' Rose's voice sharpened. 'And I don't appreciate you coming here and firing questions at me.'

'It looks like murder, Mrs Taylor.' Rose took in a sharp breath. 'Were you in touch with Lee?'

'No.' The word was spat out with such vehemence Eden recoiled.

'When did you last see him?'

'Twenty-five years ago.'

'You didn't keep in touch with him? This boy you fostered for a year?'

'No, I didn't.' Rose clenched her hands together tightly in her lap.

The woman on the settee cast her an anguished look, then got up and left the room. Her footsteps went up the stairs and across the room above their heads, then there was the creak of a bed.

'Who would want to harm Lee?' Eden said.

'Any number of people,' Rose said. 'He was into all sorts of things. Drugs, probably, knowing him. And he knew some rough people. If you play with fire, you get burned.'

'You're not sorry he's dead?'

Rose hesitated, then said softly, 'That boy ruined my family.'

'What happened?'

Rose glanced up at the ceiling as if afraid the woman upstairs could hear. She dropped her voice when she said, 'Before he came here, I had two lovely children and a wonderful husband. And a year later I had a son in prison and a daughter … pregnant. At sixteen!'

'And it was Lee Jones' fault?'

'He was a bad lad before he came here, I knew that. I didn't realise he'd get my Tom involved. I thought he had more sense, but Lee worked on him, told him they'd get away with it, no one would ever know. So Tom went along and they broke into a warehouse and stole a lot of televisions. And they all got caught, but because my Tom was eighteen, he went to prison.'

'And what happened to your daughter?'

'I promised we'd stand by her. There was no question of getting rid of the baby.' Rose's shoulders slumped. 'The baby was stillborn and the doctors told her she'd never have another. She's never recovered. She's been in and out of hospital more times than I can remember.' She lifted her head. 'So no, I'm not sorry that Lee Jones is dead, God help me.'

'You had access to his hotel room.'

'I have access to all the rooms; I'm the housekeeper.'

'So you could have gone into his room.'

'And attack him? Why should I do that now? Why wait twenty-five years?'

Eden shrugged. 'You tell me.'

'I will tell you.' Rose stared her straight in the eyes. 'I didn't do it.'

She was convincing, Eden granted her that, but it smelt all wrong. That instinct she'd developed when she worked undercover was still primed and alert, and it told her there was something in all this that she was missing.

Rose's story of her daughter's stillborn baby cut her. She'd lost a baby herself, had called her Molly though she'd died before she was full term. The loss of Molly had been the beginning of the end of everything. Her husband Nick, blamed her, said the stress of her work caused the miscarriage and couldn't forgive her for refusing to stop work while she was pregnant. And then when Nick was gone, she'd thrown herself into the dangerous under-cover work with Hammond's gang. Hammond, who'd found her despite her new identity. Hammond, who'd sworn revenge.

Shuddering as she remembered the form Hammond's revenge took – a messy, long and agonising death – she darted back to her car and went home. At least she could check out Rose's story.

Her flat was as she left it, the hair in place across the door-way and the drawers left open a precise amount. No one had breached her sanctuary. She let go of the deep breath she'd been holding, drew the chain across the door, and made herself a hot chocolate. It was chilly in her flat and she hiked up the heating. Outside the day had turned dank and dusk was already creeping in at the edges, like an ink stain spreading across the sky.

She took out the staff roster and DVD she'd pinched from the Imperial Hotel that morning. A quick glance at the roster showed her Rose was telling the truth: she worked the early shift yesterday, and today was her day off. It didn't mean that she hadn't snuck back and clobbered Lewis Jordan, though. Let's face it, she had every motive for doing so.

Eden slid the DVD of the hotel's CCTV into her laptop and pressed play. The picture appeared as four squares: the entrance to the hotel, the car park, the garden at the side where they served afternoon tea in summer, and the staff entrance at the back. The picture was grey and grainy, and had a date and time stamp in the bottom right-hand corner.

Lewis left the Cultural Heritage Unit before six yesterday, and was with his mother shortly afterwards. He left her around seven or seven-thirty, according to Tracey. At seven thirty-three, Lewis Jordan stepped out of a taxi and bowled into the hotel. Eden kept watching, fast forwarding through the footage and jabbing the play button any time someone entered the hotel through either the staff or main entrances.

There was no sign of Rose so she went back to six o'clock and viewed the DVD footage again. At six-thirty, she saw herself entering the hotel and coming out again a few minutes later when it was apparent Lewis wasn't in. A few minutes later, someone she recognised entered the hotel. She paused the DVD, rewound, and ran it again. At six fifty-two, a woman entered the hotel. Now Eden knew who it was she'd heard in Lewis's hotel room the night he was murdered.

CHAPTER
THIRTEEN

Wednesday, 28 October 2015

16:15 hours

'Aidan, Mark Savage is on Skype.' Mandy's head appeared around his office door. 'They've got the isotope results.'

'I'm coming,' Aidan said. He took off his spectacles and folded them into the breast pocket of his jacket. Not that he'd got any work done that day. Since Eden had swept out of his office like a tornado with anger issues a few hours before, he'd sat and stared at his computer screen, praying it would miraculously flash an answer at him. Lewis Jordan was dead, and Eden suspected him of having a hand in his death.

He unfolded the paper swan she'd found in Lewis's hotel room, smoothed it out, and started to remake it, his hands trembling. He knew how that swan had got there, and it terrified him.

'Aidan?' Mandy again. With an effort, he pulled himself together and went into the office she shared with Trev.

Mark Savage grinned out from Mandy's computer screen. Aidan took the seat in front of the screen, Mandy beside him. Trev and Andy had already pulled up chairs and loomed behind him. What a bunch they were, he thought. Andy, Mandy and Trev, like characters in an Enid Blyton book. Three go mad in a trench. Four, he corrected himself, ruefully.

'Lisa got fed up waiting around. She's gone shopping,' Mandy said. 'Shall I phone her mobile and get her to come back?'

'No, this has nothing to do with her,' Aidan said. Let her keep away as long as possible. He couldn't bear to be around her right now.

'She did take the samples,' Trev commented. 'Shame for her to miss the results.'

'You can fill her in when she gets back. We could've taken those samples, it's just that she looked better on TV,' Aidan said, hoping the bitterness in his voice wasn't as stark to them as it sounded in his own ears. '*We* found the skeleton, remember? And *we* excavated it. As far as I'm concerned, this is Cultural Heritage business and Lisa is a paid outside contractor.'

'You two had a tiff?' Trev asked.

'Let's get on with it, shall we?' Aidan clicked on the button to unmute the sound. 'Afternoon, Mark, you guys don't hang around, do you?'

'Not when we're paid to rush a job through,' Mark said. 'Samples couriered here by a biker in leathers, and orders to turn it round soon as. I worked all night on this and it's going to cost you. You lot robbed a bank?'

'TV company funding,' Aidan said. 'They want everything yesterday so they can film it and move onto something more interesting.'

'They had a druid on standby,' Mandy added, muscling in at the side of the screen.

Mark pulled a face. 'OK, well I can't help you with anything like that, but I can give you some stark scientific findings if that's not too boring.'

'Go ahead.' Aidan opened his notebook and uncapped his fountain pen. He wrote 'Isotope analysis' across the top of the page in blue-black script.

Mark consulted his notes. 'The isotope samples show some interesting patterns. I've created a graph which I'll email over to Mandy when we finish up here, but there's evidence of malnourishment in his early years. A very poor diet, mostly grains and little protein. The isotopes indicate he was brought up in central England.'

'Which is where we excavated the skeleton,' Andy chipped in from the back row.

'And then it gets interesting,' Mark said, 'because it seems his diet took a sudden turn for the better. More protein, for a start.'

'What type?'

'Animal. And grains, from the same area, central England.'

'Approximate age?'

Mark sucked his teeth. 'Difficult to say with accuracy, but I'd guess very early childhood was impoverished, then around seven to twelve, give or take a few years, he got better fed.'

'And after that?'

'A very good diet: fish and meat protein, dairy products, and lots of grains.'

'Central England again?'

'No, he was eating a Mediterranean diet, and the isotopes point to a variety of areas in the Mediterranean and Middle East.'

'What?'

'He got about, your chap. He was moving around the Med for about twenty years or more.'

Aidan scribbled a note. 'When did he leave England?'

'The isotopes suggest he was in his late teens,' Mark said.

'Anything else?'

'Yes, something rather horrible,' Mark said. 'Hope you're not about to have your tea, but there's some evidence of periods of starvation and they correspond with particular proteins. Rodent, to be precise.' Mark paused. 'Your monk – if he was a monk – had periods of intense starvation, which he eased by eating rats.'

He paused while general exclamations of disgust echoed round the room.

'Any idea of the age of the skeleton?' Aidan asked, trying not to think of the roast beef and horseradish sandwich waiting for him in the staff fridge.

'Based on the isotopes and matching them with confirmed patterns on our database, your chap died around the mid sixteenth century.'

'That's great, Mark,' Aidan said. After some archaeological chit-chat he left Mandy to arrange to get the graphs and written report from Mark's lab, and went into the staff kitchen. He chucked the roast beef sandwich in the bin, switched on the kettle and hunted around for a clean mug.

Earl Grey tea, no milk, no sugar. Just as he was savouring the fragrant scent, Trev bustled in and shut the door behind him.

'What's with you and sticky-knickers?' he said.

'Who?'

'Lisa. What's going on?'

'I know her from university,' Aidan said.

'And you two got jiggy?' Trev made a skiing-thrusting action.

'Trev!' He took a sip of his tea and hoped he didn't look as embarrassed as he felt. 'We dated at uni. And now she's trying to make trouble between me and Eden.'

'Eden could take her, no problem. Let me know when the fight starts, I'll sell tickets.'

'Lisa doesn't do outright hostility; she prefers the insidious route to get what she wants.'

'But if you're not interested in her, then she's got nothing on you,' Trev said. 'You're not interested, are you?'

Aidan ran his hand through his hair. 'Of course not.'

'Then tell her to piss off. You've got a great girl there in Eden. Keeps on tripping over dead 'uns for us to investigate. Don't mess that up.'

Despite everything, Aidan smiled at Trev's priorities. 'Thanks, Trev.'

'One broken heart round here is more than enough.'

'What are you talking about?'

'Mandy. In love.' Trev rolled his eyes.

'With me?' Aidan was horrified.

'No, you sad bastard. Some bloke she was seeing. Dumped her, poor cow.' Trev shook his head. 'She's pretty cut up about it.'

'Hell, I never realised.'

'Well, you're not exactly good with women, are you?' Trev said. 'I've told her to get out there and find a new bloke.' He paused and an evangelical light came into his eyes. 'Hey! Why don't we fix her up with Mark Savage?'

'Or we could just mind our own business.' That was the last thing he needed: Mandy mooning about in love with the guy who ran their lab tests, then snarky emails and huffing on both sides when it all went pear-shaped.

The whole team was disintegrating before his eyes. Stolen artefacts, dead TV producers, women with biological clocks going nuclear, and he was supposed to be in control of it all. He puffed out his breath and longed for a moment to be a newbie archaeologist again, in a trench, digging up history. Not juggling spreadsheets and performance appraisals and scrounging for funding every five minutes.

He realised Trev was looking at him expectantly, so he said, 'Right, shall we get the gang together and see where we're up to with this skeleton?' He had something else to tell them, too. It couldn't wait any longer.

'Cake run first?' Trev said.

Aidan dug his wallet out of his back pocket and pulled out a twenty pound note. 'Go to Huffkins, and bring back the change.'

The team settled round the meeting room table. Mandy had downloaded Mark's isotope graphs and printed them out, and doled out a copy each. The cakes perched in the middle of the table.

'Bagsy the custard doughnut,' Mandy said, eyeing the box.

Aidan looked around the table. He'd have to tell them about Lewis. While Trev was on the cake run, he'd tried calling the TV company to find out what was happening, but they were as shocked and disorientated as he was and could only advise him to stand by for further instructions.

He cleared his throat to call for quiet. 'OK, I've got some bad news, everyone.' He took a deep breath and plunged in. 'Lewis Jordan was found dead this morning.'

'Dead?' Trev echoed. 'How?'

That was the question. 'They don't know right now, but suspect it might be foul play.'

A shocked silence filled the room, then everyone spoke at once, voicing disbelief and horror. Finally, Mandy raised the fear that had dogged him all afternoon. 'Is it connected to the Holy Blood being stolen?'

'I don't know,' he said, frankly.

'But it can't be a coincidence, can it?'

He shrugged. 'I don't know what to think right now.' That at least was true; his mind was a whirlwind of dread and suspicion. 'I was hoping the artefact would turn up again, but as it hasn't …' he paused to look at them each in turn.

'You thought it was one of us?' Her eyes were hurt and accusing.

'No, maybe, look I didn't know what to think,' he said, 'but I'm going to have to call the police.' A deep misery filled his soul. 'Even if it's not connected to Lewis's death, it'll cause a lot of adverse publicity for us. And for me personally.' He'd probably lose his job. Allowing a priceless artefact to be stolen from right under his nose. They'd never get funding in the future.

The others groaned. 'That's not fair,' Mandy said. 'It wasn't your fault. I bet it was one of those weird TV girls, wanted it for perfume or something.'

'Hang on,' Trev said, leaning his meaty forearms on the table. 'Can we be clever about this?'

'Go on.'

'Until the test results come back on what we're calling the Holy Blood, we don't actually know what it was that was stolen. It might be an old perfume bottle.'

'So?'

'So what if we wait for the results to confirm what it was, then we can report it stolen. No point getting the press all excited if it's just any old bottle that's gone missing.'

'And it's not the Holy Blood, anyway,' Mandy added, 'because it was destroyed in 1538.'

'So no need for a fuss,' Trev concluded.

'And what if it is connected to Lewis Jordan's death?'

'Why not see what Eden says?' Mandy said. 'She'll know what to do.'

'I bet she's already fossicking around in the background, anyway,' Trev added, with a chuckle. 'That girl loves a bit of trouble.'

You don't know the half of it, Aidan thought, wincing at the memory of her furious eyes when she confronted him over the origami swan.

'OK, I'll speak to Eden and see what she has to say about the missing Blood,' he said, not relishing the conversation.

'Artefact,' Mandy corrected.

'And for now, I suggest we carry on with our investigations into the skeleton.' He cracked open his notebook and dragged his mind back to the task in hand. 'So, what have we got?'

Trev counted off the points on his fingers. 'Male skeleton, aged around forty, dating from the mid sixteenth century.'

'Born and died in central England,' Mandy continued, 'but seems to have travelled in the Mediterranean and Middle East.'

'Used to hard labour, pronounced muscles, possibly a soldier,' Trev added.

'So how did he end up in a drainage gulley at Hailes Abbey?' Aidan asked. 'With a hole in his head?'

Lisa Greene trotted into the meeting room just as they were finishing up, a carrier bag from a boutique dress shop swinging from her arm.

'Here you all are,' she trilled. 'What are you all up to, conspiring like thieves?'

They all winced at the word 'thieves'.

'We're working,' Aidan said, staring pointedly at the shopping bags.

'Just getting a few new things for the TV cameras. It's tax deductible.'

'Good for you.' Aidan snapped his notebook shut. 'OK, team, thanks for your work. We all know what we're doing, so let's get on with it.'

He was irritated when Lisa followed him to his office.

'What's eating you?' she said, leaning against the door.

'You should go back to Oxford, Lisa,' he said. 'You won't be needed on camera.'

'What the hell are you talking about? Lewis wants to reshoot some of the footage from yesterday.'

'Lewis Jordan is dead.'

Her mouth moved silently for a moment. '*What?*'

'Very convincing, Lisa, but I know what you did last night.'

'What the fuck are you talking about?'

He shoved her aside and yanked open the office door. 'You disgust me, Lisa. Get out.'

'What the hell's the matter with you?'

He pushed his face very close to hers. He could smell cigarettes on her breath and the sweet cherry scent of her lip gloss. 'You're so desperate to have a baby, anyone will do. Even that pillock Lewis. What happened, Lisa? Get a bit rough, did it? Suddenly got the wrong sort of stiff on your hands?'

She paled, the freckles on her face glowing in stark relief. 'What do you know about it?'

He reached into his jacket pocket and drew out the origami swan. He threw it at her. 'Everything. I know everything.'

CHAPTER
FOURTEEN

Wednesday, 28 October 2015

18:02 hours

Jocasta was in the coffee lounge at the Imperial Hotel, using both thumbs to jab at a BlackBerry. Her brown ponytail was sleek, the rubber band hidden with a lock of hair wound round the shank, but when Eden called her name, she turned a face that was ravaged by tears.

'How are you doing?' Eden said gently, dropping into the seat opposite.

'Pretty devastated,' Jocasta said. 'No one knows what to do. We're just hanging around, waiting.'

'How long have you worked for Lewis?'

'About a year. It was my first proper job out of uni.'

'What was he like to work for?'

Jocasta smothered a snort. 'Infuriating, but I liked him.' A tear swelled at the corner of her eye. 'Really liked him. Pathetic, isn't it?'

'You liked him as more than your boss?'

'It was no secret how I felt about Lewis.'

'He knew how you felt?'

Jocasta gave a bitter laugh. 'He knew all right. It amused him.'

'What happened between you?' Eden asked.

Jocasta abandoned the BlackBerry. 'It was in June. We'd been working late one night at the studio, and he suggested we go for dinner, just us two. I'd been mad about him for ages, and I thought …'

She blinked a couple of times, lost in the memory. Shaking herself back into the present, she continued, 'It was a tiny Lebanese place, not the flashy restaurants where Lewis normally went. And he made me feel like I was the only person in the world.'

The Lewis charm, Eden thought. That way he had of holding your gaze when you were talking, letting you know he had your full attention. She could easily see how captivating that would be to a young woman like Jocasta, naive to the wiles of older men.

'After dinner he took me to his apartment, and in the morning he made me breakfast,' Jocasta was saying. 'I thought that meant he really liked me, but he made it clear it was a one-off.'

'But not for you?'

'I was in love. Still do love him, despite everything.'

'Everything?' Eden prompted.

Jocasta flushed to the roots of her hair and mumbled when she spoke. 'Calling me Jo-Jo.'

'A nickname?'

'Sort of.' The hurt was raw as she said, 'I kept thinking that what we had was different. I wasn't his type; he'd taken me to his apartment, not a hotel – that meant something. And I just couldn't let it go. A few months ago I got really drunk and blurted out to him how I felt, how I thought we were destined for each other, and I told him something I shouldn't.'

Eden waited for her to smother her shame enough to confess it.

In a tiny voice, Jocasta said, 'I told him the newspapers would put our names together, like Brad Pitt and Angelina Jolie. Jocasta – Jordan: Jo-Jo.'

'And he teased you about it?'

Jocasta nodded. 'He thought it was funny, but sometimes I wondered if he was just being mean, calling me Jo-Jo in front of everyone, waiting for someone to ask why.' She glanced up, her eyes bright with pain and fury. 'I thought if he calls me that again I'm going to kill him.'

She realised what she'd said with horror. 'I didn't mean … I didn't …'

Eden chose her words carefully. 'I went to speak to Lewis last night, and heard someone with him in his room. Was that you?'

'You think I killed him?'

'I need to establish where everyone was, at what time. Was it you?'

'No, I was out with the crew until nearly midnight.'

'I didn't say what time I went to his room.'

Jocasta's neck blossomed red. 'What time were you there, then?'

'About eight. Who was out with you?'

'The film and sound guys, me and Xanthe.'

'Anyone come back early? Or leave the group at any point?'

'No, I don't think so.'

'And Xanthe, how did she get on with Lewis?'

'She wasn't one of his conquests, if that's what you're getting at.' She barked a humourless laugh. 'He'd need a totally different arrangement to interest her.'

It took a moment for Eden to work out what she was saying. 'Xanthe's gay?'

'Didn't you realise?'

Some private eye I am, Eden thought, mentally kicking herself. 'Could it have been Xanthe I heard last night?'

'I said she was out with us,' Jocasta snapped.

Eden changed tack. 'Do you still have Lewis's laptop?'

'Yes, he gave it to me when we finished filming. Said he was off to see some woman.'

Eden decided to give the girl a break. 'It was his mother he went to see,' she said, gently.

'Oh.' The relief on Jocasta's face was heartbreaking: despite everything she knew about Lewis, she still yearned for him. Eden pressed home her advantage. 'Can I borrow the laptop, please?'

'Why?'

'It might have information on it that will help us find who killed him.'

'Sure.' Jocasta nodded. 'It's in my room. I'll fetch it. Just a mo.'

She hurried away, ponytail swinging like a metronome, and returned shortly with a laptop bag which she handed to Eden.

'You won't be able to get into it, though,' Jocasta said.

'Password protected?' The work of minutes to crack it.

Jocasta laughed, genuinely this time. 'Lewis couldn't ever remember passwords. He used his fingerprint. Only he can get into it.'

18:54 hours

First stop her friend Judy's house, a three-storey Victorian terraced house close to the railway station. Eden searched for a parking space and found one at the top of the road. Tucking her jacket round her, she walked back down the street to a neat house painted pale blue with cream window sashes and sills. The door was a deep midnight blue with a knocker in the shape of a dolphin, a clipped bay tree in a blue pot beside it. The overall impression of grown-up elegance was undercut somewhat by the wheelie bins clogging the tiny front yard, and the plastic dinosaurs wedged in the pot's soil.

Eden rang the bell, and not hearing a chime within, banged on the knocker. Judy answered, filling the doorway with her Amazonian physique.

'Can't get enough of me, eh?' she said, hugging Eden to her in a rib-crushing embrace.

They had met up at their usual Tuesday night Zumba class the evening before and gone to the pub for a drink afterwards, as they always did. 'To put the calories back on,' as Judy always exclaimed.

'I'm here in a partly official capacity,' Eden said.

'Ooh, goody, are you going to arrest me?' Judy said. She leaned forwards, and in a stage-whisper hissed in Eden's ear, 'I could do with the rest, to be honest. Make sure you bang me up for a good long time. Until the boys are at university would be fine.' She jutted her wrists forwards for the cuffs.

'That onesie should get you ten years at least,' Eden said, eyeing the black and white velour all-in-one panda leisure suit.

'Horrible, isn't it? My mother-in-law bought it. I'm sweating like a pig in here.'

'Thanks for the update.' Eden went into the hall, took off her jacket and hunted for space on the pegs to hang it. They groaned with coats and hats and scarves, so she slung her jacket over the newel post and followed Judy into the kitchen, poking her head into the sitting room to say hi to Marcus, Judy's husband, and her three young boys.

'Are you staying for dinner?' Judy asked.

'I didn't mean to invite myself,' Eden started.

'It's chicken bites, potato waffles and beans,' Judy said. 'Can't be bothered with grown-up food tonight. I think I'm coming down with something. I probably need a long time in bed being nursed by someone big and hunky with bulging muscles and a large …'

'I get the idea,' Eden said. 'Have you tried a cold shower?'

'Spoil sport,' Judy said, jiggling the kettle to assess how much water was in it and flicking the switch. 'Now, what do you want?'

'Firstly, a balloon,' Eden said, shifting a pile of books from a kitchen chair and sitting down.

'Is this some kinky thing I don't know about?' Judy said, hauling open a kitchen drawer and dragging out handfuls of rubber bands, pens, coupons and assorted junk. 'Long and thin or a fat one?'

'Fat one, please.'

'Red, blue or yellow?'

'Any.'

'Here, have a red one.' Judy slung over the balloon. 'What do you need it for anyway?'

Eden hefted Lewis's laptop onto the table. 'To get into this. It's got biometric security on it.'

'You're shitting me!' Judy breathed. She leaned over to see. 'You can do this?'

'Never tried, but I know the theory.' Eden opened the laptop, careful to keep her hands away from the screen. She angled it to the light until she could see the smudges clearly. 'Here goes nothing,' she said, inflating the balloon slightly and rolling it over the screen. She pressed the power switch, and when the laptop bloomed into life, she pressed the balloon's surface over the fingerprint reader. 'Fingers crossed.'

She rolled the balloon over the reader again, and the laptop screen changed colour and displayed the start-up menu.

'I'm in,' Eden said, letting go of the breath she'd been holding.

'You alright, Eden?' Judy asked. 'You look terrible.'

Eden scrubbed her hands over her face. 'It's been quite a day.'

Judy muscled into the seat next to her. 'Budge up, what we looking for?'

'Anything that will lead us to a murder.'

Judy gawked at her.

'My client was murdered last night,' Eden said. 'I found him, and I'm going to find who did it.'

She filled Judy in on the day's adventures while the laptop's hard drive whirred and clicked. When the desktop was presented to her, she selected documents and reviewed the folders. There was a lot of dross on the laptop: research notes for old TV documentaries; lists of contacts for each programme; and contracts for the sound and technical guys. There were also half-baked plans for future documentaries, including one called, 'Zombies in Cardiff: Fact or Fiction', and some outline costs for making it.

One folder was named 'Accounts'. She clicked it open and found separate sub-folders for each documentary, helpfully named by the same title as the programme. She flicked through all the spreadsheets, not really knowing what she was looking for but just hoping that some anomaly would shoot out of the page at her. Nothing.

The sub-folder called 'Tax' was more interesting. In it were PDF copies of Lewis's bank accounts: current, savings and credit cards. The credit cards were maxed out: like mother, like son, she thought, recalling the unpaid bills and astronomical pay-day loan statements stashed in Tracey's biscuit tin. Lewis paid the minimum on each card every month, and when he needed more money, he simply applied for a new credit card with a higher balance and transferred the lot across.

'Blimey!' Judy exclaimed, peering at the bank statements. 'I worry when I've got more than a hundred on my credit card.'

The savings account had under thirty quid in it, but the current account had more going on. A regular going-in and coming-out of salary, utility bills and mortgage payments. Then two weeks previously, Lewis had deposited thirty thousand pounds in cash. Immediately after, there was a bank transfer of thirty thousand pounds to T. Jones.

'That's weird,' Eden said, pointing to the transaction. 'Where would you get thirty grand in cash?'

'Are you sure it was cash?' Judy asked.

'Counter transaction – says cash on the statement.'

'Drug deal?'

Eden screwed up her face.

'Sold his car and was paid in cash?'

'Who pays for anything in cash these days? It's easier to pay by PayPal or bank transfer.'

'Obviously dodgy then?'

Eden thought of her old life, hunting down scumbags: drug dealers, gun runners, fixers, human traffickers, slavers and sex traders. 'It looks like money laundering,' she said. 'You put it in the bank, declare it on your tax return, and that money is clean.' She had a thought. 'Or bail money. You pay that in cash and get it back in cash and that makes it clean.'

'Did he use cash to pay the people he was filming? You know, bribing MPs to ask questions in parliament,' Judy asked.

That was a point. Eden dug her notebook out of her bag and made a note to ask Xanthe and Jocasta how they paid informants. But the fact remained that the money went into his account in cash, and was transferred straight out to T. Jones, his mother. So if the money was for paying informants, it didn't reach them. Had he embezzled it?

Eden thought for a moment. 'You've got a friend who works for the BBC, haven't you?'

'Natasha. You met her at my party last Christmas.'

'Would you mind ringing her up and asking her some delicate questions?'

'Proper PI stuff?' Judy's eyes gleamed. 'Do I get to wear a mac and trilby and smoke on street corners?'

'If you want to. Though you might want to change out of your fancy dress costume first.' Eden twitched an eyebrow at Judy's disgraceful onesie.

Judy grabbed the phone from its holster. 'Right, Columbo, what do you want to know?'

'Roughly how much a TV producer gets paid. Specifically, are they likely to have a spare thirty grand lying around in cash.'

'If they do, I'm jumping ship and getting myself a TV producer,' Judy said, pressing the number. She cocked her head to listen as it rang. 'Natasha, it's Judy. Fine, thanks. And you? Got a quick question, it's going to sound odd but it's for my PI friend, you know? Yes, that one. Question number one: how much does a TV producer earn? Ri–ight. So are they likely to have a spare thirty grand lying around? Possibly in cash?' Judy held the phone away from her ear so Eden could hear the sarcastic laughter.

While Judy chatted with Natasha, Eden browsed the remaining folders on the laptop. Nothing sprang out. Just as she was about to close it down, she checked the recycling bin. Drafts of contracts. Research notes. Documents that had gone through numerous versions and were patriotic with red and blue track changes and comments. And then an untitled document that made her heart miss a beat:

Keep looking over your shoulder, sick boy

There were several other untitled documents that had been AutoSaved. Eden opened them one by one:

**You think you're so clever but I know what you really are.
  Prepare for the end
You can't escape. I know where and what you are
One word from me and your life is over
Ready to die, sick boy?
You don't deserve to live
I'll tell the world what you are
You should be ashamed of yourself. You don't deserve to
  live**

'Bloody hell!' Eden cried. The poison pen letters Lewis had received. She flicked through the pages of her notebook. According to Lewis, the first note he received was 'You don't deserve to live', which he got on 17 September. According to the file details, it was created two days earlier, on the 15th. The second letter, 'I'll tell the world what you are', was received on the 24th of September, and created on the 23rd. All the other letters were created on 1 October.

Judy was back in the seat beside her and goggling at the letters. 'Have you ever thought of having a normal job?' she asked.

'No one would employ me,' Eden said. 'What do you make of these?'

'Most of them written on the same day, and I guess they were printed out at the same time because none of them have file names but have been AutoSaved.' Judy reached over. 'Check the document properties.'

She did a right mouse click on the first document and pulled up the properties: the number of words, the number of lines, the date and time it was AutoSaved, and the name of the person who created it.

Jocasta Simpson.

21:10 hours

Eden was settled on the settee, listening to a radio play, when her doorbell rang. Instantly she froze, yesterday's phone call from Hammond chiming in her memory. Had he sent someone to frighten her? Abduct her? Her scars, a daily visible reminder of Hammond's reaction to people who crossed him, prickled.

She peeped through the spyhole and her stomach lurched. Aidan. Tall, handsome, clever. He was raking his hand through his dark hair and glancing up and down the corridor. She considered not opening the door, but relented and let him in.

'Hello,' she said.

'Hello.' He shuffled about uneasily.

'Want a drink or anything?'

'No, thanks, I …' He shoved his hands deep into his coat pockets. It was a long, black woollen overcoat, and she knew that he often carried volumes of poetry or philosophy about with him, in case he had to wait in a queue or was stranded without something to read. 'The gang suggested I should come and see you.'

'The gang?'

'Trev and Mandy.'

'What about?'

'Look, can I sit down a minute?'

'Sure.' She stepped aside and he perched on her settee, still with his hands in his coat pockets.

'We've got a problem,' he said.

'We?'

'The Cultural Heritage Unit. You remember when we excavated the skeleton we found a bottle that looks like the Holy Blood of Hailes?'

'The thing that caused all the fuss and brought Lewis Jordan here and now he's dead? Yes, I vaguely remember that.'

He flinched at her tone. She stared right back at him.

'The thing is, last night, when everyone packed up, they found it was missing. They rang me straight away but …'

'Hang on.' Eden held up her hand. 'What do you mean "when everyone packed up"? Weren't you there?'

'Er, no, I'd left.' His eyes skittered away from her face and she was instantly on alert. 'Trev rang me and said the Blood had gone. It's been stolen.'

'What time was this?'

'Trev called about half six. Maybe a bit after.'

'And what did you do?'

'Went back to the Unit to help search for it.' Aidan stood and paced around the room. 'Look, Eden, I don't think you've quite grasped the right bit here. Someone has stolen the Holy Blood and you're questioning me like you want to know where I was all evening.'

That did it. She exploded. 'That's because I found an object in a murdered man's room that could only have come from you,' she shouted. 'And now you tell me that the Holy Blood was stolen. The only person who's likely to have stolen it is Lewis. And he was killed only hours after you discovered it was missing.' She sucked in a deep breath. 'Have you told the police?'

'About the Blood? No. I'm telling you because the gang thought you'd know what to do.'

'What I should do is make a citizen's arrest right now, on suspicion of the murder of Lewis Jordan.'

'What the hell are you talking about?'

'You've got motive and opportunity, Aidan,' she said, her face very close to his. 'And you left your calling card behind.' She was so angry she could hit him. 'Still saying you don't know anything about that paper swan?'

He looked away, the muscles in his jaw working. 'No,' he said at last. 'I have no idea how it got there.'

Liar.

CHAPTER
FIFTEEN

Hailes Abbey, October 1538

It was warm in the infirmary: there were always good fires there, even when there were no sick to be attended to. Brother John insisted that they be ready at a moment's notice to receive a poor ailing soul, and kept the fires well stoked. He also ignored the rule of silence which applied to the infirmary as much as to the rest of the Abbey, insisting that he could hardy instruct Matthew in the apothecary's art through mime show.

Brother Sebastian perched on a stool in the middle of the floor, his robes untied and his arms bared. He was the Abbey cook, a ruddy-faced, vile-tempered man who seasoned the broth with the sweat from his brow. He gritted his teeth as Brother John applied the knife.

'Ready with the bowl, Matthew?' Brother John asked, as the knife cut into the flesh on Brother Sebastian's forearm, and the blood started to flow. Matthew placed the bowl under the Brother's elbow, and watched the dark blood drop into it.

When a puddle of blood covered the bottom of the bowl, Brother John released the cord fastened around Brother Sebastian's forearm. 'That's enough,' he said, pressing a wad of linen against the wound. 'Take this, Matthew, for one moment.'

Matthew kept up the pressure on the wound while Brother John took the bowl of blood away. By the time he returned, the wound had stopped bleeding and was ready for bandaging.

'Now rest,' Brother John said, tucking Brother Sebastian up in bed. 'Sweet Matthew will bring you some herb broth to help you recover your strength.'

As Matthew turned away, Abbot Sagar entered the infirmary. Tall, broad shouldered and imposing, his very shadow made the heart quake.

'I heard voices,' the Abbot said, his black eyes switching between the brothers and Matthew.

'A prayer, Brother Abbot,' Brother John said, smoothly. Brother Sebastian nodded in the bed and held up a string of rosary beads.

Abbot Sagar snapped his attention back to Brother John. 'I have told the other brothers, and now I'm telling you, that the abhorrence known as the Holy Blood is to be taken away.'

'Taken away?' Brother John echoed. 'Where?'

'To be tested and then destroyed, I hope,' the abbot said. 'I shall be glad to see the end of it.'

'The Blood has not been displayed for some time now,' Brother John said. 'Why remove it?'

'Because that is what His Majesty wishes.'

'And you would know the contents of His Majesty's heart, being his chaplain?' Brother John said, smoothly.

Abbot Sagar flushed with anger. 'Enough! The thing is a fake, a trick to deceive poor credulous souls and I'll have no more of it.' He visibly took a breath. 'The commissioners will be here within days to take it away. That is all.'

And with that he nodded curtly and swept out of the room.

'Taking away the relic?' Matthew echoed.

'So it would seem,' Brother John said.

'But the relic … it can't go,' he said. 'All those people …'

'Hush boy, we must do as our Brother Abbot orders,' Brother John said, and led him away.

Matthew knew the power of the Blood, had seen Brother John wield it and summon miracles on many occasions since he'd come to live at the Abbey. A woman who lay dying of fever suddenly sat up in bed and shouted, 'Praise the Lord!' and the sweat dried on her brow and her heart beat regular and slow when Brother John revealed the Holy Blood to her.

And then there was a man who had been gored through the leg by a ram, the wound green and festering with putrefaction. The dead flesh fell away revealing pink, whole flesh beneath, and he got up and walked, as sound and firm as a youth once in the presence of the Blood.

Never mind the babies that refused to turn in the belly, and the sweats that threatened to extinguish a family. They all succumbed to the power of the Holy Blood.

'They can't take it away,' Matthew stammered again. 'How will the people be cured if you don't have the Blood?'

Brother John closed the door to his workroom firmly. 'Now listen, Matthew. We have work to do. You must hurry to the smith and request of him his best work yet. Describe the Holy Blood to him, how the vessel is adorned with silver and precious gems. Get him to make its twin.'

'But he's a simple village smith,' Matthew protested, 'he won't have precious gems and silver and gold.'

'He doesn't need them. The gems and metals themselves will not be tested, only the contents of the vessel, and for that, Brother Sebastian has provided an answer.' He pointed to the bowl of blood on the workbench. 'Better it impersonate the Blood than feed the sluice.'

Matthew hesitated.

'Are you afraid, Sweet Matthew?'

He nodded. 'What if Abbot Sagar finds out?'

'He won't. He will be long gone before the commissioners get here. To one of his fine residences, no doubt. He won't want to witness the surrender of our precious relic, for all he's told Cromwell he doubts it.' He held Matthew's gaze. 'Now go! Hurry!'

And Matthew fled.

The lane to Winchcombe was baked hard in the sun, jarring his legs as he ran. He paused only once on his journey, when his lungs screamed for mercy and he was forced to pull up and rest his hands on his knees until his vision cleared and he had enough wind to start running again. He hurtled up the main street, skirting wide to avoid the butcher's shop, and turned into the lane where the smell of hot iron singed the air.

'Are the dogs of hell at your back, young Lazarus?' the smith asked, dipping a glowing rod into the water trough. It gushed with steam.

'Brother John needs your help,' Matthew said, spitting out each word with a cough from burning lungs.

'Brother John?' A shadow crossed the smith's face and he left the hot metal in the trough. 'He's not hurt?'

'No.' Matthew shook his head. 'But he … we … are in trouble. Great trouble.'

'Come along inside, boy,' the smith said, and led him into the cottage. He shooed away his wife and their three children. The oldest boy was Matthew's age, and had been saved by Brother John's skill when a horse kicked his head and shattered his skull. The midwife had come with winding cloths to lay out the body, and was sent away empty handed when Brother John locked himself in a room with the boy and pressed the Holy Blood to his lips. The moment the vessel touched the boy's skin, he was restored to life.

'The commissioners are going to take the Holy Blood,' Matthew said, heaving for breath. 'We can't let them. The Blood … it's …'

The smith laid a heavy paw on his shoulder. 'Aye,' he said, grimly. 'What does Brother John need from me?'

'A vessel that resembles the Blood itself.' The idea was so shocking, Matthew whispered the words, but the smith merely nodded.

'Can you draw it for me, boy, and describe it to me in detail? I have only glimpsed it once, and then but for a second.'

Matthew took a stick and drew in the dust on the floor of the cottage. The smith crouched at his shoulder, nodding and seeking further clarification.

'It shall be done as soon as I can manage, if I have to work all day and all night,' the smith said.

'But how will you make it look like precious gold and silver and gemstones?' Matthew cried. They would be caught out in their deception, he knew it, and they would all hang.

'Leave that to me,' the smith said, his mouth set in a grim line.

Less than a week later, he smuggled the counterfeit into the Abbey. Side by side, his vessel was no match for the Holy Blood, but for those who had never seen it, the imposter was convincing enough.

'And now for the Blood,' Brother John said. The blood taken from Brother Sebastian was dried now, but he mixed it with hot water, oil, honey and saffron, and made a substance that looked akin to fresh blood, which he poured into the thick, dark glass bottle and sealed it with the metal stopper the smith had made.

'Take this and put it in the church,' Brother John said, handing it to Matthew. 'Make sure no one sees you.'

He crept down the infirmary stairs with it hidden under his robes. Past the refectory where the lay brothers were sweeping the floor and scrubbing down the long wooden tables.

He slunk past the door to the kitchens; the baker often called to him and pressed a misshapen loaf into his palm. He must be invisible today and hunched deep into his robes, dreading hearing anyone call his name.

He clutched the vessel tight with one hand, his fingers growing slick with sweat. Past the cloister, where two ancient brothers paced side by side, old bones creaking, then into the church.

The gloom swallowed him the moment he stepped inside. It was a dull day, and no sun lit the coloured panes in the windows. Though the stone arches and walls were painted with bright reds, blues and gold, today the colours were flat, and the walls pressed in upon him.

He stood motionless for a moment, ears straining for the rustle of robes on the herb-strewn floor or the murmur of prayer. Nothing. He inched forwards, casting a glance at the door to the dormitory stairs, heart banging against his ribs in case a brother came clattering down. Nothing.

Another few inches. No one in the nave of the church. He tiptoed further, towards the altar that had housed the Holy Blood. The dais was empty, had been empty for a long time, and the screen that concealed the Blood long since put away. But he remembered being a child and taken to witness the Blood, being held high in his father's arms to see as the screen was slowly lowered and a keening sigh came from the press of pilgrims before the altar.

All gone now. No travel-stained pilgrims had stood in awe and terror on this spot for years.

Matthew stole past the dais, heading towards the trunk at the side of the nave which housed old vestments. The Blood had been consigned to this fusty grave long ago. The metal fastenings on the trunk screamed when he raised the clasps. His eyes darted about the church, his heart loud in his ears, afraid the scream would bring people running. He froze, his hand on the lid of the trunk, for what seemed an eternity. When his heart slowed, he lifted the lid.

A gust of mouldy air. The stink of soiled clothes, long abandoned to mouse and moth. No place for the Blood. Matthew dug out the top layer and slid the vessel from under his robes, took a last look at it, then slid it into the trunk and piled rusting velvet over it. He lowered the lid and snapped the clasps shut, wincing at the echo in the empty church.

His knees cracked as he stood, startling him. He turned to leave the church, and walked straight into Brother Sebastian.

'What are you doing here, boy?' Brother Sebastian said, his piggy eyes searching Matthew's face.

'Brother John kindly allowed me some time to come and pray.'

'And you were praying to that trunk?'

Matthew thought fast. 'He asked me to put some wormwood in there, to ward against the moth,' he said, his words tripping over themselves.

'I see,' Brother Sebastian said. He folded his arms and waited.

'Brother?'

'You came to pray? So pray.'

Matthew swallowed, then walked slowly towards the altar. He halted a respectful distance from it, feeling Brother Sebastian's stare drilling through his spine, then slowly sank to his knees, brought his palms together, and began to pray.

By the time he returned to the infirmary, the Holy Blood was gone.

'I have it safe,' was all Brother John would say.

The commissioners came two weeks later and raided the church. The brothers assembled as they scooped up the relic with a sneer of disgust and stuffed it in a saddlebag.

When they were gone, the church seemed empty, as if all the air had been sucked out of it. Some of the older monks had tears on their cheeks as they knelt to pray and beg forgiveness. As Brother John had predicted, there was no sign of the Abbot.

CHAPTER
SIXTEEN

Thursday, 29 October 2015

08:54 hours

Eden approached the Imperial Hotel through the park. Most of the flowerbeds had been dug out and left as humped bare earth, only a sickle of bedraggled begonias remained. The grass was wet and long, still bearing the scars of the marquees from the Literature Festival a few weeks before.

On the far side of the park, smoke curled from a litter bin and Eden went over to investigate. Someone had set it on fire; fortunately, the contents were damp and it hadn't gone up taking the nearby tree and bench with it. She scooped up a handful of wet leaves and doused the fire. Poking from the top of the pile was a crushed white envelope, only partly burned. Enough remained to show it had been addressed to Lewis Jordan at the Imperial Hotel. No stamp or postmark. Eden fished it out and found a charred match caught in the fold. The envelope had been slit open and inside was a single sheet of paper.

Ready to die, sick boy?

She bundled the letter back into the remains of the envelope and put it in her bag, then excavated the contents of the bin.

Crisp packets half-full of water, fag ends, a stinking nappy, and a matchbook from the Waa-Waa Club. Two of the matches had been torn out.

Eden pocketed the matchbook and set off down the street, thinking. A letter shoved under Lewis's door, a letter half-burned in a bin. A set of letters composed on a laptop that Lewis had access to.

The Waa-Waa Club on the Promenade nursed a dejected air during the day. She went up the marble steps into a Regency building laid out in a series of small interconnecting rooms. She hunted around upstairs, trotting from room to room and getting disorientated, then descended into the basement.

'You here for breakfast?' a young man behind the bar called to her. He had a tattoo of a snake winding around his neck.

'No. Were you working on Tuesday evening?'

'Yeah. So?'

'Was it busy?'

'On a Tuesday evening? Give me a break.'

'Good.' She hitched up a bar stool and plonked herself down. On the bar was a glass bowl full of matchbooks. She took one: it was identical to the one she'd found in the bin. 'Who was in?'

'You're kidding, right?'

She flashed her ID and he screwed up his face to assist the thinking process. One more brain cell and he'd have two to rub together.

'A couple who got engaged,' Mastermind volunteered at last. 'Sat in that corner there. A mum and dad and posh kids, bit of a nightmare.' He sniffed and rubbed his nose with the back of his hand. So much for the hygiene rating. 'All had allergies. And there was a noisy group who sat upstairs and drank cocktails – the girls were alright but the blokes were wankers.'

'Wankers? How?'

He snorted. 'Tried to get free drinks by telling us they worked in TV.'

'How many of them?'

'Two girls. Wouldn't say no to either of them. Two blokes, nerdy tossers.'

'Thanks.' She jumped down from the stool then turned back with more questions. 'What time did they get here?'

'I dunno. Seven? Seven-thirty?'

'And when did they leave?'

'We had to kick them out.'

'What time was that?'

'Almost midnight. The place was dead except them. We all wanted to go home so we stacked up the chairs around them. They got the hint.'

So much for the hospitality industry. She wandered back out onto the Promenade and headed to the Imperial Hotel, where she spoke to the receptionist.

'Has any post come for Lewis Jordan?'

'Yes, something came this morning. We weren't sure what to do with it.'

'I'll take it,' Eden said.

The girl handed over the envelope, evidently relieved to get rid of the responsibility. It was another large white envelope. Again a single sheet of paper:

You think you're so clever but I know what you really are. Prepare for the end

It had been posted early the previous morning, when Lewis was already dead.

She dug her notebook out of her handbag and flicked through her notes. There had been drafts of eight letters on the laptop. Four were sent to Lewis before he arrived in Cheltenham. 'You can't escape. I know where and what you are' had been shoved under Lewis's hotel room door the morning he died. 'You think you're so clever but I know what you really are. Prepare for the end' had been delivered that morning, and 'Ready to die, sick boy?' was half-burned in a bin.

While she sat there, contemplating the letters, Detective Inspector Ritter came through the revolving door into the hotel. He did a double take when he saw her, and sauntered over, his hands in his pockets. Both he and his suit were so creased they looked as though they'd been through a mangle. Together.

'Miss Gumshoe,' he said. 'What are you doing here?'

'Everyone's got to be somewhere,' she said. A whiff of cigarette smoke came off him. That probably meant he was in a better mood, so she took the chance to ask him, 'What was the pathologist's report on Lewis Jordan?'

'Is that any business of yours?'

'He was my client.' She lifted her shoulders and made an attempt at winsome. 'Please.'

Ritter sighed. 'Cause of death was a fractured skull. Blunt instrument to the back of the head.'

'When?'

'He died around one in the morning, but he could have been attacked before then.'

'The bloody fingerprints on the carpet,' Eden said. Poor Lewis, clawing his way across the room. She shivered inside at the thought of him bleeding out, unable to summon help. 'And his eyes?'

'Ammonia in his eye drops. Probably from a standard oven cleaner.'

'Shit!' she breathed. 'And his mouth?'

Ritter's mouth quirked. 'Ah yes, his blackened mouth. Very Gothic.' He held the suspense for a moment then laughed. 'Liquorice.'

He rocked on his heels at her surprise. 'Now you can help me,' he said, reaching into his pocket and handing her a crumpled sheet of paper. 'We found this in his jacket pocket. Any idea what it's about?'

Eden scanned the paper, her heart beating faster. 'I asked him to write down anyone who might have a grievance against him, to give me a start on the poison pen letters he was getting.'

The note was handwritten on hotel notepaper. Across the top, Lewis had put, 'People who might hate me'. Underneath was a single name: Jocasta Simpson.

Xanthe and Jocasta were outside the hotel when Eden left. Jocasta was applying a lighter to a cigarette, her hands trembling. Her face was swollen and blotchy: no amount of foundation could disguise a night's heavy weeping.

'That policeman has just told us about Lewis,' Xanthe said. 'Something in his eye drops, he said.' She shuddered. 'I've never seen anything so horrible.'

'He said they think one of the chambermaids was clumsy when they cleaned his room,' Jocasta added, breathing out a long stream of white smoke.

Bollocks, Eden thought. If the police really thought ammonia in Lewis's eye drops was a clumsy accident, then they ought to be policing Trumpton, not Cheltenham. No, they suspected foul play all right, but they weren't going to tell this pair. Probably hoping they'd spread the word and get whoever doctored the drops to make a mistake and reveal themselves.

'What's going to happen about the documentary?' Eden asked.

'A new producer is coming tomorrow and we're going to try and catch up with the filming schedule,' Jocasta said. 'It won't be the same without Lewis.' She smudged her cigarette out with her boot and fled inside, her hand shielding her face.

'Poor Jocasta,' Xanthe said, her eyes following her. 'She's so cut up about Lewis.'

'She was in love with him.'

Xanthe puffed out her cheeks. 'And he was a brute, he really was.'

'She told me he teased her for feeling that way about him.'

'Taunted, more like. Called her Jo-Jo in front of everyone. Even called her Joanne sometimes.'

'Joanne? I don't understand.'

Xanthe hugged her jacket closer around her. 'Joanne is her real name. She changed it to Jocasta when she went to university. Every time Lewis called her Joanne, he was reminding her of everything she was trying to escape.'

'Which was?'

'Being ordinary. She changed her name to reinvent herself.' Xanthe shrugged. 'We all do it, don't we? Only Lewis wouldn't let her forget who she really was, under the skin.'

The rain had not improved the smell of damp in her office, nor had her absence from it for the past two days. Eden hefted the door open and quickly made a pot of coffee, letting the aromas do battle for supremacy. It was cold and dank inside, and she switched on the electric heater, adding the stink of singeing dust to the ambience. *L'eau de* brassick PI.

Logging on to her computer, she went to a credit ratings site, and ran a search on Lewis Jordan. That thirty thousand pounds came from somewhere. His credit report made interesting, though depressing, reading. He had numerous debts from store cards, credit cards and bank loans, plus an eye-watering mortgage for his London flat, and he'd defaulted on all of them at some point in the past few months. Robbing Peter to pay Paul; more going out on credit repayments than was coming in, so he juggled which ones he paid and which he left fallow for a month or two.

Over the past few months, Lewis had applied for loans of varying amounts, from fifty thousand pounds to a hundred thousand pounds, and several banks and lenders had run credit searches on him. None of them had been approved, and his credit score had diminished each time. At the bottom of the list was a credit search carried out about a month previously. It wasn't done by a bank or lender, but carried only by an identifier number, similar to the one Eden herself used as a private investigator. Time to find out who it was.

She rang the credit reference agency and summoned her credentials from when she worked in Revenue and Customs. No one had been diligent enough to cancel all of her old accesses when she died and she soon got through the initial checks using her old username and passwords.

'I can see that someone ran a check on my person of interest,' she told the operative at the other end. 'I need a reverse ID on who ran the search. Yes, I'll wait.'

She recited the identifier number and listened to a tinny version of 'The Magic Flute' until a voice came back on the line.

'It was a private investigator search,' she was told. 'Name of Bernard Mulligan, offices in Birmingham. Help you with anything else?'

'Not right now,' Eden said. 'Thanks for your help.'

She hung up, her mind churning. A month before Lewis died, a private investigator ran a credit check on him. Part of a routine financial and pattern of life analysis? But if so, who was the client, and why were they interested in Lewis? Or did Lewis himself employ Bernard Mulligan to fossick around and see who was sending the poison pen letters? He might well have run a quick financial check on his flashy client.

A quick Internet search brought up Bernard Mulligan's office address and phone number. A phone call later and Eden was heading up the M5 to Birmingham.

Mulligan's office was in the old jewellery quarter of Birmingham, a part of the city that Eden adored for its

Victorian buildings and tiny workshops. She could easily imagine how it was in its heyday: a scramble of little shops, the glare of blowtorches and the smell of hot metal. Leaving her car in the multi-storey car park, she checked her phone for directions and walked past the old cemetery with its catacombs to a tall, narrow Victorian building at the end of the street. A jigsaw of plaques beside the front door showed Mulligan shared the building with a tax accountant, a web designer and a recruitment firm.

She opened the door into a clean, plain hallway with its original Victorian tiles in black, red, green and yellow. A sign pointed her up the stairs to Mulligan's office. When she knocked, the door swung open and she faced a short, stocky man in grey slacks, white shirt and black V-necked sweater. He was in his late fifties, she guessed, and had pepper and salt hair cropped close to his head, and the biggest, droopiest bags under his eyes she'd ever seen, giving him the look of a basset hound.

'Mr Mulligan?' she said. 'I'm Eden Grey. I called earlier.'

He stepped aside for her to enter a large, high-ceilinged room painted in cream with a biscuit-coloured carpet and oatmeal soft furnishings, like a counsellor's therapy room. Discrete, pallid watercolours were placed exactly central on each wall. There was a filing cabinet, a modern desk and a chair specially fitted for lower back problems.

'You've just driven here from Cheltenham?' Bernard asked. He had a pleasant, deep voice with traces of a Geordie accent. 'You'll be needing a cup of tea.'

She waited a second for him to offer coffee, too, and when it didn't materialise, said, 'Please. White, no sugar.'

'NATO standard minus two,' Bernard said, clicking on a kettle in a small kitchen unit in the corner. 'Copy that.'

He brewed a strong cup of tea and indicated they should sit on the comfortable chairs at the far end of the room rather than at the desk. A low table placed between the chairs was piled with folders.

'Your name rang a bell so I went back through my files,' Bernard said. He picked up a pen from the top of the folders and clicked it on and off.

'I wondered how you knew I'd come from Cheltenham,' Eden said. On the phone she'd requested an interview with him and given no further details.

Bernard tapped the side of his nose. 'I am a detective,' he said, deadpan.

Eden decided she liked him. 'My turn,' she said. 'You were in the forces, then joined the police. Right?'

'Bang on.' He gave her an appraising look. 'Usual route for private eyes, but you're a different kind of fish altogether.' He slapped his hands on his knees. 'We won't go there. To business. How can I help?'

'I have a client, Lewis Jordan, who engaged me to investigate some poison pen letters. I'd only just taken the brief when he turned up dead in his hotel room. The police are playing the robbery-gone-wrong line, but it stinks of murder.'

'Irritating when the client gets bumped off before you can invoice them.'

'Lewis had huge debts, yet he paid his mother thirty grand not long before he died. When I ran a credit check I saw you'd also run a financial check on him, and I wondered why.'

Bernard slurped his tea. 'It's a funny one, Eden. A month ago someone came into my office – no prior phone call – and asked me to run background checks on a list of people. When I started digging, I twigged they were all connected to that find at Hailes Abbey earlier in the year.'

'Can I see?'

Bernard opened the top file and took out a sheet of paper. A list of names was typed on it, with brief descriptions. She looked down the list with rising shock. Aidan, Mandy, Trev, Jocasta, Xanthe, the sound and technical guys, Lewis, and Eden herself were on the list. Bernard was right: everyone connected with the skeleton found at Hailes.

Bernard tapped the files. 'So I got cracking.'

'What was your client looking for?'

'He didn't say exactly, but it seemed to me he was looking for a weak point to exploit. He wanted me to go into finances, family background, sexual past, everything. I think he wanted to find leverage somewhere.'

'For what purpose?'

Bernard shrugged. 'Never said. He was a close one alright. Tight as a gnat's chuff. But he twitched a bit when he saw Lewis Jordan's file.'

'What did you turn up on Lewis?'

'Who he really was, his brushes with our boys in blue, and his financials. You saw them: a lot of loan applications that got turned down. Looked to me like a man who was desperate for money.' Bernard drained his cup and banged it down on the table. 'Yours was interesting, too.' He held her gaze for a moment. 'I couldn't find a thing about you. It's almost as if you don't exist.'

She stared right back and didn't answer. 'Who was your client?'

'No idea.'

'You must have!'

'Not a sausage. He turned up without an appointment and paid a deposit in cash up front.'

'So how did you report back to him? You must have had a contact number.'

'He told me he'd be back in ten days' time and expected results by then. Paid handsomely, too.'

'How could you take a brief from a client who won't even give you his name?'

'Times are tough, Eden. Sometimes you do stuff that stinks a bit. And running background checks on people isn't dodgy.'

'It is if you're not sure how they're going to use the information.'

'My responsibility began and ended with the brief.' Bernard collected up the empty mugs and carried them over to the kitchen unit. 'I can't be the conscience of all my clients.'

'When did the client first approach you?'

Bernard licked his forefinger and riffled through the pages of a desk diary. '21st September. He was back here on the 1st of October for my report.'

'What did he look like?'

'Tall, gaunt looking. Early forties I'd say but not ageing well. And that air that powerful people have. You know, they expect to be obeyed.'

'Anything else?'

'Not really, he was just a suit,' Bernard said, then laughed, 'had a sweet tooth though, ate a whole bag of sweeties while he was here.'

CHAPTER
SEVENTEEN

Thursday, 29 October 2015

10:00 hours

A pall of mist veiled the ruins of Hailes Abbey. Aidan stood at the entrance, breathing deeply, a profound peace settling over him. He'd escaped for a few hours from the seething passions that smouldered in the Cultural Heritage Unit. Mandy was still mooning and lovesick; Trev was still trying to fix her up with the guy from the lab; and Lisa … well, he mostly fled the office to avoid Lisa.

Lisa had strutted in first thing that morning and announced she was going to re-examine the skeleton and scrutinise the isotope analysis, letting everyone know about the work she'd done excavating a war grave a couple of years ago.

Mandy had snapped, 'You're not my boss, Lisa, you're just a paid consultant,' when Lisa had ordered her to make her a coffee and take dictation of her observations on the skeleton. Even Trev had rolled his eyes when Lisa swanned around in surgical scrubs, ostentatiously snapping on rubber gloves and declaring that she was 'going back to the victim'.

To his immense relief, Lisa was giving him the cold shoulder after he'd bollocked her the day before. But the silent treatment was getting embarrassing: Trev and Mandy noticed that

Lisa sucked in her breath and turned away whenever Aidan addressed her. It was not good for his dignity as Director.

A job he might not have much longer, he thought, ruefully. Not with a possibly priceless artefact missing and the fact he had still not reported the theft to the police. The thought of that interview filled him with dread. It was as Eden said: the theft of the Blood meant he had a motive for confronting Lewis Jordan, and he didn't have an alibi for the night Lewis died. The irony of the situation wasn't lost on him: if he'd given in to Lisa and spent the night with her as she'd wanted, he'd have his alibi and his origami swan couldn't have turned up in Lewis's room to point the finger of suspicion at him.

He took a quick walk around the Abbey ruins, glancing into the gulley where he'd excavated the skeleton. The Abbey's water flowed off the hills behind it into several fish ponds, then ran into drainage channels to flush away the waste from the latrines. He squinted back down the line of the drainage ditch, seeing the path the water must have taken. It led back to the site of the old infirmary. Nothing remained of it now except a number of grassy lumps suggesting where it might have been.

Time to get on with it. He walked over to the visitor centre and through to the storage rooms at the back. The Abbey kept facsimiles of several documents relating to its history; the originals were housed in the National Archives. He arranged his notebook and pen on the table, fetched the records and started to scan the text. After an hour, he'd sketched out the buildings and drainage channel and calculated that the skeleton was most likely dumped in the infirmary fish pond, then heavy rains washed the remains into the drainage channel, and eventually into the open gulley where Eden found it.

Funny how remains can stay hidden for centuries and then come to light, sometimes resisting waves of archaeology and then making their presence known. Spooky, at times, how you dig and re-dig an area and find nothing, then go back and reveal treasure, almost as if the finds themselves had decided the time was right for them to make a reappearance. Aidan recalled a dig when he was an undergraduate. The area had been dug by students every summer for over twenty years, and all that came to light were shards of pottery and the occasional musket ball. Yet on the last day of the dig, when he was checking the site for abandoned tools, he felt a strong urge to go back and look at a post hole he'd excavated earlier. All that remained was a dark circle of earth marking where the post had been. He'd dug it out and knew there was nothing left to find, yet he felt compelled to go back and dig again. His trowel scraped over the circle, again and again, and suddenly chimed against something solid. He took the layer back and there it was, a golden torc. A band of twisted golden threads that had decided to reveal itself after a thousand years hiding in the soil.

And now this skeleton at Hailes had come to light, after being buried for nearly five hundred years, and he was no closer to identifying who it might be or what had got him killed.

Aidan wandered out and found the site curator. 'Have you got any records about what happened to the Abbey after the Dissolution?' he asked. 'Did any of the monks stay here?'

'It was all sold off or given away,' the curator said. 'We've got some plans from the 1570s, when the west range was developed. There might be something there.'

She fetched the records and Aidan holed himself away again. The plans were dated 1576 and showed how the Abbey had changed since it had been dissolved. Much of the stone, lead and glass had gone, and most of the Abbey buildings had been demolished. The large infirmary buildings were gone, with only a cottage remaining, to the side of a physic garden. The west wing of the Abbey, which had housed the lay brothers, was being converted into a manor house.

Attached was a planting scheme for a new garden at Coughton Hall, dated 1569. A comment scrawled on the top stated, 'Following the pattern of the physic gardens at Hailes'. He studied the plans: the garden was walled, and shaped like the temples he'd seen in Malta with a narrow entrance opening into a wide, circular, womb-like area. Details were given in tiny writing, but he made out some of the names: rosemary, lavender, Alchemilla, sage, sorrel, feverfew.

His mind fastened onto the patterns and symmetry of the garden, and the anxiety of the past few days ebbed. His mind always sought order, and he often found himself counting over and over again, seeking the middle letter in words, rearranging tiles and wallpaper patterns into regular blocks. There was comfort in counting, in regular patterns, and this planting scheme was perfect.

The symmetry soothed him, and before he knew it he was counting. One sage, ten Alchemilla, one lavender; one sage, ten Alchemilla, one lavender. Rosemary, sage, three Alchemilla and a lavender on the narrow path up to the wide circular bed. Five sets of Alchemilla, sage and lavender around the circle.

He stretched and yawned. Lunch time. He left the archives and went to his car, and listened to the car radio while he ate a sandwich. Tavener's *The Protecting Veil* filled the space, the notes soaring, the vibrato on the cello mesmerising him into an altered consciousness. It was a piece of music he loved intensely, holding his breath at the beauty and transcendence of the piece. The first time he'd heard it, he'd found tears in his eyes as his mind whispered, unbidden, 'This is the voice of God.'

It never failed to affect him the same way, no matter how many times he heard it. He leaned his head back against the headrest and let the music inhabit him, and for the second time in as many days his mind filled with old, familiar words, long unused yet undimmed. Our Father, who art in heaven. I believe in God, the Father Almighty. Hail Mary, full of grace.

Tavener ended and *Autumn* from Vivaldi's *Four Seasons* started, yet the words continued to chase each other. Suddenly the pattern he'd been studying for the past hour resolved. He had to check whether he was right. He scrunched up his sandwich wrapper, scrambled out of his car and sprinted back to the archives.

He spread the garden plans out on the table and studied them again. One sage, ten Alchemilla, one lavender. Five sets. He took up his pencil and jotted down the pattern, assigning a new identity to each plant. Now he knew he was right, and ran to find the curator.

'Can I check something on the Internet?' he asked.

'Sure, what is it?'

'What sort of plant is Alchemilla?'

She smiled. 'I love that plant, I've got tons of it in my garden. Lady's mantle.'

'Lady's mantle.' He leaned against the doorframe as ideas rushed at him. 'Come and have a look at this planting scheme. It's got a secret code embedded in it.'

She left her desk and followed him back to the archives. 'How exciting! What have you found?'

'There's a pattern to this planting,' Aidan said, breathlessly. 'Each plant stands for a prayer. As you walk around the garden, you say the prayer.' He showed her the code. 'It's the rosary,' he said. 'The garden plan is the rosary.'

'Good God, you're right,' the curator said, poring over the plans. 'But this garden was planted in 1569, based on the garden here …'

'When practising Catholicism and owning a rosary were illegal,' Aidan finished for her. He glanced back at the plans. 'You had a heretic in your midst.'

His spirits were light as he parked his old black Audi in the space outside the Cultural Heritage Unit; spirits that sank as he saw Lisa's car in his parking space. It was a dinky electric-blue Mazda MX5, a metaphor for Lisa herself: dainty, fast and uncompromising. When he went inside, she was in the common room, sipping a takeaway coffee and regaling Trev and Mandy with stories from the war graves investigation she'd done.

'Haven't you gone back to Oxford yet?' he asked, pleased to see how Mandy and Trev scrambled out of their seats and set about making themselves look busy.

'The TV company called,' Mandy said. 'A new producer is turning up tomorrow to reshoot some of the footage.'

He groaned. Not that pantomime again.

'They say they'll pay us again for the re-filming,' Mandy added. She picked at the scraggly end of her plait. 'Only problem is, they want to reshoot the bits with the Holy Blood.' She looked as though she was going to cry.

'Brilliant,' Aidan said, his heart sinking. 'Don't you worry about it, Mandy, it's not your problem. But I've got something for you. Can you get a rough idea of where the major Catholic families were in this area, during Elizabeth I's reign?'

'Sure, but why?'

'Something cropped up in the records at Hailes. If you could cover a twenty-mile radius from Hailes that would be great.'

Mandy perked up and hurried away to start the research. Aidan turned to Lisa. She was perched on a chair, legs crossed, swinging her foot. In her navy shift dress and matching navy sling-backs, and with her short, reddish pixie haircut, she looked eminently respectable, like a solicitor or a tax account-ant. The Lisa who taught him the filthiest songs he'd ever heard was centuries away.

'Find anything new on the skeleton?' Aidan asked.

'I've recorded every single wound on the bones,' she said. 'Every nick, every healed fracture. He'd been through the wars, our chap. I'm surprised he lived so long, to be honest. Quite a few of those injuries could have killed him, never mind the risk of infection.'

'What do the injuries suggest about him?'

'Apart from the fact he was almost indestructible – until someone bashed his head in – I'd say he was a soldier. A professional soldier, by the injuries. I don't think he was just called into his local lord's service as and when. I think he spent his life fighting.'

'A mercenary?'

'I'd be happy with that conclusion,' she said, crisply.

'That fits with the isotope analysis.'

'Mandy showed me the graphs. He'd been around a bit. If it weren't for the injuries, I'd say he was a commercial traveller.' She slugged the coffee. 'Or one of Walsingham's spy network.'

'Maybe we can interest the TV company in that instead of the mumbo-jumbo and the druids,' Aidan said. 'Might distract them from the fact I've inadvertently lost the Holy Blood.'

He kicked out a chair and flopped down into it, puffing out his cheeks. 'Right bloody mess this is. A documentary about the Holy Blood and the fucking thing has vanished.' He scrubbed his hands over his face. 'That's a much better story for the TV company, how we had this artefact and lost it. I'm going to look like a right idiot.'

'Have you told the police yet?'

'No. I was hoping it would turn up again.'

'Who do you think took it?' Lisa said.

'Lewis Jordan,' Aidan said, without hesitation.

Lisa drained her coffee. 'Me too. The way he looked at it, like it had magical powers.' She laughed. 'You know, I wouldn't be surprised if he believed that it would give him eternal life.'

'Didn't work for him then, did it?'

'No.' She pursed her lips. 'What would you do to get it back?'

'Not kill him, that's for sure.'

'I didn't say you did. Though you were quite happy to accuse me.' She cocked an eyebrow. 'So go on, Aidan, what's it worth to get the Holy Blood back?'

He shrugged. 'Right now it's costing me my job, my reputation, probably my whole career and the future of the Heritage Unit. So that's everyone's job on the line. Plus Eden thinks the missing Blood makes me suspect number one in Lewis's death.'

'Oh dear,' Lisa drawled, 'trouble in paradise?'

'Don't start.'

'I can make this mess go away, you know.'

'What are you talking about?'

'The reason the Blood didn't give Lewis eternal life is because ...' she reached into her bag, 'I stole it back.'

And there was the Holy Blood: the deep crimson jewel phial with its silver stopper. For a moment, Aidan couldn't breathe.

'How the hell did you get that?' he whispered.

'I told you, I stole it.'

He stared at her, his mind racing with questions.

Lisa dragged her chair closer to his. 'When you said the Blood was missing, I knew it must have been Lewis who took it. So I went to his hotel room and pretended I wanted to talk about the documentary and, well, flirted with him.'

'You slept with him to get the Blood?'

She reared back. 'You think that of me? I'm not a whore, Aidan.'

He breathed hard through his nose. 'I'm sorry. How did you get it?'

'I pretended I'd got grit under my contact lens and went into the bathroom in his hotel room to sort it out. The Blood was in his washbag so I pinched it.'

'But how did you know it was in the bathroom?'

'I'd already searched his jacket pockets while he was ringing room service for drinks.'

He ran his hands through his hair. 'You're amazing,' he said, at last.

'True. So how about you stop being such a bastard to me?'

'I'm sorry. Eden found that origami swan I made in the pub in Lewis's room and asked a lot of awkward questions about how it got there.'

Lisa ran her tongue over her teeth and regarded him for a moment. 'What did you tell her?'

'I lied.'

CHAPTER

EIGHTEEN

Hailes Abbey, September 1571

Lazarus followed Brother John out of the physic garden and towards the old workshop. When he had known it, many years before, it had adjoined the infirmary. Beyond it were the fish-ponds that supplied the Abbey's table; as a boy he'd dabbled his fingers in the cool water for the fish to nibble. As they rounded the corner, he was dismayed to see the infirmary buildings torn down, not a stone remaining, the workshop standing alone in a sea of bare earth. The fishponds were clogged with weeds, and a rank stench hung over them like a miasma.

'How is it you are still here?' he asked.

'I stayed to treat the sick, and was allowed to make my home in the workshop,' Brother John replied. 'When they took down the infirmary, they left my house standing, thank God.'

'You never thought to move away?'

'There was much to do here.' Brother John pushed open the door. 'And where would I go?'

Lazarus shrugged and ducked his head to enter the house. There was a narrow bed in one corner, a leather chest, and a fire with a pot hanging from irons beside it. The rafters were festooned with bunches of dried herbs. One wall was lined with shelves crammed with glass beakers and pottery jars.

'Every medicine for every ailment,' Brother John said, seeing Lazarus eyeing the shelves.

'As always,' Lazarus said.

Brother John poked a stool into the middle of the room with his toe. 'Sit, and let me tend those wounds, my friend.'

Lazarus shook off his cloak and jacket, and pulled his shirt over his head. His skin mapped his life's journey: every fight, every kill was marked there. Brother John came close, his breath feathering on his naked skin as he examined him.

'You have seen great danger and survived, Sweet Matthew.'

'They still call me Lazarus.'

'Earned more now than ever before, I see.'

Brother John fetched down two pottery jars and a glass phial of dark green liquid. He mixed up a potion in a beaker, topped it up with water from the pot, and pressed it into Lazarus's good hand.

'Drink. It will help this wound in your leg, though I must wash it to take out the poison.'

Lazarus gulped down the hot liquid. It looked and tasted as vile as a frog boiled in ordure. He gritted his teeth and forced it down. When he dared breathe again, he caught the merry blue eyes of Brother John on his face.

'You have indeed grown into a man of great courage,' Brother John said. 'Now let me see this wound.'

Pain knifed through him when Brother John washed the poison from his festering wound and Lazarus dug his finger stumps into the meat of his thigh to stop himself screaming. The stink of it made him ashamed. He dared not look at the mess that spewed forth, but he felt its hot trail down his skin. Brother John pressed the wound again, probing it for pockets of poison, only sitting back on his heels when he was content that the wound was fully drained and clean. He went to the chest and drew out a length of linen, packed the wound with herbs and ointment, and bandaged it tight.

'It is bad,' Brother John said, wiping his hands clean on a square of linen. 'But I pray it will resolve itself. Come back in two days and I will drain it again.'

Lazarus pulled his breeches back on. 'I do not know where I shall be in two days.'

'You'll be here,' Brother John said, and fixed him with a stare that penetrated to his soul. 'I would offer you lodging here, Sweet Matthew, but I fear that would not suit you.'

'I need to be free to make my way how I see fit,' Lazarus said. He dug some coins out of his purse and slid them onto the workbench. 'For the physic.'

As he stood to go, Brother John said, 'I'm glad to see you, Matthew. When you disappeared, I feared for you, and searched for you for a long time.'

'You had no need to do that.'

'I did. You were under my protection. I could never forgive myself if you had come to harm.'

Lazarus swallowed. 'A long time ago.'

'Indeed. But some things never change.'

Hailes Abbey, Christmas Eve 1539

A crowd had already gathered in the cloister. The usually quiet precincts were rowdy with townspeople and rank with ale-seasoned breath. There was a moment's hush then a great roar when Abbot Sagar appeared in the cloister with Dr London at his side. Dr London, in his long black robes and with a narrow lawyer's face, glared out at the rabble like an eagle contemplating a juicy rabbit. In his hand was a scrolled document. He brandished it at the crowd and spoke, not raising his voice and thus forcing the mob to shut up so they could hear him.

Matthew, shrouded with misery, made out only a skeleton of his words. *His most gracious Majesty ... in his great mercy ... end of monstrous deceits and heresies ... a noble day for us all ... live in honesty ... His Majesty's loving subjects.*

Beside him, he could feel Brother John shaking, though whether that was due to anger, or fear, or the wet snow that had started to fall, he could not tell. Across the cloister the other lay brothers huddled, shocked and afraid; like him, uncertain of where and how they would live from now on. Of the monks themselves, twenty-one remained, wide-eyed and trembling.

The document was unfurled on a table that had been dragged across the cloister flagstones, and Abbot Sagar signed it and shook sand over his signature. He swept up the document and waved it at the brothers.

'The Abbey is surrendered,' he told them. 'You are released from your vows.' As an afterthought, he called after them, 'Apart from your vow of chastity, of course.'

The drunk crowd jeered at this, swallowing up whatever it was that Abbot Sagar added in a howl of derisory filth.

At the proclamation, Matthew felt the air gust out of his body, as though he'd been kicked in the stomach. His eyes darted around the Abbey precincts, at the honey-coloured stone walls that had sheltered and nurtured him; at his home.

Abbot Sagar turned now to Dr London and handed over the seal of the Abbey. For a moment, his fingers clenched the great seal as if he were parting with a lover, then he relinquished it and stepped back to watch Dr London place the seal on the table, and smash it in two with a hammer.

Dr London held up the pieces of the Abbey's great seal, and Matthew bit back the wail that was forming in his throat. As if he sensed it, Brother John rested his hand on his shoulder. 'Be strong, Sweet Matthew, the Lord is with us,' he whispered.

Dr London shoved the broken seal and the document of surrender into a saddlebag and turned to go. His horse and that of Abbot Sagar were ready. Both men mounted and were at a canter through the gate as the auction started. As if the dogs of hell were yipping at their heels, Matthew thought, watching the billowing black gowns recede.

A beefy, ginger-haired man heaved himself up on the table, planted his feet in a manner that tolerated no nonsense, and yelled, 'Auction of the property of the place formerly known as Hailes Abbey.'

Two men hauled in the door to the chapter house, its hinges still screwed to the wood and flapping. Behind them, a team of men set about dismantling the Abbey and collecting every pot, spoon, bucket, blanket and ladder they could set hands upon.

'This fine door here,' the auctioneer shouted. 'What am I bid?'

Two men approached the clutch of monks. 'Strip,' they said.

The brothers gaped at them.

'Your robes are property of the Abbey and it's all being sold. Strip.'

Seventy-year-old Brother Hereward – crooked of back, cloudy of eye, and childish in his wits these past five years – mashed his gums at them. The men grabbed him and tore off his habit. He shielded his nakedness with his arms, his skin pale and welt with the marks of mortification he'd inflicted on it over the years. Beside him, his fellow brethren slowly disrobed and handed over their garments to be sold.

One of the dismantlers came up to Brother John. 'You too. Get them off.'

'Leave him!' Matthew jutted his chin forwards and lifted his fists, ready to fight. Brother John steadied him with his hand on his shoulder.

'It matters not,' he said, and started to remove his monk's robes.

'Brother, take this.' It was the smith, pushing through the crowd and untying the laces on his cloak. He swept it around

Brother John's shoulders. It was a rough thing, patched and torn, but Brother John stroked it down and smiled at the smith.

'Thank you, my friend.'

The snow was falling harder now, a pale wetness that rimed the pots and plates and jars and shelves that were stacked in the cloister waiting to be sold. Matthew shivered and rammed his hands up the sleeves of his coat.

They were selling the refectory benches now. Gone for a few pence and dragged away by a ruffian and his ill-featured son. Matthew saw the feet of the benches scuffing along on the cloister slabs and pain sliced through him. How tenderly the Abbey furniture had been kept: scrubbed clean and polished with beeswax. To see it treated so roughly was almost too much to bear.

And what of him? He was also property of the Abbey. A lay brother bonded to Brother John, who was no longer a brother but a mere man, and neither of them with a place to live nor a groat to call their own. How could Brother John stand there, silent and yielding, as their lives were dismantled around them?

'Brother?' Matthew said. 'What is to become of us?'

'We are free men now, Matthew.' The answer came out on a deep sigh. Freedom given in this way was unwelcome indeed.

'But what am I now, Brother?'

No answer. Brother John was staring at the auctioneer, who was now holding aloft a pair of candlesticks that had once graced the high altar. Brother John's throat bobbed, and he covered his eyes with his hands.

On the other side of the cloister was a rumpus, a pocket of noise and growled threats. Matthew looked across and his heart banged in his throat. The butcher, the man who had half killed him, was only feet away from him.

As if he sensed Matthew's gaze, the butcher looked about him, and his eyes fastened on Matthew's face. His mouth twisted into a noiseless roar, and instantly Matthew was a child again, cowering against the butcher's boot in his ribs.

He ducked behind Brother John, then slid away, weaving his escape between the legs of the crowd until he was behind the infirmary. The auctioneer's men were dragging down the beds and tossing the blankets out of the windows. He snatched up a blanket and ran, hurtling round the Abbey wall and across the fields, not stopping until he was sure there was no one in pursuit. Then he drew up and looked behind him. The Abbey squatted like a tawny toad in the valley. Pain pricked his heart again, and he turned, spread the blanket about his shoulders like a cape to shield him from the snow that swirled fast and thick about him, and trudged over the fields to meet the road to Gloucester. He would not be noticed there, in the city. He knew how to use a knife; he could slit a pig and bleed it dry; he knew how to tend plants and mix physic. He would make his own way, somehow.

CHAPTER
NINETEEN

Thursday, 29 October 2015

16:32 hours

An accident on the M5 on the way back from Birmingham trapped Eden in bumper-to-bumper traffic, unable to move an inch. The car radio was tuned to a local radio station, which had a phone-in on the badger cull. Listeners, who evidently had nothing else better to do than compete for five minutes of local fame, were ringing in and yakking about anything but the badger cull. Eden lost patience and snapped the radio off.

Drumming her fingers on the steering wheel, she reviewed the case and her meeting with Bernard Mulligan, mentally constructing a timeline and slotting in what she knew. She started with the skeleton at Hailes Abbey, which had thrown up an artefact remarkably like the Holy Blood of Hailes when it was excavated. This discovery brought Lewis and his crew running to Cheltenham, where he used to live and where he had old enemies amongst his former foster mother and her family. Not that he was short of disaffected former lovers and their husbands who might wish him ill. Stranger was the fact someone hired Bernard Mulligan to background check everyone even remotely associated with the archaeological find. The Holy Blood was stolen and Lewis Jordan found dead in his hotel room, his eyes burned out with ammonia, his mouth blackened, and with a hole bashed in the back of his skull. The poison pen letters that Lewis had been receiving for some time before he came to Cheltenham continued to arrive, some of them posted after he was dead, and drafts of those letters were on Lewis's own laptop.

Love, lust, lucre: those were the motivations for murder, and here there was plenty of each, sowing suspicion onto pretty much everyone associated with Lewis.

There were too many suspects: Jocasta and Xanthe, who could have sent the poison pen letters as they knew Lewis's movements, but both were out on the town at the time Lewis died. Lewis's foster mother, Rose Taylor, who resented him for wrecking her children's lives, and who worked at the hotel where Lewis was killed, but not on the night he died and there was no sign on her on the CCTV. Lewis's mother, Tracey, burdened with debt she had no hope of ever paying off, stood to inherit Lewis's London apartment. That would see her right for the rest of her life. And then there was the mysterious thirty grand Lewis paid into his bank account in cash and immediately transferred to Tracey. Did it come from a money lender who charged interest in blood and pain?

She sighed and thumped the steering wheel in frustration. Too many suspects, and that was without factoring in Aidan, who probably suspected it was Lewis who stole the Holy Blood, and who didn't have an alibi for the evening Lewis was killed. And then there was the origami swan in Lewis's room, which bore every sign of being made by Aidan, down to the nick in its beak. She didn't believe for a moment that Aidan had killed Lewis, but there were questions she couldn't answer right now. Did Aidan visit Lewis and challenge him about the Blood? How did that origami swan get into Lewis's room? And where was the Blood right now?

Her mobile rang, interrupting her thoughts. She answered it using the hands-free and a voice spoke straight into her ear.

'Found you at last.'

Her breath caught. Hammond.

'I've been calling your house. Your lovely, safe home, but you're not there. Where are you, I wonder? How would I find that out, hmm?'

'What do you want?' she said, her throat spasming with fear. His voice, in her earpiece, in her head, here – imprisoned, alone and vulnerable in the car. For a mad moment she thought he could see her, was watching her from the road bridge up ahead.

'That's no way to speak to an old friend, is it?' Hammond said. 'I just wanted to check you were alright, not getting into any trouble.'

'How the hell did you get this number?'

A laugh; a nasty, taunting laugh that filled her veins with ice. Escape was impossible. It was just her and him, his voice, bound together.

'You do get yourself into trouble, don't you, Jackie?' Hammond said. 'Don't worry, I'm looking out for you.' The line went dead.

She yanked the earpiece out and threw it into the foot well, her breath coming in sharp gasps. Fighting the urge to fling open the car door and run out into the road and down the motorway, she switched the radio back on and let the banalities fill the space until her heart had steadied and her breathing was no longer ragged.

Car engines started around her. The traffic was moving. The brake lights in front of her flashed then the car pulled away. She turned the key in her ignition and followed, her mind in turmoil. Would she ever be free of Hammond?

17:36 hours

It was dark when she pulled into the car park in front of her flat and the sky was blanketed with cloud, smothering the stars. A gusty breeze hurried through the trees and shook more leaves to the ground. Gaudy lights twinkled from one of the balconies: someone had put their Christmas tree up.

As Eden reached into the car to get her bag, she had the distinct impression she was being watched. Years ago, when she started surveillance training, she was taught never to focus on the target, but keep them in the corner of your eye, only glancing at them occasionally. An atavistic instinct warns people when they're being stared at, and that instinct prickled in her now. Stretching her peripheral vision, she scoured the area. No one in the car park; no one standing at the windows of the flats; no sudden movement of a curtain. The trees on the lawn concealed the flats from nosey passers-by, but also meant she couldn't tell if there was anyone lurking there. Taking her hefty torch from the glovebox, Eden headed back up the drive to the street, all her senses alert.

Facing her was a square of blank-faced amber Regency buildings with wrought-iron balconies, one draped with plastic wisteria. At the far corner, a line of women queued to enter the church that had been converted into a restaurant. Opposite was a Victorian villa quarantined by security fencing. No sign of movement there. No one on the street. She patrolled the perimeter of the square: all quiet.

Still with the uneasy sensation she was under surveillance, Eden went back to the flats and let herself in. The foyer was empty, the lift was empty, and the corridor outside her flat was empty. The hair she always left across her doorway was still in place, and when she opened the door and stepped into her flat, the air shifted to accommodate her. No one had been in this space since she left that morning.

Out on the balcony, she scanned the street, car park and square. Nothing. She released a pent-up breath, aware how Hammond's phone call had unsettled her. Miranda had warned her he'd been moved out of a high-security unit, and knowing Hammond, he'd rule not only the wing, but the whole prison. She imagined the comfort of his cell, the privileges he never had to work for, the lackeys cleaning and fawning over him. The drugs he had smuggled in and favours he arranged on the outside to maintain his position as top dog. Untouchable.

She switched on the TV for the comfort of the sound and flickering picture rather than the content, and closed all the curtains in her flat, startling herself with her own reflection in the windows. It had been a hell of a day. What she needed was a hot bath, a long read and a good sleep. Just as the bathroom was filling with scented steam, the doorbell rang.

The image that met her eye when she peered through she spyhole made her gasp and stagger back in shock. She peeped again, just to check her mind wasn't playing tricks. The last person in the world she thought ever to see again.

The bell rang again, and a voice called, 'I can hear you.'

Slowly she drew back the bolt and opened the door. A man stood outside. Medium height, dark-blonde hair, square-built. He stared back at her, his mouth working silently.

'It is you,' he said, at last. 'They told me you died.'

'Hello, Nick,' she said.

His face crumpled. She stood aside to let him in, then went to turn off the bath taps, snatching a moment to breathe deeply, aware her heart was galloping. When she returned to the sitting room, he faced her with a countenance full of shock and disbelief.

'Sara,' he said, then faltered. 'I don't know what to say except, why are you alive? And that sounds wrong.' He folded his overcoat round him as though cold and attempted a smile but his lips caught on his teeth. 'Where's your long hair gone?'

'It went a long time ago, along with everything else.' She saw he was shivering, knowing it was shock, not cold, that made him tremble. 'Sit down, Nick, I'll get us a drink and something to eat.'

Thank goodness the kettle took so long to boil and the toaster was slow to heat up. It gave her precious time to try and collect herself, to decide what she could say to him, this ghost from her past. She made a pile of toast and loaded butter, marmalade and Marmite onto a tray.

'Do you still like marmalade?' she asked.

'Yes. I see you haven't got over your Marmite addiction.'

She slid a mug of tea towards him. He sipped and winced at the scalding liquid, and put it back down again.

'It's been a long time, Sara.'

'I'm Eden now.'

'What happened?'

She hesitated. Telling him would put her life in danger, but then, he'd already found her, and Hammond seemed to be able to taunt her whenever he felt like it. Her new life and identity hadn't lasted long. 'I worked undercover with a gang, and when they went to prison I had to have a completely new identity. I left London and came here. I'm a private detective now.'

'That job!' Nick groaned. 'I said it would be the death of you.'

She flinched. 'It almost was,' she said. 'The gang found out I was working undercover and tried to kill me.' Her mouth was dry and her tongue clicked against her teeth. 'The ringleader is still after me.'

Nick stared at her for a long minute, evidently at a loss what to say. What was there to be said? To cover his confusion, he took a slice of toast and slathered it with marmalade. It reminded her of the early days of their marriage: breakfast in bed, coffee from the thick pottery mugs they'd bought on honeymoon, their whole lives ahead of them. How little time they had actually had together.

'How did you find me?' she asked.

'I saw something on TV about a skeleton, and there was a woman on camera who looked exactly like you. I thought it was just a coincidence; it couldn't be you, you were dead, but for some reason I couldn't let it go. I found the footage on the Internet and played it over and over, and the more I saw it, the more I knew it was you, crazy though it seemed. I rang your old office, said who I was, and eventually I spoke to someone who told me to leave it. And that frightened me.'

'Because if I really was dead, they'd just have said sorry for your loss. So much for my cover.'

'Exactly. So I kept on digging.'

'How did you find where I live?'

'I went to your office and started asking around. Someone said they thought you lived here, so I came to check it out. The post in the pigeonholes told me which flat.'

'You should be a private eye yourself,' Eden said.

'How did you come up with the name Eden Grey?' he asked.

She stretched her legs out in front of her. 'An in-joke, really. When I worked undercover I became Jackie Black. Sara White to Jackie Black, so when I needed a new name, I mixed the two to get Grey.'

'And Eden?'

'Saw it in a book and liked it. And sometimes clients aren't sure whether I'm going to be a man or a woman, and that can be useful.'

Nick polished off the last slice of toast. 'That was nice, Sara, but hardly filling. Let's get dinner.'

'I've had a hell of a day and I can't face going out again.' Besides, how could she sit opposite him, making polite restaurant conversation when they were divorced and she was dead?

'Takeaway? I saw there was a Thai place just along the road, are they any good?'

'Food's wonderful, but I can't afford it right now.' She pulled a face. 'Sorry to be a wet blanket, but self-employment isn't making me rich.'

'My treat,' he said. 'The least I can do.'

She fetched a takeaway menu and they pored over it, heads together, the way they used to when they were married. The memory jagged her heart. She'd lost so much. She remembered the day Nick left, the pain in his eyes as he blamed her work for the loss of their child, and his despair that she wouldn't give up her career for him. He never understood how important her work was to her: making a difference, however small that difference was.

'Are you still working for Price's?' she asked, when the order was rung through.

'Made partner a couple of years ago,' he said.

'That's great. I'm pleased for you.' She hesitated before she asked the next question, but she'd already registered the flash of gold on his finger. 'And you're married?'

'Four years ago.'

So he hadn't mourned the end of their marriage for long. Maybe he'd a replacement wife already pencilled in while they were still rowing.

Nick continued, 'She's called Naomi. I met her at work.' He fished in his wallet and pulled out a photo. 'That's her.'

A willowy blonde with long straight hair. Nick always had a thing for long hair. He would've gone mental if he'd seen the hairstyle she wore when she was undercover: one half of her head shaved and a tattoo on her scalp. Naomi's arms held a baby.

'That was taken ages ago,' Nick said. 'This one's more recent, but I love the light on their faces in the other one.'

He handed over another photo: the same willowy blonde with a little girl with fair hair and a sunny smile. Both of them fed by Waitrose and dressed by Boden.

'This is your daughter?'

'Yes, she'll be three at Christmas. Born on Boxing Day so we called her Holly.'

Pain ripped through her. Holly. Their little girl was Molly. Molly, who didn't carry full term, who was born dead, a wax figure, a perfect dead little doll.

'Holly and Molly,' she said, her voice tight.

'It was a way to remember her, I suppose.' He took the photos back. 'And you? You're not married, I take it?'

'No.' The takeaway arrived at that point and saved her from elaborating further. Nick went to the door and paid, and she gathered plates and spoons and forks and arranged them on her dining table, shoving aside the papers scattered there.

Over dinner, they reminisced about the old days. Though it hurt to recall how things had been between them, the pain softened the more they talked, and Eden realised that she had stopped loving Nick a long time ago, even before he left her, and she felt a sudden surge of gratitude that he'd been brave enough to end it for both of them.

'That holiday in Budapest!' Nick said at one point. 'You were speaking Russian and no one could understand a word.'

'I thought Hungarian must be similar. How wrong I was!'

'And our hotel room? So small we couldn't walk round the bed and there was nowhere to put the suitcase.'

'And you banged your head on that sloping beam every time you got out of the bath.'

'And that cafe that did the honey pastries. We must have eaten dozens of them that weekend.'

'I was only talking about that cafe the other day,' Eden said, remembering her conversation with Gabor. 'In Oktogon Square.'

'You mean Tordai Street,' Nick corrected her.

'No, it was on Oktogon Square. Not far from our hotel.'

'I went there six months ago with Naomi. It's in Tordai Street,'

Nick said, putting down his fork. 'Dig out that guidebook you had, that'll settle it.'

'I don't have the guidebook,' Eden said. 'I had to leave everything behind: all my clothes, books, pictures, certificates. I have no photographs of Mum and Dad. I had to create an identity from scratch.'

Nick stared at her, speechless, for a long moment. 'What happened to all your things?'

'As I'm supposed to be dead, I imagine they gave it all to Mum and Dad,' she said, trying hard not to think of the pain that must have caused her parents, sorting through her belongings, deciding what to keep, what to give to charity, what to throw away.

'Jesus!' Nick breathed. 'I never thought about how … complete it was.'

She hesitated before she asked the next question. 'Did you tell Mum and Dad that you'd seen me on telly?'

Nick's eyes met hers. 'No, I didn't want to hurt them more than they are already.'

'Are you going to tell them now?'

He tore off a chunk of naan bread and wiped it over his plate. 'No. I know that you wouldn't just disappear unless there was very good reason.'

Tears pricked her eyes and she blinked to clear her vision. 'Thank you,' she said.

'I always liked your parents,' Nick said. 'I don't want to hurt them. Or put them in danger.'

She scraped up the last of the curry. 'Thank you for dinner, Nick,' she said. 'This was lovely. Just what I needed after today.'

'Tough one?'

'You have no idea.'

As she collected up their plates, her doorbell rang. She froze, afraid it was someone sent by Hammond, then crept to the door and peeped through the spyhole. Aidan, clutching a bouquet of flowers. She opened the door and he came in, bringing with him the scent of cold night air.

'I wasn't sure if you'd see me, seeing as last time we saw each other you accused me of murder, but there's something you need to know ...' his voice trailed away as he caught sight of Nick.

'Good evening, Aidan,' Eden said. 'This is Nick, my ex-husband. Nick, this is my boyfriend, Aidan.'

The two men shook hands, eyeballing each other.

'I didn't realise you had company,' Aidan said. 'I'll go.'

'No, it's fine,' Nick said, picking up his overcoat. 'I've got a long drive home. Nice to meet you, Aidan. Look after her, won't you?' He turned to Eden and seemed to be weighing up whether or not to hug her. In the end, he simply touched her elbow and said, 'Take care, Sara.'

And he was gone.

Aidan collected up all the takeaway containers and washed them out, dried them, and stacked them in ascending order of size on the kitchen counter. He tipped away the washing up water and ran fresh, giving it a good squirt of washing-up liquid, then washed the plates and cutlery, the plate with the toast crumbs, and the buttery marmalade knife. Eden watched in silence as he put away the cups, repositioning everything on the shelf so all the handles pointed south-east, and as he rearranged the cutlery so the forks spooned each other and the knives all faced the same way in the drawer, as if to prevent them chatting to each other in the dark.

As he folded and hung up the sodden tea towel, he said, without looking at her, 'So that was Nick.'

'Yes, that was Nick.'

'I didn't realise you were still in touch.'

'We're not. He tracked me down and turned up unexpectedly.'

Aidan faced her. 'Tracked you down? Why would he do that?'

She balled her fists. 'Not for the reason you think,' she said. 'But as he was told I was dead, and for all I know attended my funeral, he was a bit surprised to see me on TV at Hailes when I found that skeleton.'

'Why did he call you Sara?'

'Because that's my name. My real name.'

'How many names have you got?'

She barked a short laugh. 'Too many. But now, only one.'

'What did he want? Nick?'

'To find out why I wasn't dead.' She picked at a bit of loose skin around her thumbnail. 'What are you doing here, anyway?'

He opened his mouth as if he wanted to say something, then closed it again. 'There's something you should know. It's about Lewis Jordan.'

She flopped into an armchair. 'Go on.'

'He stole the Holy Blood.'

'Tell me something I don't know.'

'How did you know?'

'It was obvious from the way he was around it.'

'That's what Lisa said.' Aidan crouched down beside her. 'She told me she went to his hotel room and stole it back.'

Eden sat up straight in her chair. 'It was *her*? Not you?'

'Not me.' He took her hand. 'Don't get mad, but we went for dinner after the filming, there was a flyer on the table and I folded it into a swan. She must've pinched it and then dropped it in Lewis's room.'

'So it *was* your swan.'

He nodded.

'Why did you lie?'

'I knew it must've been Lisa in Lewis's room, and I was frightened she'd killed him.' He puffed out his cheeks. 'I was trying to protect her.'

Eden stared at him. 'Even though you thought she'd committed murder?'

When he didn't answer, she scrambled out of the chair. 'I need to speak to Lisa.'

'I don't think …'

'Don't you understand? She might be the last person who saw Lewis Jordan alive.'

CHAPTER
TWENTY

Friday, 30 October 2015

07:14 hours

She awoke to a grey sky and squally rain rattling against the window pane. She'd slept badly, dreaming she was still married to Nick and they were taking Molly to the park, the zoo, her first day at school. Each time she jolted awake, she remembered anew that Nick and Molly were long gone, yet when she slept again, the film reel continued.

Finally, she crawled out of bed and switched on the television news. Normally she liked the intimate chuntering of the radio, but this morning she wanted colour and flashing images, and the mix of the deadly serious and the locally heartening. Her muscles were stiff and her back creaked when she stretched. Maybe a run would clear the fog in her head.

Eden tugged on her running gear and plugged in her earbuds, zooming up the volume so her head filled with pop music. Cheesy, but it had a good beat, and she pounded along the pavements, her hands blooming red in the cold, and her gloom lifted. Down to the university campus, around the lake and along the paths through the gardens, past the Bath Road shops and back through the Suffolks. She did a quick lap of

Imperial Gardens and was about to head for home when she wondered if any more letters had come for Lewis Jordan.

Jerking the buds out of her ears, she went through the hotel's revolving door and into reception. There was a man at the desk, youngish yet looking like a refugee from an Evelyn Waugh novel in a green three-piece tweed suit with purple flecks. On his feet were shiny brown brogues. One glance and she knew exactly what he was. Posture a little too erect. An air of self-confidence and swagger about him. He was from her old life – a spook.

He was leaning on the reception desk and saying, 'I know it's not that valuable, but it's the principle. Someone's been in my room and taken something.'

'I'm so sorry to hear that,' the receptionist said. 'Are you sure you couldn't have misplaced it? All our staff have the best references, I'm sure no one would have stolen anything.'

Hah! Eden thought. The hotel manager had told her that there had been a spate of minor thefts from guests' rooms. Nothing particularly valuable, but thefts none the less.

The casualty of Waugh reddened. 'It's missing. I've checked everywhere and it's gone. Now what are you going to do about it?'

'Would you like me to phone the police?'

'No, it's not worth it, but I'll speak to the manager. Petty pilfering is a bad sign.'

As he moved away from the desk, Eden approached him. 'Excuse me?'

He swivelled on his heel to face her. 'You are?'

She stuck out her hand. 'I'm Eden Grey, I'm a private detective, and I overheard that you've lost something.' She lowered her voice. 'You're not the only one. Have you got a minute?'

He looked her up and down, taking in her running clothes and evidently weighing up whether or not to believe her.

'I can come back later with ID if you want,' Eden said, 'or you can check with the girl on reception. She knows who I am.'

He had a brief chat with the girl on reception, who nodded vigorously, evidently glad that the theft was now Eden's problem. He came back to Eden and steered her into the coffee lounge.

'I'm Will Day,' he said. 'What do you want to tell me?'

'Can you tell me what's been stolen?'

'Nothing valuable, really, just a pair of gloves.'

'Anything else?'

'No, but the last time I was here I lost a DVD. Again, not expensive, not worth reporting to the police, but annoying.'

'It fits the pattern,' Eden said. 'Small, relatively inexpensive items going missing from the rooms. Not worth bringing in the police about.'

'Someone nicking for kicks?' Will suggested.

'Maybe.' She noted again the tweedy suit and ultra-shiny brogues. 'Do you always stay here when you're in Cheltenham?'

'Yes.'

'Business?'

'Yes, I'm a management consultant.'

Eden hid a smile. Like hell you are. 'And your colleagues, do they use this hotel, too?'

Will leaned back in his chair and regarded her for a moment. 'Yes, they do,' he said slowly.

'I'll do some digging,' she said.

'I'm not sure it's worth your time,' Will said. 'I'm not going to pay you to investigate a pair of gloves.'

'I think there's more at stake here,' Eden said. Lowering her voice, she leaned forwards and said, 'You're from south of the river. I know you can't make a fuss.'

'I really don't know what you're talking about.'

Still whispering, she said, 'I used to be one of you. There's a Hockney on the second floor, near the lifts. The canteen always serves roly-poly pudding on Fridays, but uses apricot, not strawberry, jam.'

Will said, 'I think you've mistaken me for someone else. Now I must get on,' but when he stood and walked away, she found he'd left his business card on the seat. William Day, Management Consultant. It had a mobile phone number and no email address.

'Gotcha,' she said to herself.

There had been no further letters for Lewis Jordan: evidently whoever was sending the poison pen letters had desisted once news of his death came out on Wednesday morning. Eden left the hotel and went home to shower and change, and to prepare for what could be a tricky interview.

Aidan was grey when she went into his office, and dark circles under his eyes betrayed a broken night's sleep. She wondered whether it was meeting Nick and being confronted by her past, or the fact that he suspected his ex-girlfriend of murder that had unsettled him. He was frowning at a computer screen when she came in, and when he saw her, he snatched off his glasses and folded them into his breast pocket.

'I like you in glasses,' she said.

He didn't reply. They stared at each other for an awkward moment, before Eden said, 'Lisa's here? I saw her car outside.'

'I told her you wanted to speak to her. She says she's busy with the skeleton but frankly I think that's a ploy. If she examines it any more closely she could file a paternity suit against it.'

'In the basement?' Eden asked.

'I'll come with you.'

Lisa was in the lab, the skeleton laid out on a gurney before her. She wore a green overall and rubber gloves as she handled the bones. As they came in, she was holding the skull and peering at the teeth in the upper jaw.

'Rehearsing for *Hamlet?*' Aidan asked.

She put the skull down. 'I thought the TV people might like a bit about tooth wear and dentition,' she said. 'It was crucial in one of the war graves cases I handled.'

'I'm sure they'd find that fascinating,' Aidan said. 'Meanwhile, Eden wants to ask you if you killed Lewis Jordan.'

Lisa blasted him with an icy glare.

'Aidan,' Eden said, 'why don't you go back to your office? I'll come and find you before I go.'

He swivelled his head from Lisa to Eden. 'You'll be OK on your own?'

Lisa rolled her eyes. 'There's not going to be catfight on the bones, if that's what you're worried about.'

With a backward glance, he left them alone.

Eden dragged over a plastic chair and took her notebook out of her backpack. 'Aidan says you saw Lewis Jordan on Tuesday evening. Start from the filming and tell me what happened.'

Lisa sucked in a breath through her nose and looked her over like a snake calculating the strike range to its prey. 'I left here about six with Aidan. He said he wanted to take me for dinner. He knows I love Thai, so we went to a little place he knows down the High Street.'

'The pub?' Eden said, without looking up from the notebook.

'Er, yes. We ordered and had a drink. Lots to catch up on, as you can imagine. We've been friends for over a decade – golly how old that makes me feel – then Aidan got a phone call and had to leave.'

'Why?'

'What?'

'Why did he have to leave?'

'You know that.'

'Tell me anyway.'

'The Holy Blood was missing. When Andy Pandy and Weed or whatever they're called packed up after the filming, the

Blood was missing. They called Aidan and he rushed back here. He told me to stay and have my dinner, but I thought it was most likely Lewis who pinched the Blood so I went to see him.'

'What made you think it was Lewis?'

'Puh–lease! Eyes as big as millwheels when he looked at it. He believed all that shit about it making people immortal.'

'So you went to see him? When was this?'

'Nearly seven.' That tallied with the CCTV. Eden had instantly recognised that sprightly figure trotting up the steps to Lewis's hotel. 'He wasn't in so I had a drink in the bar then tried his room again. That was about half seven. We talked about the documentary – he said I could have my own series. Lisa Greene Investigates. Cold cases from history, that sort of thing.'

'And?'

'Maybe a syndicated series with the US but he —'

'I meant what else did you and Lewis do, in his hotel room?'

'We had a drink. He rang down to the bar.'

'What did you drink?'

'I had a vodka and tonic, he had a red wine.'

Eden looked up. 'You're sure?'

'Yes.' A tetchy note crept into Lisa's voice.

'What time did you leave?'

'About half past eight.'

'How did you pinch the Blood?' Eden asked.

'I searched his jacket pockets while he was ringing room service. No Blood, so I went into the bathroom and hunted through his washbag. It was hidden in there, so I pocketed it.'

'Did you see Lewis's eye drops?'

'There was one bottle in his jacket – I thought it was the Holy Blood at first. There was another bottle in the bathroom.'

'Did he use his drops while you were with him?'

'Yes, the bottle in his jacket.'

'And how did he seem?'

Lisa put her head on one side. 'Excited, and a bit mischievous. His phone kept on ringing and sometimes he just refused to answer it and at others he answered and told whoever it was he'd be there in his own good time.'

'Who was calling him?'

'No idea.'

'Anything else spring to mind?'

'When I first went in, he was a bit distracted. He told me someone was sending him poison pen letters and he'd just picked up another one. He showed it to me – it wasn't nice.'

'What did it say?' Eden asked.

'"Ready to die, sick boy?".'

'Just that?'

Lisa nodded.

'And what did he do with it?'

Lisa shrugged. 'Put it back in the envelope and left it on the table. His phone started ringing about then and that seemed to cheer him up. When he switched off his phone he said "filthy lucre" and sort of laughed to himself.'

'The envelope was left on the table?'

'Yes. Is it important?'

Eden closed her notebook and snapped the elastic around it. 'Might be,' she said. When she discovered Lewis's body on Wednesday morning, there was no envelope on the table, and the letter Lisa described had the same message as the one she'd found charred in a bin in the park. Who had taken it, and were they the last person to see Lewis alive?

CHAPTER
TWENTY-ONE

Friday, 30 October 2015

09:47 hours

Mandy hovered in the doorway, clutching a notebook. Her sallow cheeks were tinged pink with excitement.

'You know you asked me to check out the Catholic families around Hailes?' she said. 'I found something.'

Aidan capped his fountain pen. 'Good stuff, Mands. What have you got?'

Mandy sidled into his office and closed the door behind her. She dropped into the chair opposite and flicked her plaits over her shoulder. For a moment he had the impulse to urge her to cut her hair, get rid of those little-girl plaits with their frizzled ends and to chuck away the unnaturally bright hair dye. Then again, it would probably be construed as sexual harassment, and there was enough sexual tension curdling the team right now.

Mandy plonked her notebook on his desk and hunched over it, crowding his space. He leaned back in his chair, trying hard not to flinch.

'I've mapped out the locations of known Catholic families,' Mandy began, tugging out a map and unfolding it on the desk. 'Obviously I can only find the big families, but you can see there were a few of them in the area. The biggest one was

Coughton, but there was also a family called Ashford, who lived a few miles from Winchcombe.'

'Not far from Hailes,' Aidan added, scouring the map. 'Is the house still there?'

Mandy shook her head. 'House was demolished after the First World War. But I did find this.'

She produced an old black and white photograph of a manor house: medieval at the core, and much altered and extended by subsequent generations. 'This was it.'

He tugged at his lip while he thought. 'What happened to the records? Account books, letters, diaries?'

'Not sure, but I can find out.'

'Please. Anything else?'

Mandy's face brightened. 'You said to search a twenty-mile radius, but I extended it because Coughton was so important. Anyway, there's a reference to Hailes in the Coughton papers.'

'Really? The garden plan I saw yesterday was from Coughton, but it was copying a garden at Hailes.'

'Just a brief mention, but there might be more.' Mandy checked her notes. 'Coughton was a bit of a vortex for plots over the years, and hosted several Catholic priests. It's got a number of priest holes for them to hide in. There's a letter that suggests a priest from Hailes visited Coughton and hid in one of them for over a week.'

Aidan thought of being enclosed, shut in the tiny space, scared to breathe in case you gave yourself away, and went cold. Being squashed in the drainage tunnel at Hailes had freaked him out. It gave him a new respect for the sort of faith that enabled men to put their lives on the line for something they believed in.

'When was this?' he asked.

Mandy ran her finger down the page. '1568.'

'Any mention of who the priest was?'

'No, too dangerous, I guess, if the letter was intercepted. All it says is that the priest was formerly a monk at Hailes, and he came to Coughton to minister to the family.'

Aidan picked up his fountain pen and doodled a swan on his notepad. 'Doesn't sound like our skeleton, does it?'

'Not really. The skeleton probably wasn't a monk. Knees not flat enough for a start.' She tucked the end of one of her plaits into her mouth and sucked it. 'Want me to keep on digging?'

'You have the time?'

'Sure.' She hesitated for a moment. 'What am I looking for?'

'I don't know,' he said. 'There's just something about that garden plan that's set bells ringing.' He shrugged. 'Probably not connected to the skeleton at all, but I'm just intrigued.'

Mandy nodded. A seasoned archaeologist herself, she understood how powerful instinct could be, however much she swore allegiance to science. 'I'll see what I can find,' she said.

The new TV producer arrived at ten o'clock. Pamela Salway was tall and slender, with piercing blue eyes and a single diamond ring of about four carats on her middle finger. In her fifties, she wore a sapphire blue hobble skirt and a black biker jacket, and used a ring binder and pen rather than a smartphone, Aidan was reassured to see. She had a calm, business-like manner and got straight down to work.

'We've got footage of the examination of the skeleton and of the Holy Blood, but we'll reshoot the material where Lewis is visible,' she said in a deep, musical voice. 'And I'm not happy about this druid angle. A lot of tosh if you ask me,' she added in a stage whisper to Aidan, who warmed to her instantly. 'I don't know what these silly young girls were thinking of, letting him get away with it. I know Lewis was into the sensational, God rest him, but I'd rather focus on the science and the history.'

'Sounds good to me,' Aidan said. 'We've got the isotope analysis results, which Mandy can talk you through.'

Pamela scribbled a note in her ring binder. 'Anything else?'

'I've been doing some digging in the records at Hailes, and I've come up with something potentially interesting,' he said.

'Oh?'

'A post-Dissolution planting scheme.' Aidan fetched the plan he'd made. 'There's a pattern here, and it seems to match the rosary.'

Pamela gazed at the drawing. 'You're right,' she said. 'I'm not sure what this has to do with the skeleton or the Holy Blood, but it's original and interesting. I'd like to include it. Will you go on camera and explain it?'

Aidan felt himself flush. 'Me? Lewis seemed to think I wasn't ... er ... eccentric enough.'

'Bollocks to that,' said Pamela. 'I want experts talking about their area of expertise. We'll mike you up and go in five.'

The rest of the day passed quickly, Pamela issuing brisk orders and the technical guys jumping to perform her commands. Even Xanthe and Jocasta seemed more focussed on the job. Jocasta had voiced a protest about the new direction the documentary was to take, but was soon disabused of any expectations that it would continue to follow the Holy Grail and eternal life crap that Lewis was so enamoured of.

Even Lisa fell into line when confronted by Pamela's curt efficiency. She tied on her surgical scrubs and was poised and ready to explain the dentition on the skeleton without a single flounce or pout.

'We're filming today and today only,' Pamela informed everyone. 'So we get it right first time, every time. Got that? There will be no extender fees if we're back here on Monday. Understand?'

At six o'clock that evening, Pamela declared, 'It's a wrap. Thank you, everyone.'

She approached Aidan with her hand extended. 'Thank you for putting up with us. I'll get you to come and check the footage once I've cut it, just to make sure I've got the history right.'

'No problem,' Aidan said, impressed that she cared to get the history right. 'Nice working with you.'

They packed away the skeleton, wrapping it in bubble wrap and placing it in a long cardboard box. Strange to think that a full-grown human could occupy so small a space. The technical guys wound up their cables and packed their equipment in record quick time, anxious to be home before they lost any more of the weekend. Even Lisa seemed keen to be back in Oxford, calling, 'Bye, everyone. Hope to see you again soon, Aidan,' as soon as her re-shoots were done. She held his eyes for a second too long, raising her hand in farewell, then her shoulders sagged a little and she was gone.

The bright lights and relentless pace of the day had taken their toll, and pain sliced from the top of his head, through his eye sockets to his jaw. Now Aidan wanted nothing so much as a cool bath and the poems of Catullus to soothe his mind. What a bloody week it had been. Murdered TV executives, stolen artefacts and Lisa in the frame for all of it, but now at last there was a return to normal. Whatever passed for normal in the Cultural Heritage Unit these days. He prayed that on Monday morning they would all be back to their usual routine. He switched off the basement light and clattered up the metal stairs to the ground floor to find Trev and Mandy waiting for him.

'All done?' he said.

'All sorted,' Trev said. 'See you Monday.'

They trundled off down the street to the pub, leaving him to lock up. Aidan went home, his head screaming in pain. He stretched full length on the settee, and fell asleep.

He awoke an hour later, his head still banging and his tongue with the tell-tale numb tingling that meant a migraine was on the way. He eased himself up from the settee, wincing at the pinch in his neck. His stomach clenched with foreboding. Something was wrong. It was a moment before he realised what. He'd forgotten to lock the safe. He remembered handling the Holy Blood for the filming, and remembered wrapping it and putting it in a box, and lodging it in the safe. And he remembered closing the safe door, but there his memory clouded. Did he lock the safe?

He grabbed his coat and ran back to the Cultural Heritage Unit, fumbled with his keys and finally got the door open. His hands were shaking with cold and fear. Leaving the Blood in an unlocked safe! He prayed he was wrong, that the Blood was in the safe and the safe was locked and secure.

He flicked on the lights as he went in, slammed the front door shut behind him, and headed down the metal stairs to the basement. The safe was in the corner of the finds room: a shoulder height, weighty monstrosity with a dial on the front and a hefty lever to open the door. He tried the handle. The door didn't budge.

He collapsed against the door, relief flooding through him. Locked. He'd locked it, after all. Better just check the Holy Blood was inside. He twizzled the dial and yanked the heavy handle. The door swung open, slow and stately. There was the box, right at the back. He brought it out and opened the lid. Gently, he started to unwrap the Blood from its protective cocoon, knowing he'd never rest until he was convinced it was safe.

A noise above made him jump. He held his breath for a moment, listening, but was unable to hear anything apart from the beating of his own heart. He placed the box back in the safe and pushed the door to, then went to investigate. Probably just a mouse. It was a wonder they weren't overrun and explaining themselves to the council rat catcher, the amount of biscuit crumbs Trev scattered over the carpet on an hourly basis. No vacuum cleaner could keep pace with him.

He went down an avenue of shelves stacked with boxes of human remains, an army of the dead flanking him, and up the stairs to the ground floor, aware he was tiptoeing. Aware, too, of the pulse pounding in his throat. In the entrance hall, he checked the front door. Shut, but unlocked. Did he forget to lock it in his hurry to check the Blood was safe? The migraine was burning away his memory like acid. He dropped the snib on the front door and went to check the rest of the building.

The staffroom was empty, the mugs rinsed out and left upside down on a tea towel on the draining board to dry. A sheet of plain paper bearing the half-reconstructed remains of a Roman amphora stood on the table: Andy's latest jigsaw. A rustle behind him. He whipped round, stifling a cry. No one was there, just an old crisp packet, crunched up and tossed in the bin that had chosen that precise moment to unfurl. He swore softly. Heart failure induced by crisp packet, he chided himself.

The office shared by Mandy and Trev was also empty. A green light glowed on the computer monitor, an evil sprite lurking. He clicked on the overhead light and winced at the sulphur glow it cast over the room. He flicked it off again and went to his office. The door was closed. He grasped the handle and opened the door and a jolt punched him in the chest. Someone had been in here. His pens, which he always left in a neat line in ascending size order at the side of his blotter, were muddled up, and his blotter was no longer exactly parallel with the edge of the desk.

He crossed to it. The drawer was slightly open, too, the contents stirred about. And papers that he had filed in the bottom drawer were now in a pile on the top. He hurried to the filing cabinet and tugged at the top drawer. It flew open. He always locked it. He dipped into the top files, searching to see if anything was missing.

A step behind him. He turned, a cry of surprise, then an incredible pain in his head. He fell, striking the edge of the desk and slumping to the floor. Another blow and all went black around him.

CHAPTER
TWENTY-TWO

Friday, 30 October 2015

19:24 hours

Eden could hear the screaming when she was still two houses away. The noise intensified when the door opened, and she stuck her fingers in her ears. Judy grabbed her and yanked her into the hallway.

'Please take me away,' she begged. 'I can't stand any more.'

She pushed open the door to the sitting room and Eden peeped in. Three small boys surged round the room, armed with a range of plastic weaponry, all of them screeching at the tops of their voices. The sofa cushions had been dragged onto the floor and fashioned into a barricade, which they alternately leapt over and crouched behind making machine-gun noises, aiming the guns at the TV, which was playing an episode of *Doctor Who*. The Daleks didn't stand a chance.

Eden pulled the door shut. 'Where's Marcus?'

'Hiding in the kitchen.'

Eden went down the hall and found Marcus at the kitchen table, noise-cancelling earphones rammed on his head, a pile of paperwork in front of him. She waved at him and he hitched the earphones back.

'Hello, Eden. How you doing?'

'Fine thanks, Marcus. Can Judy come out to play?'

He cast an anguished glance at the sitting room door. 'Er …'

Judy bounded over and planted a kiss on his cheek. 'Thanks, sweetie. Come on, Eden, where are we going?' She clattered down the hallway with Eden in her wake, and grabbed a jacket from the heaving racks. 'Give them another ten minutes, then it's calm down time, story, bath and bed,' she shouted back towards the kitchen.

'Thanks, Marcus,' Eden called. 'Have a good evening.'

They were out on the pavement before he could reply.

Judy let out a deep breath that fogged in the chill air. 'Freedom. This is what freedom smells like.'

'It was your decision to have three children.'

'The first one was an experiment,' Judy said, buttoning her coat. 'And the other two were a cruel joke by pixies.'

They clambered into Eden's car and set off into the centre of Cheltenham. 'Mind if we're cheap and cheerful?' she asked. 'Nothing on my books after I finish this case.'

'Fine by me. I'll tell Marcus we went somewhere posh and spend the difference on a new handbag.'

'I'll borrow Aidan's parking space,' Eden said, pulling into the space in front of the Cultural Heritage Unit. The building was shrouded in darkness, the windows blank.

'Not seeing him tonight?'

'No, I'm cross with him right now,' Eden said.

'What's he done?'

'Lying about what he was up to, and trying to shield his ex from a murder charge.'

'Blimey! You two don't do things by halves, do you?' Judy said. 'Let's get inside and you can tell me all about it.'

At the corner of the street was an old pub that had been turned into a café. During the day it was haunted by yummy mummies and outsize prams clogged the doorway, but in the evening it was the venue of choice for students. The menu was varied, the prices cheap, and the portions generous. The café maintained a functional interior, with exposed pipes and rough woodwork giving it an industrial look, which all contributed to its hip and trendy vibe.

Eden and Judy found a table and draped their coats over the seats, then went to the counter to order from the multi-pierced server. Back at their table, with drinks in jam jars with handles, Judy said, 'So what's this about Aidan and do I need to go and thump him for you?'

Eden smiled. Judy was always in her corner. 'It's a bit complicated,' she began, 'and it's to do with this client of mine who was killed.'

Judy's eyed widened as she sucked on her straw. 'Have you ever thought of having a normal job, you know, in an office from nine to five, whingeing by the water cooler instead of clients dropping dead all over the place?'

'Who would employ me in an office?'

'True. Go on.'

'When I found the body there was a paper swan in the room. It was exactly the same as the ones Aidan makes. He's got a thing about origami at the moment. It looked like he had been in the victim's room so I asked him about it.'

'Confronted, more like, I imagine,' Judy added.

'And he said he had no idea how it got there. Later it turns out he went out for dinner with Lisa, his ex, and made one of those swans and she picked it up, and she was the one who left it in Lewis's hotel room.'

Judy ducked her head forward to whisper, 'And she killed him?'

'She says she was just there to steal back the Holy Blood.'

Judy put down her drink. 'Hang on a minute. Steal back the Holy Blood?'

'All-day breakfast and a kedgeree and a side order of chips.' A waiter materialised beside them, armed with plates.

'Thank you,' Eden said.

'There are sauces over there.' He pointed to a table with an array of ketchup and mustard bottles.

'Thanks,' she said again. She waited until he'd gone, then said in a low voice, 'There's this artefact, found with the skeleton. It looks just like a religious relic called the Holy Blood. Lewis stole it while they were filming. Lisa says she went to get it back.'

'And she killed him?'

Eden shook her head, mouth full of chips.

'Why not?'

'Because he was receiving poison pen letters, and they started before she'd even met him. And because someone doctored his eye drops.'

'How?'

'Put oven cleaner in them. Whoever did that knew he was always putting drops in his eyes. Lisa wouldn't have known that. Not in time to mess with the drops, anyway.'

Judy grabbed a chip and dunked it in the egg yolk in her all-day breakfast. 'So who did know about his drops?'

'Anyone who worked with him, his mother, his foster mother, anyone who had a relationship with him, and there's no shortage of suspects there.'

'So one of them killed him.'

'The people who worked with him all have an alibi. They were all out together that evening.'

Judy's eyes gleamed. 'Like *Murder on the Orient Express*,' she said. 'They all provide alibis for each other.'

'And they all trooped into his room and bashed him?'

'I thought you said his drops were poisoned?'

'They were, but that's not what killed him. Someone bashed his head in.'

Judy speared a bit of sausage and chewed it thoughtfully. 'So our murderer writes a load of poison pen letters. "You're going to die, sonny Jim", that kind of thing. Then they poison the drops. Then they come along and bash him on the head. Talk about overkill.'

Eden paused with her fork part way to her mouth. She'd been blind, absolutely blind. Love, lust, lucre: those were the motives for murder, and in this case, she had all three. She'd been working on the wrong timeline and looking for a single motive. No wonder nothing fitted: she needed to start again.

21:49 hours

Eden and Judy came out of the warm fug of the café into the cold shock of the street.

'Are we going to a strip club now?' Judy asked, tucking her hands in her pockets.

'How about a hot chocolate at my place then I'll drive you home.'

'An excellent alternative. Those posing pouches only make me laugh. Maybe it's because I've got three boys, but I don't find willies very interesting any more.'

Eden chuckled. 'No, Judy, it's called middle age.'

'Cheek! You're only a few years younger than me, remember.'

They reached Eden's car. 'Is that a light on in the Cultural Heritage Unit?' Eden said.

'Someone's working late.'

'On a Friday night? No way. Besides, I'm sure it was dark when we parked.'

'It'll be the cleaners.'

Eden shook her head. 'No, they come in earlier. I'm just going to check it out.'

'Burglars don't put the light on!' Judy called after her, as she headed up the stone steps to the front door.

Eden pushed at the front door. It swung open. She sprinted back to the car and fetched her heavy torch. 'Stay here,' she said to Judy. 'Something's wrong. I'm going to check it out.'

'Not on your own you're not,' Judy said. She hustled up close behind Eden and together they went in.

Eden froze in the hall, straining her ears for a sound. Nothing. Light came from the basement. She crept along to the stairs, then inched down them, scouting for movements and tensing her senses for signs they weren't alone. The strip lights were harsh in the low-ceilinged room, casting sharp shadows on the walls. She moved from room to room. Everything seemed in place: the skeletons in their brown cardboard boxes filed on the shelves; the finds boxes with their labels facing outwards; the metal shelves in neat parallel lines.

As she reached the far end of the finds room, she stifled a cry. The safe was open, the door swinging wide, the contents of the safe scattered over the floor. She spun around and charged back up the stairs to the ground floor, Judy breathing hard behind her. The staffroom was empty, so was the first office. The door to Aidan's office was shut. Gripping the torch tightly, she seized the handle and burst in.

It was a moment before she saw him. A foot, sticking out from behind the desk, his body slumped on the floor in a pool of blood. A broken pot lay in bloodied shards beside him. She ran to him and turned him over, her heart gripped with fear.

'Aidan! Can you hear me?'

'I'm calling an ambulance,' Judy said, pulling her phone out of her pocket. 'Is he breathing?'

Eden tilted her cheek close to his mouth. 'Just. But he doesn't look good.'

'Conscious?'

'Aidan, Aidan!' No response. She tapped his cheek. 'Aidan! Can you hear me?'

He groaned and opened then closed his eyes. 'Eden,' he croaked. 'What happened?'

'The ambulance is on its way,' she said. 'Just hold on.'

'The Blood,' he said. 'Is it still there?'

'Don't worry about that now.'

'You must go and check. It's in the safe.'

Judy bent over him. 'What does it look like?'

'Like a red perfume bottle with a silver stopper,' Eden said.

Judy touched her shoulder. 'You stay with him. I'll go and check.'

She disappeared and her footsteps clattered down to the basement. There was a hiatus then she reappeared again, shaking her head.

'It's gone,' she said.

The corridor was painted in pale green and had a dark blue lino floor. A nurse squeaked towards them and they glanced up, anxious for news, deflated when she walked past without a glance in their direction.

'What was he doing there?' Eden said. 'It was after nine o'clock, for God's sake.'

Judy tucked her arm around her shoulders. 'Try not to worry. He'll be fine.'

'You can't tell with head injuries,' she said. That was the trouble with the training she'd had, years ago: she knew too much. She'd known colleagues who'd arrested a suspect and thought they were fine to be interviewed, only to find they collapsed a few hours later from an injury that had been assumed to be minor. Death in custody, every officer's nightmare.

'The police will find who did it,' Judy said.

Eden snorted. 'That wretched relic.' She huddled deeper in her jacket, though it was roasting in the hospital. Aidan, in a pool of blood on the floor. Thank God they'd seen the lights on in the office and gone to investigate, otherwise he could have lain there until Monday morning. A victim of the Holy Blood. So much for eternal life.

A doctor in a flapping white coat came towards them, and they rose from their seats. Anxiety coopered Eden's chest. Please let him be OK.

'Relatives of Aidan Fox?' the doctor asked.

'That's us,' Judy said. She tucked her hand into Eden's and squeezed it.

'He's taken quite a bash on the head, but he's conscious and there are no signs of intra-cranial bleeding. We want to keep him in for observation for a few days, just to make sure that the injury is stable, but there's no reason for concern.'

'Can we see him?'

The doctor pursed his lips. 'For two minutes. And don't upset him.'

'Thank you, doctor,' Judy said, as he hurried away.

Aidan looked like a little boy in the hospital bed. His face was ashen, stark against his dark hair, and his eyes were huge and moated with purple. A bruise spread from his hairline down to his cheekbone. Dressed in the blue hospital gown, he was vulnerable and sick.

'Aidan!' Eden rushed towards him. 'Oh God, look at you.'

'All in one piece,' he croaked. 'Christ, my head hurts.'

She grasped his hand and massaged the knuckles. Shame washed over her at the thought of the last few days' mistrust and bickering.

'How you doing?' Judy said. 'You look awful.'

'Thanks, Judy. I feel worse than I look. What were you two doing in my office?'

'We saw the lights on,' Eden said. 'What were you doing there?'

'I thought I'd forgotten to lock the safe. I went back to check.'

'What happened?'

'I don't know. Someone had searched my office; all my stuff was moved about. I was checking it when I heard a noise.'

'See anyone?'

He shook his head and winced. 'I can't remember. Where's the Blood?'

She patted his hand. 'Don't worry about that now. Concentrate on getting better.'

He struggled to sit up and she pressed him back down against the pillows. 'Stay there, buster.'

'But the Blood; I can't believe I've lost it again. God, what a mess.'

'Leave it to me,' she said. 'I'll get it back.'

CHAPTER
TWENTY-THREE

Saturday, 31 October 2015

09:14 hours

Eden slept badly and awoke with a headache pounding her skull to sand. She dragged herself out of bed and padded into her sitting room, drawing back the curtains and gazing out over the tops of the trees to the square. Another Christmas tree had sprouted on the balconies, its pink, yellow and green lights winking in the morning gloom. The sight was overwhelmingly depressing.

Her mobile rang while she was making breakfast. She froze at the first ring, her throat taut. What if it was Hammond, taunting her again. Her next thought was it was the hospital. Aidan. Fear churned inside her. When she finally answered, her voice cracked.

'Eden Grey?'

'Who is this?'

'It's Will Day. We met in the Imperial Hotel yesterday. I'd had some gloves stolen.'

Was that only yesterday? It seemed a lifetime ago. 'Yes, I remember. How can I help you?'

'I wondered if you were free for brunch today? I'd like to talk to you about the missing gloves.'

'Sure, but can we make it a late-ish one?' Aidan needed pyjamas and a washbag, and no doubt a pile of reading to keep him entertained while he was in hospital.

They fixed up a time and place to meet, and Eden hung up. She ate, showered and dressed quickly, then grabbed her car keys and went to Aidan's flat. It was in an imposing Regency building in Lansdown, one of a crescent of stone houses that had been converted into flats. She let herself in and went up two flights to his flat, half afraid that she'd find the place turned over. Her breath came out in a whoosh when she opened the door and saw the calm, though eccentric, order that ruled Aidan's home.

Everything was symmetrical: the arrangement of objects on the marble mantelpiece; the placing of easy chairs and coffee table; the ordering of pictures on the walls. His bookcases were set into the alcoves either side of the chimneybreast, and were arranged in size and colour order. A shelf of old orange Penguins, a line of black-spined classics, philosophy, poetry, mythology. Aidan had a magpie mind: his interests were eclectic and once he'd heard or read something, he never forgot it. He was a deadly weapon on pub quiz teams.

She took a pair of pyjamas out of the chest of drawers, and unhooked his dressing gown from the back of the bedroom door. In the bathroom, she gathered washing and shaving kit, adding a bottle of aftershave to cheer him up and combat the disinfectant stink of the hospital.

With a final check that she'd got everything, she locked up and drove to the hospital, parking in a side street nearby so she didn't get stung by the car park charges, and walked to his ward.

Aidan's black eyes had developed overnight and were spreading down his cheeks. Some of his hair had been shaved away and the stitches stuck out like false eyelashes. His eye sockets were hollow and she was alarmed by how poorly he looked.

'How you doing?' she asked, kissing his forehead.

'Terrible,' he said. 'I don't know what he hit me with, but it was heavy.'

'He?' She unpacked the bag into the bedside cabinet.

'I've remembered I saw his shoes. Long, slim feet in leather brogues. Looked expensive.'

'Remember anything else?'

He waggled his head. 'No. I saw his feet go past and I blacked out.'

'Did he say anything? Smell of anything?'

'No. Nothing.'

'OK, don't worry, just try to rest.' She slid the books onto the bedside cabinet. 'I wasn't sure what you'd want with a head injury, so I brought Dorothy L. Sayers, Celtic legends, and some Horace.'

'Brilliant, thank you.'

She perched next to him on the bed and twined her fingers in his. 'I'm sorry the Blood has gone again.'

'Someone must really want it.'

'Is it valuable?'

He shuffled himself higher on the pillows with a grunt. 'As a medieval bottle made from a gemstone with a silver topper, it's not worth that much,' he said. 'But if it is the Holy Blood, one of the most important religious relics in history, it's priceless.'

'But who would want it?'

'People like Lewis, who think it's got mysterious properties. Or people who just get off on thinking they own a bit of Christ. Makes them feel powerful.'

'But you don't know what was in that bottle yet,' Eden said.

Aidan let go of a deep sigh. 'That's not the point. It might be real, so I guess for someone it's worth taking the risk.'

'Who would want it that badly?'

'There are relic collectors out there,' Aidan said. 'You can buy relics online.'

'You can buy bits of dead saints online?' Eden echoed.

'It's illegal to trade in the relics themselves,' Aidan explained. 'You can only sell the thing it's held in, the reliquary, and the relic itself is passed off as a gift from the seller to the buyer.'

'If you sell it openly,' she said, catching his eye.

'Yes, if it's sold openly.' He coughed and grimaced. 'But there's a black market in relics, too.'

She shouldn't be surprised. There was a black market in all sorts of things, from exotic animals to weapons to Nazi memorabilia. Her time at Revenue and Customs had taught her that people would go to extraordinary lengths to obtain the objects they desired. Danger and suffering only added value to the item, to the wrong person.

'How much would the Holy Blood cost?' she asked.

'How do you put a figure on something like that?' Aidan said. He fingered the side of his bruised eye. 'But we know he's prepared to kill for it.'

The café was in the Suffolks area of Cheltenham – narrow streets of independent boutiques, a favourite haunt of arty types – and was full of men in three-quarter length wool coats and long stripey scarves, and women in green velvet skirts and clattery bangles. Will modelled his off-duty clothes of deep pink moleskins, pale blue polo neck and a navy blazer: the perfect image of a cavalry officer in civvies, and the favoured weekend look for a spy.

He'd bagged a leather sofa towards the back of the café, and stood and waved when Eden entered.

'You've not gone back to London for the weekend?' she asked him.

'No, I'm here for a few days.' Will leaned back in his seat and spread his arms out along the back of the sofa. 'I've done a bit of asking around since we spoke yesterday.'

'Oh yes?'

'I checked with some of my colleagues, and a few of them also said they'd lost stuff when they stayed at the Imperial Hotel. Nothing worth making a fuss about. Some of them reported it to the hotel manager, but none of them wanted to take it further and involve the police.'

'Too many awkward questions?'

'And too much hassle, to be honest. It's not worth having to make a statement and possibly come back to Cheltenham to give evidence, just for gloves and shoes and toiletries.'

'No one's thought to stay elsewhere?'

Will sniffed. 'The bookings are done by our travel team, and until you cropped up no one realised there was a problem with the Imperial.'

'So the bookings are made centrally?'

'Yes.'

Eden mashed butter into her croissant while she thought. 'Security there is pretty slack. They've had lots of little thefts, pilfering really, yet they're careless about where they leave access keys for the rooms.' She'd found a pass key in the pocket of an overall. Very handy both for nosy private investigators and minor thieves.

'What are you doing at the Imperial?' Will asked.

'I was investigating some poison pen letters sent to a client, and when he turned up dead, I hung around. That's how I know about the thefts.'

'You think the death and the thefts are linked?'

'Not sure, but my guess would be it's more in your line of work.' She caught his eye. 'Any known foreign interest here?'

Will paused before he answered. 'Russian and Chinese. We know that some of them have bought flats conveniently close to certain assets.'

'You ever take a camera, phone or laptop when you stay there?'

Will slumped as he said, 'Yes. Bugger!'

'And you leave them behind in your room when you visit certain assets?'

'But no one's had a phone or laptop stolen.'

'The thief doesn't need to.' She polished off the last of the croissant. 'I'll keep on digging and let you know if I find anything. But I have to tell you, Will, I wouldn't stay at the Imperial any more if I was you. And I'd warn your colleagues to steer clear, too.'

'Point taken.'

Her mobile rang as she finished her coffee and was debating whether to have another. 'Aidan, what's the matter?' she said, when she heard his voice. She listened for a few moments, sighed, and hung up. 'I've got to go, Will,' she said. 'That was my boyfriend. He's discharged himself from hospital.'

The nurses weren't at all happy about Aidan leaving, and told Eden repeatedly that he was not to be left alone and that if he became groggy or confused at any point, she was to bring him straight back to hospital.

'I only saw you a couple of hours ago,' she grumbled, as she helped him into her car. 'All you had to do was lie in bed and be quiet.'

'I can do that at home,' he said. 'I was bored. And the curtains had got swirly bits on that just wouldn't line up and I couldn't make the tiles fit any sort of pattern.'

She started the engine. 'All right,' she sighed. 'But you're not going home, you'll have to stay at my place.'

'I promise I'll behave myself.'

She snorted as she pulled away. 'That'll be the day.'

She settled him on the settee while she stripped the bed and remade it with fresh sheets. Aidan always loved the feel of crisp sheets: another thing that calmed his mind and stopped his thoughts from whirring. With the pillows plumped up, and the sheet yanked tight, she helped him undress, wincing at the bruises on his back, arms and neck, and eased him into the cold sheets. He sighed with relief when his head met the chill pillow.

'No coffee for you,' she said, drawing the duvet up to his shoulders, 'but I've got plenty of green tea. And I bought you a present.'

She took a purple paper bag out of her drawer and handed it to him. Inside was a hardback copy of Victorian fairy tales.

Aidan swooped on the book with a cry of delight. 'Brilliant! Thank you! Where did you find it?'

'That bookshop in Suffolk Square. It was in the window. Thought it might cheer you up.'

'Thanks, Eden.' He was already turning the pages and sinking more comfortably into the pillows.

She lay down on top of the covers beside him. 'I've got some work to do. Will you be OK here while I get on with something? I'll only be in the next room if you want me.'

'Yeah,' he said, evidently not listening and already engrossed in the book.

She left him to it and went to her dining table where she spread a huge sheet of blank paper. In the middle she drew a circle and wrote Lewis Jordan's name, then drew circles around him, labelled them with the people in his life, and drew connections between them. She added in the events of the case: the poison pen letters, the thefts from the hotel rooms, Lewis' murder, the stolen Blood, and the attack on Aidan. Then she started to compile a timeline of everything that had happened, back to when she rescued the boy and discovered the skeleton and the Holy Blood of Hailes.

Aidan shuffled out of the bedroom a few hours later, bleary eyed and with his dark hair sticking up at the back. He pulled out a chair at the table and looked over the mind maps and timelines Eden had drawn up.

'What's this?' he asked.

'Everything I know about Lewis Jordan.' She scrubbed her hands over her face. 'It doesn't make sense. Poison pen letters, large amounts of money paid into his account that immediately go out again, background checks on everyone, thefts from the hotel, oven cleaner put in his eye drops, Lewis killed, the Holy Blood stolen.'

'You think it's all linked?'

'It can't be. Too much going on. The trouble is, the key people seem to have alibis.'

'Can you corroborate any of them?'

She snapped her fingers. 'The CCTV. At least it will help to confirm the timeline.'

'Want some help with it?'

'You should be resting.'

'I'm going a bit mad with all this resting. Come on, Sherlock, break out the CCTV.'

She dug out the DVD she'd stolen from the hotel's security office and slotted it into her DVD player. 'May as well watch it on the big screen,' she said.

'Do we get popcorn?' Aidan asked, making himself a nest of pillows on the settee.

'Coming up.' She scavenged a large bag of crisps and a block of fruit and nut chocolate from the kitchen. 'Budge up.'

For two hours they skipped through the CCTV footage, noting the arrivals and departures of everyone who went through the revolving door. Aidan's sharp eyes and photographic memory were a blessing with this chore: despite his head injury he could remember faces, no matter how blurry, and recall when he'd seen them coming and going before.

Eden paused the DVD. 'That's everyone. We've seen Lisa arriving and leaving, before Lewis was killed, and we've had the film crew staggering back, after he was killed.'

'What was the time of death?'

'The people in the room next to his heard a rumpus at ten. I think that was when he was attacked.' Her words tailed away. 'But we don't know whether he died immediately. In fact, they said they also heard a scream at about midnight.'

'Does it make a difference?'

'Yes, because the rumpus could have been him lumbering around after he'd put in his eye drops.' She sat for a moment, fiddling with her bracelet. 'The corrosive in the drops didn't kill him, but it must have been agonising. And there was no sign of that in his hotel room when I found him.'

'What do you mean?'

'There was no turned over furniture, no evidence he'd blundered about crashing into things while his eyes burned out. Only some bloody handprints on the carpet.' She jumped up from the sofa. 'He could have been killed later. We could be working on completely the wrong time of death.'

'Where are you going?'

'I need to check his hotel room.' She planted a kiss on the top of his head. 'Won't be long.'

She grabbed her jacket and bag, and hurried out of the flat.

The Imperial Hotel wasn't far away, and soon she was pushing through the revolving doors and heading across the black and white marble floor to the staircase. Gabor was clearing tables in the bar and gave her a wave when she walked past.

'Hello, Gabor,' she said. 'I was only talking about Hungary the other day. And talking about that café we were discussing, the one in Budapest.'

'Ah yes, the café, with the best coffee in the world!'

'And the best honey pastries,' she said. 'The one in Oktogon Square.'

Gabor kissed his fingertips. 'The thing that makes me sick for home. Those honey pastries from Oktogon Square.'

'Good to see you, Gabor. Maybe I'll see if that café will do international orders.'

She trotted up the stairs and headed to room 204. Blue and white police tape was strung across the doorway. Checking the corridor was empty, she pulled out her library card, slotted it between the door and the frame, tugged the door towards her sharply, and it swung open. She ducked under the tape and went inside, closing the door swiftly behind her.

The curtains were open but the room was gloomy. She switched on the light and took a good look. A large brownish stain on the carpet, with a blackish stain next to it. The bed had been stripped: no doubt the police were swabbing it for bodily fluids. Splodges of fingerprint dust coated every surface. Eden pulled on a pair of latex gloves and set about re-examining the room where Lewis Jordan met his death.

She started by the door, sliding open the drawers of the bedside table and stirring the contents before moving on to the wardrobe, the bathroom and the minibar. The teabag in the bin had dried and hardened into a lump, stuck to the empty sweet packet. The heavy stone lamp she'd noticed when she discovered Lewis's body was missing. Bagged by the police, she assumed, along with Lewis's belongings. Was the lamp the murder weapon?

Crawling on her hands and knees, Eden scoured every inch of carpet. There were indentations in the pile beneath the small table, slightly to the left. She lifted it and fitted the table's legs into the dents. It matched exactly: the table had been moved.

Carefully she checked the rest of the room. No other pieces of furniture had been shifted out of position. Casting a last look around the room, she snapped off her latex gloves, peeped out into the corridor to make sure the coast was clear, and made her escape.

'Hardly any crashing around after he put in his drops,' Eden told Aidan once back at her flat. 'Only one thing had been moved, and that's a little table.'

'So the killer poisoned the drops and then hit him over the head?' Aidan said.

'Why would you bother doing both?' Eden said. 'My guess is he was hit with the lamp, which suggests it wasn't premeditated. Poisoning the drops was definitely planned, and it could only have been done by someone who knew him. If they meant to kill him, they could have put cyanide in the drops.'

'I've found something odd on the CCTV,' Aidan said. 'Someone who went in through the front door at eight, and left through the staff door at ten thirty.'

'Show me.'

He flicked through the DVD until he got to the right part and pressed play. A man entered the hotel just before eight, smartly dressed in a suit and overcoat, and carrying a leather briefcase. He didn't leave the hotel again, and Eden had assumed he was a guest in the hotel. But when they switched to view the CCTV that covered the staff entrance, there he was, leaving in a hurry and clutching his briefcase to his chest.

'Is he anywhere else on the CCTV?'

'Not that I can see.'

'Play it again, Sam,' Eden said, grabbing a handful of crisps and flopping back against the sofa cushions. 'Gabor said someone with a briefcase waited in the bar for a date to turn up. He could have sneaked out the side entrance if he was embarrassed about bumping into her.'

'A blind date he didn't like the look of?' Aidan suggested.

He started the CCTV coverage right at the beginning, and they watched the comings and goings at the Imperial from 10 a.m. the day Lewis was murdered, flicking through it frame by frame.

'I've seen better movies,' Aidan said.

'Hold it!' Eden sat forwards on the settee. 'Go back a bit. Now play. Stop!'

The picture was grainy but she could make out the person going into the staff entrance of the Imperial Hotel at five past five on the evening Lewis Jordan was killed. The pale stripes in her hair were distinctive.

'What the hell is she doing there?' Eden breathed.

It was Gwen, the receptionist at Simon Hughes' office. The woman who told her Lewis Jordan should have been drowned at birth.

CHAPTER
TWENTY-FOUR

Winchcombe, September 1571

Whatever the physic was that Brother John gave him, it sent him to sleep as certainly as if he'd dropped magic dust into his eyes. For once his sleep was dreamless: no creeping childish hands or merry dark eyes to haunt him that night, and he awoke refreshed. Lazarus shuffled out of bed and tested his gammy leg. A groan from the wound, but not the scream of pain that had accompanied every step for the past weeks.

Hobbling downstairs, he found the innkeeper awake and busy: the glare he treated him to yesterday had obviously hit its mark, and the fellow was brisk and efficient enough. He ate in the parlour at the front of the inn, overlooking the main street. The tradespeople were stirring, throwing back shutters and dragging baskets of goods outside. While he watched, a dark figure rode past on a chestnut mare. Lazarus stared after the figure, saw it turn to call greetings, and recognised the profile with a jolt. Brother John.

He stuffed the bread and meat inside his shirt and swilled back the pot of ale in two gulps, then hurried from the inn and fetched his horse. The animal was sluggish with age, but the main street was long and straight, and he easily kept the figure in sight. Beyond Winchcombe, Brother John urged his horse to a canter and headed north, Lazarus in pursuit. After about eight miles, he turned to enter through a pillared gateway and trotted up to a fine manor house built in the old style.

Lazarus lurked by the pillars and watched as Brother John dismounted and handed his reins to a boy of about twelve, pale and skinny as a sapling. Then Brother John went into the house through the main door. Not the kitchen, he noted with interest. And the boy coming to meet him suggested he was expected. A wealthy patron in need of physic? But surely there was physic to be had closer than this?

He clambered down from his horse and walked up to the house and went round the back to the stables. The boy he'd seen take Brother John's horse was there, brushing the sweat from the animal.

'Boy!'

The lad jumped and balked when he saw Lazarus's face, but soon twitched his features into a blank mask.

'Master?'

'Boy, I am ashamed that I am lost. What place is this?'

'Ashford Grange.' He looked astonished that anyone could fail to know this place. 'Where are you heading?'

'I am servant to Master John. My horse took a stone and he went on ahead.' He looked at the mare as if for the first time. 'Ah! God favours me, that's his horse! I have found him!'

'He is inside.'

'Who is it that is sick in this house?'

'Sick? None is sick.'

'I beg pardon, I assumed that Master John was here to tend someone who ails.'

The boy frowned. 'John Ashford? He is with his family inside.'

It took a moment for the words to sink in. John Ashford. He had never thought of him as anything other than Brother John, but all men hail from somewhere. Even him. He looked again at the manor house and recalled Brother John's learning. A younger son, farmed out to the Church, it was a familiar story.

'And you, boy, what do they call you?'

'Edgar.' The boy's eyes darted to his face and away again, as if he couldn't believe the wounds there and had to keep checking his eyes didn't deceive him.

'Can I get a drink, boy?'

Edgar showed him to the kitchen door, and told the cook there that he was Master John's servant. The cook went to the buttery to fetch ale for him. He gulped it thirstily, watching her, and when she busied away into the herb garden, he slipped out of the room and into a corridor. It skirted the great hall and led to a staircase to the upper chambers. The house was unnaturally quiet. Apart from Edgar and the cook he had seen no other servants. There should have been maids scurrying along with piles of bedlinen and pails, boys fetching in firewood, and men stationed at the main door. Lazarus's senses prickled.

He loped up the stairs and headed along the passageway. A small door opened onto a minstrels' gallery, the screens to the great hall closed but rackety enough to allow the sound of voices to drift through. Lazarus insinuated himself into a dark corner and pressed his eye to a crack in the screen. Below, he could make out a large rectangular room hung with tapestries.

There were five people in the room: Brother John, a man a few years older than him and sharing the same large nose and protuberant blue eyes, a young man of thirty, an old woman in her sixties, and a priest. Lazarus caught his breath when he saw the priest. While he watched, the priest opened a leather bag and pulled out an altar stone, which he set down on a table, resting on it the communion vessels, the bread and wine. When he held up the bread and declared it transformed into Christ's body, Lazarus shrank back, afraid.

Here was treason. All the ways of the old religion were outlawed, and there were many tripping over themselves to turn in neighbours and cast doubt on honourable men. The hangman and the fires were kept busy scouring the land free of the pestilence of popery. Should anyone betray them, everyone in the house would be hanged, from Edgar the stable lad to him, peeping at heresy. The priest would be torn to pieces on the rack to reveal his fellow Jesuits. Cold fear sluiced his back. He could face a man with a sword in his hand and murder in his eyes, but secret dealings in empty houses clotted his blood with terror.

When the Mass concluded, the priest packed up his vestments and plate and the group moved to sit together at the far end of the room.

'We must act swiftly,' the older man said, 'the roads will be impassable soon. We must strike while the sea is in our favour.'

'We can only act when everything is in place,' Brother John said. 'Our supporters in the north?'

'Ready to march on London,' the youth said.

'And our Spanish friends?'

'Eager for the fight.'

'And our friends at home?'

A silence fell. Brother John glanced from one to the other, his brow creasing. 'Our friends hesitate?'

'They are afraid,' the woman said.

'But to do God's will!'

She shrugged and looked to the older man. 'Husband?'

'I have made certain promises to ensure their loyalty,' he said. He pulled a paper out and handed it to Brother John. 'They require the certainty of eternal salvation,' he added.

Lazarus shuffled closer to the screen, trying to glimpse the paper. He could make out only close writing on a scrap.

Brother John studied the scrap. 'The Blood,' he said, quietly.

The woman nodded.

'How am I to gain entry to their houses?'

'You will take physic to them, uncle,' the youth said. 'We've agreed the ailments that require your skill. They're already acting the part, and await your visit.'

Brother John pressed his fingertips together. 'And this will guarantee their support?'

'Yes, uncle.'

'And the Queen herself, has word been sent to her?'

'There's a servant there who can get letters to her lady-in-waiting. She knows she will soon be free and in her rightful place.'

Brother John was silent for a moment. 'Then there is no time to lose.'

Lazarus slid back from the screen and crept back down the stairs and outside. Walking round towards the stables, he saw Edgar lurking beneath the window of the great hall, peering in. He drew back to watch. The boy spied for a few more minutes then slipped away, keeping his head well down so he would not betray his presence. Edgar did not return to the stables but scuttled off across the field behind the house. Going to meet a sweetheart, or on a more sinister mission, Lazarus wondered, following the boy at a distance.

The lad kept clear of the paths around the house, taking for his route the bank beside a stream. Lazarus shadowed him, keeping sufficient distance that he would not be betrayed by creaking twigs or restless grass. After a distance, the boy plunged into a thicket, dark with overhanging branches. Further on, the trees thinned to a clearing, and here he stopped and loitered next to a tree. Lazarus lurked behind a thick oak and waited. After a few moments, another man revealed himself, peeling himself away from a tree where he had stood disguised as shadow play. A man who knew his trade, Lazarus thought.

'What have you for me?' he asked the boy.

'A priest in the house, and they heard Mass.'

'Who?'

'James Ashford and his wife, his brother John Ashford, and his son Joseph.'

'Who is the priest?'

'Anthony Newbury.'

'They heard Mass?'

'And talked of freeing the Queen.'

'Of Scots?'

'They didn't mention her by name, but said she would soon be free. They have friends in the north and in Spain who are ready to act.'

The man dug out a purse and handed it to the youth. 'Keep watching, boy,' he said, and melted away into the trees.

Lazarus shrank back against the oak as the boy passed, but he was too pleased with the purse of coins to look about him. He gave the lad several minutes then headed back to Ashford Grange himself.

When he turned into the stable yard, the boy was brushing his own bowed nag.

'You tend a horse well, boy,' he said.

The boy nodded and flushed, unused to compliments.

'I will take my horse now,' Lazarus said, seizing the reins.

'You're not waiting for Master John?'

Lazarus climbed into the saddle, his wounds screaming. The ride here and hunkering down in the minstrels' gallery had taken their toll. 'He has sent me ahead with a message,' he said, kicking the horse's flank and cantering out of the yard. He kept up the pace until he was away from Ashford Grange and back on the highway, then brought the horse to a walk. The animal's sides heaved in and out, exhausted by the day's ride. They ambled back to Winchcombe and had just reached the inn when Brother John rode past on his chestnut mare, his face set and his eyes staring straight ahead.

'You play a dangerous game, my friend,' Lazarus muttered to himself, and turned away.

The next morning, Lazarus was awake and up before anyone was stirring in the inn. He unbolted the door and crept out into the dark street and made his way out of Winchcombe and towards Hailes Abbey. He slipped through the ruined gatehouse like a shadow and headed towards the church. The stones had been torn down, like the stripped carcass of a slaughtered bull – reduced to bare ribs and nubs of gristle. He stood now amongst the bones.

The walls were smudged with paint here and there, a ghost of its former self. The altar that had held the Holy Blood remained as a solid lump of stone, but the screens and curtains and gilding were all gone. As he stood there, he felt the press of pilgrims at his back, smelt the sweat and dust of garments that had journeyed long to be here, heard the cries of grief and awe as the Blood was revealed.

When he opened his eyes, he was shocked for a moment to be confronted by the jagged broken walls of the church, and a shard of anguish penetrated his heart. He circled the ruins and came to stand in the spot the trunk had occupied, the trunk that held the Holy Blood. There was nothing there now to show it had sheltered so sacred a relic, just a square of muddy grass in a pile of broken stones.

Lazarus ducked out of the back of the church and crept towards Brother John's cottage. A thin light shone through the cracks in the shutters. He squatted down behind a pile of shattered masonry and settled himself to watch.

He didn't have long to wait. The light was extinguished and the door opened. Brother John slung a pack across his shoulders and went to the field, whistling softly. The chestnut mare came to him, nuzzling at his hands. He saddled her up and was away, galloping across the fields towards the highway.

Lazarus eased open the door of the cottage and stepped inside. Dawn was chasing away the night and he opened the shutters wide to let in the light. He set to work, fanning the pages of books and Bibles, taking down every bottle and jar from the shelves, stripping the bedlinen and lifting the mattress and running his fingers between the ropes of the bed.

The Holy Blood was nowhere to be found. In the pack that bounced on Brother John's back, no doubt. But hidden at the bottom of a jar of dried rosemary was a scrap of paper folded many times into a tiny square. Lazarus smoothed it out and took it to the door to examine it. Squinting in the weak light, he read a list of names, houses, and illnesses. The paper that John's brother had handed him the day before, the names of supporters, fellow traitors.

He refolded the paper and slipped it into his glove, poking it deep inside one of the empty fingers. Then he returned the cottage to rights, using the circles of dust to replace the jars and bottles exactly so Brother John would suspect nothing amiss. Finally, he fastened the shutters and pulled the door closed behind him. Armed with information that could send Brother John to the scaffold, he went back to the inn.

He was no stranger to killing for love.

He met Theresa in the Holy Land. She was every man's and no man's and he loved her instantly for her dusky skin and dark, mischievous eyes.

He was stumbling from a tavern one black night when he heard muffled screams, and followed the sound through a maze of tiny alleyways to a stinking yard. A man built of muscle and bone had a woman, fragile as a bird, pressed up against the wall, his thick forearm against her neck. She had a knife to his throat.

Lazarus sobered in a trice and ducked back into the alley for a weapon. A length of wood, not sturdy enough to kill, but sufficient to stun. He hefted it in his hands and ran back into the alleyway, striking the man on the back of his head.

He fell into the filth of the courtyard. Not dead but groaning. The woman peeled herself away from the wall, the knife pointed towards Lazarus.

'You let me go or I kill you,' she said.

'Get out now before he wakes up,' Lazarus said, moving to take her hand.

The knife was swift. A line of blood bubbled along his wrist.

'You bitch!' he shouted. 'I was trying to save your life. Run, if you've a mind to live. Or stay here and let him kill you, if that's what you want, I don't care.'

He kicked the lump on the ground in the ribs. It slithered and grumbled.

'You save me?' she said, the knife wavering.

He held out his hand again. 'Hurry,' he said, and she grabbed his hand and together they fled.

She took him to her house, to bathe the wound she'd given him. Her home was a simple daub hut, homely enough with bright woven rugs and cushions on the floor. He sat, cross-legged and self-conscious, in the middle of the floor, while she poured scented oil into a bowl and wiped the blood from his hands.

Her hair was long and loose, and as she brushed past him its warm sandalwood scent entranced him. The tickle of it on his bare skin sent rivers of fire streaming through his veins and his mind blurred. To lie tangled in that hair. To feel its silken journey along the length of his body. To wake imprisoned within its scent.

'You are mended,' she said, and took the bowl outside the hut to toss the soiled dregs into the gutter.

Lazarus stayed on the cushion, loathe to leave yet unsure how to stay. As he sat, his warrior's senses prickled. He was being watched. Slowly, he got up from the cushion and prowled round the hut. So many rugs and tapestries and hangings, there could be an army concealed behind them. He twitched them back in turn, the skin on the back of his neck alive. Hidden in a pile of cushions at the back of the hut, he found his observer.

A child. A little girl of about four, with dark solemn eyes and long black hair. She stared at him and he stared back. Then she started to whimper.

'Hey now, mistress,' he said, softly. 'No need for crying. See what I have here.'

He dug in his jacket and pulled out a rag. He twisted the end of it into a knot and slid his finger into it, making a puppet. He bounced it along his forearm.

'Mister Rabbit on his way to market, see child,' he said. 'You want to see him?'

He held out the rag to her, his finger still inside it. After a moment's hesitation, she slid it from his finger.

'Now you put your finger here. There, now there's Mister Rabbit.'

The child crawled out of her nest and came to sit beside him, bouncing the rag along his arm and over his shoulder, bolder with every bounce. When the woman came back into the hut, the child was in his lap, and the rag puppet was exploring his beard.

'Mariam,' the woman said quietly.

'Mama,' the child answered, and held up the puppet.

'You are kind,' the woman said to Lazarus.

He'd never been called kind before. A good fighter, yes. Strong, of course. But kind? Never.

'Can I come back tomorrow?' he asked, dreaming again of the scent of her hair.

She shrugged.

Lazarus clambered to his feet. 'Tomorrow, then,' he said.

He was with her for two years. For two years he visited her hut, played with the child, and spent his nights tangled in the perfumed nest of her hair. She was not his alone, and his jealousy curdled and roiled inside him but he could not leave her. After a while he realised it was the joy of the child that drew him back and made him shove his jealousy aside.

There were many days when he and Mariam were alone in the hut while Theresa was out, doing what and with whom he cared not to contemplate. He pushed aside the thought of her with other men, and fought to think only of the time when he would be with her, trapped in her honey-coloured thighs and drowning in her dark eyes. When she was absent, he took the child out to explore the city, and hand-in-hand they went together to the gardens and markets, adventurers in a new land together.

'A flower for you, my lovely,' he said, plucking a rose from the garden and tucking it into her smock.

She bent her head to smell it. 'Thank you, Dadda,' she said.

Dadda. She had never called him that before. He must be an old man with an old man's soft heart to be turned so by the sound of a single word, but turned he was. Dadda. He squeezed her hand and they walked to the market and he bought her a doll, just to hear her say it again.

He was sent away to fight, and was gone for three months. He returned alive but scarred, both in body and mind at the horrors he had witnessed. Other men's wars, he thought grimly to himself, as the image of a pile of bodies filled his mind. The crones digging through the corpses, stripping them of rings, clothes, teeth: anything they could sell, until all that was left was a stinking pile of flesh without dignity who no one cared to bury.

As he approached Theresa's hut, a man lumbered out, fastening his breeches. Theresa was in the doorway, tucking coins into a purse, and in the back of the hut was Mariam, eyes huge and tears trickling into her mouth.

'What's this?' Lazarus said.

'You know what I am,' Theresa said, wrapping her hair around her hand and tying it back from her face with a scarf.

'You, yes, but the child!'

Theresa shrugged. 'She needs to learn.'

Her words felled him harder than any sword.

'What?'

'She has to make her living. I cannot feed us both.'

'But I'm here now. I'll take care of you.'

Theresa fixed him with a look, and he shuddered at the hardness in her eyes. 'You have been away, fighting, killing. I do not know when you will return, or if you are dead. We need food. I cannot wait for a man who might already be dead.'

'You sold her?'

'She will go when she is seven.'

'You sold her?'

Theresa squared up to him. 'She is my daughter. She is mine. I will do as I wish.'

'She is too young!'

'She is the same age I was.' Theresa bent to rearrange the floor cushions. They released the stench of male sweat.

'No,' Lazarus said, catching her arm. 'How much? I will buy her myself.'

'You can't. It is arranged. If I do not give her they will kill me.'

'Give them the money back. Say she is sick, dying. Don't do it, Theresa.'

Her shoulders slumped. 'You think you can hide her? Here? Where everyone knows what everyone is doing? And if you take her away, where will you go? Who will protect her while you are fighting?'

The truth of what she said only fired his desolation. 'I'll give up fighting, set up in my own business.'

'Doing what?' she said. 'You know of nothing but death.'

It was all he had known his whole life: death. Of pitiful creatures, of other men's enemies, of strangers he was contracted to kill. His blood raged, churned by impotence into a frothing despair. He didn't know what he did; only that Theresa's head snapped back and she fell to the floor. Her teeth ground against her lips as she struggled, and when it was done her mouth was bloodied. A squeal from the back of the hut brought him to his senses.

'Mariam,' he said, gently. 'Come to me. I shall protect you.'

He coaxed her from her nest of cushions and she came to sit on his lap, her head against his chest. He crooned to her and wiped the tears from her face, sang her silly stories until a smile dawned at last. Beside them, Theresa lay limp and still.

'You know I love you more than life itself?' Lazarus whispered to the child.

'Yes, Dadda.'

'And that I would do anything to protect you, my precious?'

'Yes, Dadda.'

'Go to sleep now, then, and may the angels guard your rest.'

And he put his hands on her head as if in benediction and with a quick twist snapped her neck.

When it was done, he sat for a long time with her in his arms, weeping. His tears fell onto her face and washed her tiny hands. Safe with Jesus, he repeated to himself. He could not protect her, only send her to one who could protect her for eternity. He prayed hard over her body, the words remembered from another lifetime in an Abbey in Gloucestershire, echoed now in a hut in a hot and dusty country, far from home, over the dead bodies of the only people he loved in the world.

CHAPTER
TWENTY-FIVE

Sunday, 1 November 2015

05:46 hours

Aidan groaned and whimpered in his sleep, startling her awake. She rubbed his back and soothed him into sweeter dreams, but sleep eluded her and she lay staring into the darkness, thinking over the case and worrying what to do next. By the time early morning light crept at the edges of the curtains, she was sweaty and narky, and knew the only thing was for her to get up and run herself into a better mood.

Eden slipped from the bed and found her running gear. She stroked Aidan's shoulder until he stirred.

'You OK?' she whispered.

'Hm-mm,' he groaned. 'Head hurts.'

'Very bad?'

'Uh-huh.'

'I'll get your painkillers.'

She fetched a glass of water and his tablets, and helped him sit up and take them. His skin was clammy and the musty scent of illness clung to his pyjamas.

'Will you be alright for an hour while I have a run?' Eden asked.

'Yes, I'll be fine. Just need some rest.'

She tucked him back in and watched him surrender to sleep, then left the flat. She froze at the entrance, Hammond's phone call echoing in her mind. He was out to get her; had a network of scum that would be only too happy to scoop her up and deliver her to her fate. Was he behind Aidan's attack? For a moment her courage failed and she half turned to go back inside, then a spurt of anger fired her. Damn him! If she cowered inside, too afraid to leave the flat, then he would have won. A life half lived was no life at all. She wouldn't let him crush her.

She stretched her legs then set off at a steady pace, keeping her senses on high alert. The Sunday streets were silent. She pounded down to the university campus through streets of large, elegant villas set in mature gardens. Painted shutters, amber stone and lilting ironwork all attested to the continued wealth of the area. The university campus itself was a delight: swathes of lawn clouded with early morning mist, and punctuated with stately trees. She ran a circuit of the lake and ornamental gardens until a stitch in her side brought her up short, and she did some stretches until it eased, surveyed by a pair of bright eyes.

'Hello, pussycat,' she said, and the green eyes blinked.

She and Nick had wanted to have a cat, but somehow the time was never right. That was the problem with undercover work: the hours were irregular. She never knew when or even if she'd be home. Nick hated that. And now he had a new wife, and a little girl. Holly. Underneath the hurt, she was pleased for him, glad he'd managed to create a normal life after the train wreck of their relationship.

'You know what I want, pussycat?' she said, doing some side bends and feeling a nip in her back. 'One of those pastries from the café in Budapest.'

As she set off running again, she wondered if they really did do international orders?

She headed down the narrow streets behind the town hall and made a few laps of Imperial Gardens. There had been a party in the gardens that night, judging by the pyramid of empty beer bottles in the centre of an empty flowerbed. She passed the litter bin where she'd found the half-burned poison pen letter to Lewis Jordan and headed for home.

As she approached the Imperial Hotel, she saw Jocasta and Xanthe huddled on the pavement. Xanthe had her arms crossed, hugging a faux fur jacket about herself. Jocasta was sucking on a cigarette. Eden jogged over.

'Hello,' she said. 'I thought you'd gone back to London.'

'The others have,' Xanthe said. 'We decided to stay a bit longer.'

'Oh?'

'We had a spa day, a bit of pampering, just us two,' Xanthe said. She turned to gaze at Jocasta and her eyes moistened.

'That sounds nice,' Eden said.

Jocasta dropped her cigarette butt and ground it out with the toe of her boot. 'It was. After everything that's happened.'

Her words choked and she looked away, blinking rapidly. She fumbled with her cigarette packet and drew out a fresh cigarette and a silver lighter with trembling fingers.

'Oh babes!' Xanthe cried, putting her hand on her wrist. 'Sweetie, don't get upset.'

Jocasta replaced the cigarette. 'I can't believe he's gone.'

An anguished look haunted Xanthe's face. 'I know,' she said, her voice catching. 'That's why I wanted us to have a nice couple of days.'

'I'm glad I've bumped into you, actually,' Eden said. 'You remember you lent me Lewis's laptop?'

'Yeah,' Jocasta replied.

'How long had Lewis had it?'

'Not long,' Jocasta said. 'Two, maybe three weeks before he …' her voice caught.

'And was it bought new?'

'No, it was my work laptop,' Xanthe said. 'He commandeered it when he left his in a pub somewhere.'

'And how long had you had it?'

She shrugged, thin shoulders moving inside the coat. 'A year?'

'So why is Jocasta's name down as the document owner?'

'Jocasta installed all the software,' Xanthe said. 'I'm useless at that kind of thing.'

Eden made a rapid calculation. 'Can you give me a minute in private with Xanthe please, Jocasta?'

'If you want.' Jocasta flicked her ponytail over her shoulder and disappeared into the hotel.

Eden watched her go, then faced Xanthe. 'How long have you been in love with her?'

Xanthe's face crumbled. 'Too long. I know it's hopeless – she's straight. But ...' She shrugged to demonstrate the vagaries of the human heart.

'Is that why you sent Lewis those poison pen letters?'

Xanthe recoiled as if she'd slapped her. 'I didn't ... I wouldn't ...'

'The drafts were in the recycle bin on the laptop.'

Xanthe tucked her hands up her sleeves. 'He used her and dumped her like a tissue he'd sneezed into. And then when he started calling her Jo-Jo, well, it was just cruel.' Her shoulders drooped in defeat. 'I sent the first one as a sort of revenge because he'd been taunting her. Then I thought I'd send one every time he was a shit to her. Teach him a lesson.' Her head jerked up. 'I didn't kill him.'

'You were in his room, though, weren't you?'

Xanthe sucked in a sharp breath. 'How do you know?'

'Because one of the letters was in Lewis's room earlier in the evening, and I found it half-burned in a litter bin in the park here,' Eden said. 'There was a box of matches in with it, from the club you went to with the tech guys. It wasn't Jocasta, because she smokes and has a lighter. I think you took the letter from Lewis's room and tried to get rid of it.' She paused to let the words sink in. 'What happened?'

Xanthe swallowed. 'I'd had too much to drink. I came back from the club, and when I walked past Lewis's room I thought I'd tell him what I thought of him. I knocked on the door and it wasn't shut properly, the door just swung open, so I went in.' She hesitated.

'Go on,' Eden said.

'He was on the floor, face down. There was blood all round his head.'

'You turned him over, didn't you?'

'How …?'

'You told me how shocked you were when you saw his eyes,' Eden said. 'But you could only have seen them if you'd been in his room. The police didn't let you see his body.'

A tremor ran through Xanthe and she hugged her coat tighter. 'It was horrible. His eyes all burned and his mouth black. I dropped him, and he flopped back onto his face.'

'What did the room look like?'

'What do you mean?'

'Was anything knocked over?'

'No. There was just Lewis on the floor,' Xanthe said. 'And then I saw the letter on the table. I'd pushed it under his door earlier, trying to frighten him, so I grabbed the letter and ran, and the door locked behind me.'

'Was Lewis dead when you found him?'

Xanthe's face worked and she was unable to speak for a moment. 'Yes.'

'What did you do with the whisky glasses?'

'I thought …' Xanthe's voice cracked and she visibly pulled herself together. 'I thought Jocasta had killed him, so I took the glasses and put them on a tray in the corridor so the police wouldn't have her DNA.' She looked up at Eden, her eyes dark with fear. 'Did she kill him?'

Eden didn't reply.

Aidan was still sleeping when she got home, and on a whim she powered up her laptop and ran the name of the Budapest café into a search engine, determined that if they did international orders she'd buy herself some of those honey cakes as a Christmas present. Judy would love them, too, she thought, imagining a girly evening with honey pastries and a bottle of sticky wine.

Tordai Street. That wasn't right. It was in Oktogon Square. She'd argued with Nick that it was definitely in Oktogon Square. She'd talked about it with Gabor in the hotel, and he should know, it was his home town.

She clicked on the link. It was definitely the right place, she recognised the picture. Nick was right and she had got the street wrong. And that meant that Gabor had got it wrong, too. Alarm bells sounded. How had he got it wrong? She replayed their conversation and recognised that Gabor never volunteered information, only agreed with whatever she said. It was what she was taught to do when she went undercover: wherever possible, follow the lead of whoever you're speaking to. And that's just what Gabor had done, but they'd both got it wrong.

And the question remained, why would the barman at the Imperial Hotel need a cover story anyway?

Aidan woke a couple of hours later, shuffling into the kitchen and grabbing the coffee pot. 'All that green tea is driving me mad,' he said, to her raised eyebrow.

'How's your headache?'

'Getting better.'

She pointed at a carrier bag on the worktop. 'Fancy a late brekky? I bought some of those pain au chocolat things you finish off in the oven.'

'Sounds great.' He poured boiling water onto coffee grains. 'What are we up to today?'

'You're resting,' she said, 'and I'm still tracking down a murderer.'

'How can I help?'

'It's just going to be grunt work. Lots and lots of Internet searches and probably not finding anything useful at the end of it.'

'I can make notes for you,' he said. 'I'm good at sifting lots of data.'

'If you're sure you're up to it.'

'Please. I need something to do.'

She kissed him. 'You're a terrible patient,' she said. 'OK, you can help, but if that headache gets worse, you stop and go back to bed.'

They sat side by side at the table, Eden driving the laptop, Aidan with a huge sheet of paper spread in front of him.

'We're looking for relic hunters,' Eden said. 'I'm going to start with auction houses and see who's buying what.'

'That could give you hundreds of people,' Aidan said. 'How are you going to filter the results?'

Eden thought for a moment. 'As someone's prepared to kill for the Holy Blood, I'll stick to the high rollers.'

'And what types of relics?' Aidan said. 'There are all sorts out there. Icons and paintings and toenails and bits of foreskin.'

Eden wrinkled her nose. 'Yuk.'

'What's your hypothesis?'

'Someone carried out background research on everyone associated with the Holy Blood; someone who was careful to conceal their identity,' Eden said. 'What if that research was to find a weak link: someone who could be bought to get hold of the Holy Blood. Two weeks before he died, Lewis was paid thirty thousand in cash. He immediately paid over every penny to his mother, even though he was in debt to his eyeballs. That suggests he knew that more, lots more, was coming in. What if he was paid to steal the Holy Blood, was given a down payment, and was going to get a shed load of money when he handed it over? But Lisa pinched the Blood from Lewis, the deal goes sour, and Lewis ends up dead.'

'So we're looking for a relic collector with plenty of cash who is drawn to physical artefacts,' Aidan said. 'We'll ignore the people who collect icons and statues for now, unless the statues weep blood or something.'

'Sounds good,' Eden said, opening a search engine. 'Let's start there.'

It was painstaking work, but as Aidan reminded her, they were both used to handling large sets of data and to sifting and analysing detail. When they took a break, they had a list of fifteen names who regularly spent huge sums on artefacts when they came up for sale in auctions. Twelve men and three women who handed over thousands on scraps of cloth that had draped saints' bodies, little finger bones, tears of the Virgin Mary, and fragments of the true cross.

'Why do they want this stuff?' Eden said. 'Surely they know it's fake?'

'They don't, that's the point. When people went on pilgrimage to places that had relics, they truly believed that it was a finger bone of that saint, or a piece of the Virgin's robe, and they knew absolutely that seeing it would give them time off in Purgatory,' Aidan said. 'That belief didn't just switch off because Henry VIII said so. I've found a Catholic house near Winchcombe during Elizabeth I's reign. They risked death every time they heard Mass, but they ran that risk because they knew what they were doing was right. That's belief.'

Eden chewed the side of her thumbnail. 'Faith,' she said, at last. 'We always used to say if you want motives look for money, love and lust. But I forgot about faith.'

And as she knew from when she used to recruit agents, belief, faith and patriotism were much stronger motivators than fear or money. As Aidan had just pointed out, people would risk everything for faith.

CHAPTER
TWENTY-SIX

Monday, 2 November 2015

08:02 hours

There was a parcel waiting for her when she came back from her morning run: a slender brown rectangle poking out of her pigeonhole. The label was printed and gave no clues as to the sender. Inside was a box of chocolates, her favourites, and a card that read, *Lovely to see you again, kiss kiss.*

Nick. He never wrote crosses for kisses, always wrote 'kiss kiss'. It was his thing, his special way of signing off every card he sent her. And her favourite chocolates. She was touched he remembered.

She tucked the parcel under her arm and smuggled it into her flat, wondering how to explain it to Aidan. He hadn't been best pleased to see Nick, the blast from her past, the other day, and now there seemed to be a truce between them she didn't want to upset it with a spike of jealousy. Fortunately, Aidan was asleep when she went in, so she left the chocolates in the kitchen and dumped the label and card in the bin.

'I've arranged a babysitter for you,' Eden said, when he woke. He was still pale and sick-looking. He never should have discharged himself from hospital.

'What? I'm fine.'

'Tough, it's sorted.' The doorbell rang. 'That'll be her.'

'Not Judy!' Aidan cried, swaddling himself in the duvet and trailing after her. 'She pervs at me when she thinks I'm not looking.'

'The poor deluded woman thinks you're sexy,' Eden said, opening the door. 'Come on in.'

'Oh bloody hell!' Aidan said.

'Morning, Aidan,' Mandy said, bustling in, a furry teddy-bear backpack slung over her shoulder. 'You look terrible.'

'How are things at the office? Was the place in a mess?'

'Don't worry about that now,' Mandy said, unwinding her long, stripy scarf. 'Me and Trev went and checked it all over with the police on Friday night, and locked everything up.' She fixed Aidan with a look. 'Why don't you go back to bed, or have a nice long bath or something?'

Aidan shot Eden a murderous look, which she feigned to ignore.

'Let me show you where everything is, Mandy,' Eden said. 'It's really good of you to come and keep an eye on him.'

'No problem, Eden. I've brought some work to do.'

'For me?' asked Aiden.

'No! You're sick!' Mandy cried.

'Fucking hell! I'm going berserk here!'

'Could he help you with what you've brought?' Eden said, showing Mandy into the kitchen and opening the cupboard doors to point out where the mugs and tea and coffee were kept.

'It's only background research on Catholic families,' Mandy said.

'Perfect. Let him do some of that. He's impossible otherwise.'

'I can hear you, you know.'

'Mind if I make a cuppa to get me started?' Mandy asked. Her mouth tugged down a little at the corners. Eden had never seen her miserable.

'You OK Mandy?'

Mandy lifted and dropped her shoulders. 'I've been a prat.'
She turned her back to Eden and filled the kettle at the sink. 'I
was seeing this bloke and he dumped me and I feel humiliated,
s'all.' When she faced the room again, tears welled in her eyes.

'Hey, Mands,' Eden said. 'That's the pits.'

'He was too good for me, really, kind of cool and I'm ...' she
glanced down at her jumper and jeans. 'Trev says if I smarten
myself up a bit I might have a chance of getting a boyfriend.'
Her eyes met Eden's. 'I'm nearly forty and look at me. No guy
my age is going to be interested in me.'

Eden studied her for a moment. Nothing hurt like unre-
quited love. It could brighten the dullest day, or it could be a
torment until your heart found someone else. 'You're you,' she
said. 'When someone comes along, he'll like you for you, not
because you've dressed yourself up as someone you're not.' She
thought for a moment. 'Would you like to come out with me
and my friend Judy some time? Judy's a good laugh, and she's
got good man-antennae. Though she did spot Aidan so she's
not infallible.'

Mandy smiled. 'Really?'

'Really.' It'd be a blast, her, Mandy and Judy on a night out.
Eden had often socialised with Aidan's team and knew they
all threw themselves wholeheartedly into having a good time.
And Judy was always up for a giggle. 'I'll ring Judy and we'll
make a date.'

Her eye fell on the box of chocolates. Dropping her voice
so Aidan couldn't hear, she said, 'And if you need cheering
up, help yourself to these chocolates. Only don't let Aidan see
them.'

'Why?'

'Present from an ex.' Eden pulled a face.

'No probs. Thanks, Eden.' Mandy's eyes fixed on the chocolates. Eden gave it two minutes before the wrapper was off.

'Right,' Eden said. 'Here's my phone number if you need me. I'll pop in later and make sure you haven't throttled him. He's a terrible patient.'

'Don't worry, Eden. I know what he's like: I work with him every day, remember.'

Eden squeezed her arm. 'Your reward will be in heaven.' She went back into the sitting room, where Aidan was watching the TV news with the sound turned off. She kissed the top of his head. 'I'm off to work. Be a good boy for Mandy, won't you.'

He mumbled something she couldn't quite hear but was probably rude, and she scarpered. First stop Lewis Jordan's mother, then to Birmingham and private investigator Bernard Mulligan.

09:26 hours

Tracey Jones opened the door a fraction and peered through the crack at her.

'Miss Jones? We met a few days ago. I wondered if I could ask you a few questions, please?'

'You're the detective, aren't you?' Tracey said, standing aside to let her in.

'I was working for Lewis … Lee, I mean.'

Tracey's sitting room was stifling, the windows running with condensation. Despite the heat, Tracey wrapped herself in a leopard print fleece and tucked herself into a corner of the sofa.

'Can I ask you about the money Lee gave you, before he died?'

'He was a good boy, always looked out for me,' Tracey said.

'He gave you thirty thousand pounds?'

'I'd run up a few debts,' Tracey said. Understatement of the century. 'Lee came into some money and gave it to me.'

'Even though he had debts of his own?'

Tracey rubbed her sleeve over her face. 'He said we'd be alright, both of us.'

'More where it came from?'

Tracey shrugged. 'I didn't ask. I was just glad he was there.'

There was another matter to clear up. Eden pulled a picture out of her bag, a screen shot from the hotel CCTV. 'Do you know this person?' she asked.

'She's aged,' Tracey said, unable to hide the triumph in her voice.

'You know her, then?'

'Another Holy Josephine,' she said. 'Her and her sister.'

'Sister?'

Tracey blinked at her. 'Her sister's Rose Taylor, Lee's foster mother.'

10:37 hours

The M5 was clogged and she had plenty of time to think as she made the journey to Birmingham. Bernard hadn't sounded surprised to hear from her when she'd called him early that morning. In his measured, dry voice he simply said, 'Hello again, what can I do you for?' and confirmed he was free to see her.

She parked again in the multi-storey in the jewellery quarter and walked to his office. Bernard was ready for her, the kettle steaming and the cups waiting with teabags inside them.

'NATO standard minus two,' he confirmed when she came in.

'You remembered,' she said, taking off her electric-blue leather jacket and folding it over the back of her chair.

'Very important in the Forces, how people take their tea,' Bernard said. 'I bet you've drunk some horrible cuppas in your time, eh?'

He fixed her with a direct gaze that told her he recognised exactly what she had been: a ghost, an undercover officer.

'Oh yes, plenty of those.' She looked again at him, noting the careful way he regarded her. 'You were in Intelligence, weren't you?'

Bernard nodded. 'Takes one to know one.'

'We spot each other, us spooks,' she said. 'Which is partly why I'm here.'

Bernard took the chair opposite hers and waited for her to continue.

'You did background checks on everyone who came into contact, even remotely, with the Holy Blood of Hailes,' Eden said. 'I wondered if I could look at the list again, please?'

'Who are you looking for?'

'Someone who works at the hotel where Lewis Jordan stayed.'

Bernard went over to a filing cabinet and pulled out a folder. He slid it over to Eden and she ran her eye down the list of names.

'Him,' she said, jabbing at a name towards the bottom. 'What did you find about him?'

Bernard hunted again in the filing cabinet and extracted a flimsy document. He turned the pages slowly. 'I remember this one. It was a bit odd. On the surface, he checked out, was who he seemed to be. But when I tried to dig further, I couldn't get anywhere at all.' He handed the paper to Eden. 'He doesn't really exist.'

She skimmed the pages. It was as she'd thought. A bubble of excitement rose in her chest: she'd found one of her targets. She handed back the document, unable to conceal a smile.

'You've got what you needed then?' Bernard said.

'For one bit of my puzzle, yes.' She dug in her bag and drew out a sheaf of papers. Each one had a photograph taken from the Internet. 'Could you look at these please, Bernard, and tell me if you recognise any of these people?'

Bernard took the pages and went through them one by one, frowning as he discarded them to one side. Finally, he looked up at her. 'This one,' he said. 'He's the one who asked me to do the background research.'

'The shy client who paid in cash?'

'That's him.'

'You're certain?'

Bernard gave her a look that reminded her he was ex-Intelligence and ex-copper, a man who had an eye for detail and understood the need for caution and certainty before acting.

'Who is he?' Bernard asked.

Eden turned the page over. She'd written the names and brief details of each person on the back of each sheet. 'Him,' she said, showing him the name.

As soon as she left Bernard's office, she made a phone call. 'Will? It's Eden Grey. Can you meet me tonight? And bring someone from your side who is authorised to make an arrest. I've found who stole your gloves.'

13:03 hours

Lunchtime, and as Eden approached Simon Hughes' office in Rodney Road, Gwen came down the steps and hurried down the street. Eden let her get ahead, then followed at a distance, careful not to stare at Gwen's back. She tracked her through the town centre and along a side street to a Catholic church. She waited until Gwen was inside, gave her a few moments, then slunk in at the back.

The scent of incense wrapped itself around her, teasing her not to sneeze. The walls were opulently painted in blue and gold, and richly coloured statues peered out at her with heavy-lidded eyes.

It took a moment to locate Gwen. She was in a side chapel presided over by a statue of the Virgin Mary. A bank of candles flickered against one wall. Gwen was in a pew towards the front of the chapel, and beside her was Rose Taylor. Eden crept in and took a seat behind them.

'I did it for you!' Gwen was muttering.

'I never asked you to!' Rose replied, her voice ripped with anguish. 'How could you?'

'You let me use your key, though.'

'Not so you could kill him!'

'I didn't!' Gwen hissed. 'I did what we agreed.'

'If I'd thought for one moment you'd kill him ...' Rose began.

'She didn't kill him,' Eden said.

Both women started and whipped around in their seats. Gwen's face was white and furious; Rose's twitched with fear.

'I wondered how it was you knew all about Lee's brushes with the law, when you've only worked in the solicitor's office for a few months,' Eden said. 'Now I know you're sisters, it makes sense. But what I want to know is why now? Over twenty years after Lee left your lives for good.'

'I don't know what you're talking about,' Gwen began, but Rose spoke over the top of her, 'He wasn't fit to see the Blood of Christ.'

'So you decided to blind him.'

'Not blind him, just ... hurt him a bit,' Rose said.

'It was oven cleaner in his eye drops,' Eden said. Rose shot a look at Gwen. 'Nasty, eh? I've seen the burns it causes on arms and hands. Goodness knows what it's like to get it in your eyes.'

'I thought you said you were ...' Rose began.

'Shut up, Rose! She doesn't know anything!'

'Only someone who knew Lewis, and knew about his drops, could doctor them. And it had to be someone who could get into his hotel room, because it was the drops in his washbag that were poisoned, not the ones in his jacket.' Eden shifted her gaze to Rose. 'Naturally I assumed it was you. You fostered Lewis, have a grudge against him, and you have a pass key to all the hotel rooms. But you didn't go into the hotel that day.'

Rose's mouth worked silently. Gwen crossed her arms and tutted in fury.

Eden continued. 'You're pretty careless with that pass key, Rose. I borrowed your overall the day after Lewis died and there it was in the pocket. Anyone could have borrowed that overall and got into as many rooms as they wanted.' She turned to Gwen. 'Couldn't they?'

Gwen tried to stare her down. 'This is ridiculous.'

'You're on CCTV, Gwen,' Eden said, 'going into the hotel through the staff entrance. Let me tell you what I think happened.'

A tear rolled down Rose's cheek to her lip. She wiped it away. 'Oven cleaner?' she whispered, staring at her sister in horror.

'There's no over cleaner in that store cupboard, so whoever doctored the eye drops took it in specially. Didn't you, Gwen?'

'You said it would be lemon juice!'

Gwen's hands curled into claws, leaving nail marks in her palms.

Eden carried on; 'You went into the hotel, found Rose's overall where she said it would be, and there was the pass key. She'd left it there for you. She'd also told you which room was Lewis's. You found his eye drops in the bathroom, and added oven cleaner to them.'

'He ruined Rose's life,' Gwen said, her hand creeping across the pew to clutch Rose's. 'And her children's lives, and all she'd wanted to do was care for him and give him a good home.' Her voice choked. 'He didn't care who he hurt.'

'So you decided to teach him a lesson?'

'He was on TV crowing about filming the Holy Blood. Actually boasted that he'd held it,' Gwen said bitterly, her face twisted with anger. 'He didn't deserve to see it. Not him. It made me feel sick to think of it.' She turned to her sister. 'It was sacrilege that monster seeing the Blood.'

Faith again, thought Eden, as she rose from the pew. And a good dollop of revenge. Gwen's eyes were defiant as she said, 'What are you going to do?'

'I'll have to tell the police,' Eden said.

'Good. I want the world to know what sort of man he was,' Gwen said. 'I didn't kill him, but I'd like to thank whoever did.'

14:23 hours

There was time to kill before she was due to meet Will Day, so Eden went home to see how Aidan was faring. As she let herself into her flat, she heard Aidan calling.

'Do you want a glass of water or something?'

'What's going on?'

'It's Mandy. She's been puking for ages.'

The sound of retching came from the bathroom. Eden hurried over and tapped on the door. 'Mandy? Are you all right?'

'A bit poorly,' came the gargled response.

'Can I come in?'

'It's not very nice in here.'

Eden pushed the door open. Mandy was slumped in a heap on the tiled floor, her face eau de Nil and sheened with sweat. Eden crouched beside her and felt her forehead, alarmed how clammy and chilled her skin was.

'How long have you been sick for?'

'It started about an hour ago.'

Eden pressed her fingers against Mandy's neck, feeling for a pulse. It was fast and weak.

'Were you feeling off-colour this morning?'

'No, I felt fine. Oh!' Mandy scuffled to her knees and was sick into the toilet bowl. She grabbed a handful of toilet paper and scrubbed her mouth clean. 'Sorry.'

'It's OK.' Eden stroked Mandy's hair back from her face. 'Is it something you ate?'

'I've only had a few crackers and fruit. And some of those chocolates.'

Eden went into the kitchen. The box of chocolates was open on the worktop. About half the chocolates were missing, their brown plastic coffins plundered. She tipped the rest out onto the worktop and turned them over. Tiny holes pierced the base of each chocolate. 'Shit!'

'What the hell?' Aidan said, as she pushed past him to the phone and dialled emergency services.

'Ambulance please. I think my friend's been poisoned.' She gave the address and Mandy's symptoms, then hung up. Mandy was being sick again. 'Ambulance is on its way.' Mandy turned a tearstained face to her as Eden hunkered beside her and put her arm round her shoulders. 'I'm so sorry, Mandy, I didn't think.'

'It's not your fault.'

Eden didn't reply. She scooped up some of the remaining chocolates and put them in a plastic bag.

The ambulance arrived within minutes and Mandy was strapped into a chair and taken to hospital. Eden went with her, clutching the chocolates. When a doctor came to assess Mandy, she handed over the bag.

'I think these have been poisoned,' she said.

'It's more likely to be gastric flu,' the doctor said, his head set at a patronising angle.

'If you look at the chocolates,' Eden said, her teeth gritted, 'you'll see they've been tampered with. And they were sent anonymously. Get them tested.'

The doctor sighed, but he took the bag. Mandy was admitted for tests and Eden sat with her, holding a cardboard bowl for her to be sick into.

'I'm so sorry about this, Eden. I was supposed to be looking after Aidan, not causing more problems.'

'You just relax and don't worry about a thing. You're going to be fine,' Eden said, praying it was true.

Mandy had fallen into an exhausted sleep by the time the doctor returned.

'Got the test results back?' Eden asked.

'I can't discuss it with you, I'm afraid,' the doctor said. 'You're not her next of kin.'

He checked Mandy's pulse and temperature, and scribbled in her notes. Eden sat and held Mandy's hand, nodding at the doctor when he left.

As soon as his footsteps receded, Eden grabbed Mandy's medical notes from the end of the bed and flicked through them. Pulse, temperature, medical jargon that said Mandy was vomiting, and then the results of the tests on the chocolates. She was right, and the knowledge brought her no comfort. It should be her in the hospital bed, not Mandy. There it was, in stark black and white:

Cause of vomiting: mistletoe poisoning.

18:06 hours

Aidan was pacing the floor, white-faced, when she returned home.

'Eden, thank God,' he said. 'How is she?'

'She's pretty poorly, but she'll be OK.'

'What happened?'

'She was poisoned.'

'What?'

Eden sucked in a deep breath. 'It was meant for me, Aidan. Mandy was collateral damage.' She dug her nails into her palm, furious. 'And I'm going to find out exactly who it was.'

He flopped down onto the settee. 'I thought it was all over,' he said. 'I thought when they put that heavy who attacked you back inside that you'd be safe.'

'I know,' she said, patting his hand. If only life was that simple. She looked at him properly: the bruise was seeping down his face, blackening his cheekbone. How pale and sick he looked. 'You pop in the shower, it'll make you feel better,' she said. 'I'll make some tea when you get out and you can tell me all about your research.'

He heaved himself to his feet, his movements those of an old man. How many more people were going to be hurt by this, she wondered. After a few moments she heard the soft percussion of the shower and went into the kitchen to make tea.

On the worktop was a message scribbled on the back of an envelope. Mandy's writing, she presumed, smiling a little at the bubble above the letter i. She scanned the note and froze. Mandy had written: *Someone called Hammond phoned. Said he'll catch you later.*

19:00 hours

Will Day was waiting for her in the lobby of the Imperial Hotel. He was back in his off-duty cavalry officer gear of pink trousers, check shirt and blazer, and his aftershave was so thick it formed a mushroom cloud. On the opposite side of the lobby was a man reading a copy of the *Financial Times*. In his forties, he was well-muscled and his suit fitted tight to his solid torso. He didn't glance in their direction, but a slight stiffening of his neck sinews betrayed he was aware she was there.

'Hi, Will,' she said. 'Thanks for meeting me at short notice.'

'No problem,' he said. 'Ready?'

'I need to check something out first, then we'll get onto the main course. Is that OK?'

Will rubbed his chin. 'I guess it'll have to be, if you're not going to tell me what's going on.'

She'd outlined the only the basics of her suspicions to him, backing up her authority with details only someone who'd been on the inside of his organisation would know. 'Trust me.'

'Not in the job description.'

She jerked her gaze towards *Financial Times* man. 'Your guy?'

'Yep.' Will nodded at *Financial Times*, who folded the paper, checked his watch, and sauntered into the bar. 'We'll give him a few minutes.'

She and Will kicked around in the lobby then wandered into the bar. *Financial Times* was in an armchair in the corner, within eavesdropping distance. He had the newspaper open on his lap and seemed to be working out the crossword. A glass of dark whisky occupied a paper doily on the table beside him.

Eden hoiked her bum onto a barstool and put her foot on the brass rail. Leaning her elbows on the bar, she said, 'Hello Gabor.'

Gabor took a moment to recognise her. 'It's you,' he said. 'Back again.'

'How is your mother?' she asked in Russian.

'She is well, thank you,' Gabor answered, also in Russian. Then he added, 'What can I get you?'

'What would you like, Will?' she asked, and ordered two whiskies with water.

'You remember last Tuesday evening, Gabor?' Eden said. 'You said there was a man in the bar, waiting for a date to turn up?'

Gabor polished a wine glass while he thought. 'Yes, the blind date man whose lady never came. I remember him.'

'Think you would recognise him?'

Gabor shrugged. 'I don't know.'

Eden took a sheaf of papers out of her bag and spread them out on the bar. 'Are any of these people him?'

Gabor looked over the photographs she'd culled from the Internet, frowning and sucking his teeth as he looked them over. Finally, he picked up one of the pictures. 'Him. I think it was him.'

'You're sure?'

Another shrug. 'I think so.'

Eden took the paper from him and checked the name on the back. 'Thanks, Gabor. You know, since our chat the other day, I can't stop thinking about those honey pastries from the café. Where was it again?'

'Oktogon Square. That's the place we talked about.'

'Oktogon Square. That's interesting, because I looked them up on the Internet and they're not in Oktogon Square at all.'

Gabor carried on polishing the glass. 'I remembered it wrong. Silly me!' And he shrugged and made a 'what am I like' face.

'But Gabor, you told me it was your favourite place in Budapest,' Eden said. 'And what I realised was this: I mentioned Budapest and the café, and you just agreed with me.'

'I try to be agreeable to my customers.' He replaced the glass and picked up another one.

Will turned to her and made a little movement with his eyes, telling her he didn't understand what was going on and what the fuss was about with this Hungarian barman. Eden ignored the signal and continued, 'But the thing that really worries me, Gabor, is that you don't seem to exist. Someone did a background check on you, and found nothing.' She felt Will sit up straighter beside her, as understanding dawned.

Gabor weighed the glass in his hands. 'I not exist?' he laughed. 'Of course I exist. Here I am!' And he turned around as if showing off a new jacket.

'The main problem I have, Gabor, is that when I spoke to you in Russian, you replied in Russian. Trouble is, Russian and Hungarian are nothing like each other.'

Gabor stilled, then suddenly lunged at her with the glass, aiming for her eyes. She dodged sideways, blocked his arm and punched him in the face, then dragged him over the bar until his bloody nose scraped along the counter.

Financial Times man jumped up and ran over.

Her face pressed close to Gabor's, Eden said, 'You've been going into guests' rooms and searching them. You knew some of them were intelligence officers and you were looking for something you could use: blackmail, pressure, or just information. But because people always know when someone's been through their things, you stole small items to make it look like petty pilfering instead of what it is. Counter espionage.' She met *Financial Times* man's eyes. 'He's all yours.'

Financial Times produced a warrant card and shoved it in Gabor's face, then read him his rights and arrested him. Two more beefy men suddenly burst in and hauled Gabor to his feet, handcuffed him, and dragged him away. Wires snaked from behind their ears into their collars.

'What the hell just happened?' Will said, and drained his whisky.

'He's not Hungarian,' Eden said, draining hers in turn. 'He's a Russian agent. And he's given me the clue I need to solve the rest of my case.'

CHAPTER
TWENTY-SEVEN

Tuesday, 3 November 2015

08:23 hours

It was a shame about Mandy, but at least it meant Eden left him without a babysitter today, Aidan thought, watching Eden slide her laptop into her backpack. She riffled through a heap of handwritten notes and stuffed those in, too.

'Call me if you feel poorly,' she said, kissing his forehead.

'I'm fine. I might go home, actually.' He glanced around her flat: the books weren't in alphabetical order on the shelves and the flowers in a vase on the table stuck out any which way.

'Send me a text and let me know, OK?' Another kiss and she was gone. He flopped on the settee, feeling a sense of peace that had eluded him for days wash over him. Order, that's what he needed. This blasted headache would never go away so long as there were mugs in the sink and eleven tiles around the edge of the bath. Eleven couldn't be grouped into any sort of pattern. Not divided into threes, or fours, and five each side and one in the middle just wasn't soothing. Eden wasn't as cluttered as some women he'd known, but even so she had seven bottles of scented gunk in the shower, and five candles clustered on the ledge at the end of the bath. What he needed was his own place, the calm of a space he'd arranged for maximum mental serenity.

He packed up his clothes and washbag, tidied up the kitchen and squared the edges of Eden's pile of magazines on the coffee table. Her dining table was covered with bits of paper: timelines and notes on suspects, business cards from William Day and Bernard Mulligan, and huge mind maps of Lewis's murder. He sorted it all into size order and piled it up neatly at one end of the table, then let himself out.

The relief he felt when he entered his own flat was instant. Home. The books in size and colour order on the shelves. The perfectly aligned radio on the mantelpiece. The rug that was exactly parallel with the skirting board. He shoved his dirty clothes in the washing machine, made a pot of coffee, scooping in an extra spoonful to compensate for days of coffee denial, and spread his research notes over his desk.

Mandy had obtained copies of letters written between Catholic families living near Hailes during the reign of Elizabeth I. He set his spectacles firmly on his nose and peered at the old writing, recalling his early days as an undergraduate, despairing that he'd ever be able to decipher any document older than a century. After a while, the handwriting resolved and the abbreviations the scribes used fell into place and he could read smoothly. The coffee went cold at his elbow as he read on, caught up in a drama that had unfolded nearly five hundred years before.

My friend in Christ, I pray you are well. We, alas, are not, my dear wife Susan being afflicted with the fever these two days past and no sign of it easing. We implore God it is not the sweating sickness. Some of the servants have fled to their homes, afraid of contagion. My manservant, a stalwart brute, has ridden to Hailes for help. Pray for my dear Susan.

Dear Sister, we were visited today and the house searched from top to bottom. They prised apart the staircase, looking for concealing places, and turned all the preserves out of the pantry to search for hidden staircases behind the shelves. They found nothing, though they poked about in the roof and jabbed the hay in the stables with pitchforks. They went away empty handed and I fear they will return.

His Holiness has put our lives in danger in excommunicating the Queen. We live quietly here, and never a harm to anyone, yet now she is cast out from the Church, we who follow the true way are called assassins and traitors. Our lives are lived on a thread. I fear for my boys.

My Susan is better today, thank God. Our friend at Hailes came to her with physic and the fever broke at once. She is resting and quiet now. He assures us he will come each day to tend to her, though at great peril to his life. God bless and preserve him.

Our friend from Hailes has come and drawn plans for our new garden, similar to his own. We like its symmetry much and can foresee many hours spent there, contemplating the wonder of God around us. We have much need of its comfort. Our friend from the north was here just days before the hunters came. Though they wrenched up the floorboards and jabbed swords down the well, they did not find their prey. God save him.

My friend in Christ, I write with sorrowful news. My Susan ails again, and I have sent my man for our brother at Hailes in desperation that he might save her. But I fear that even his skills are beyond this, and that my dear wife will soon be lost to us.

My friend in Christ. I have seen it myself, and I know it to be true. The Holiest of Holy, that was lost from Hailes, is not lost. And it was here, in my own home and abode, just these past days. Our brother at Hailes brought it to my Susan, as she lay dying upon the bed. As soon as he produced it, she rose up from her pillow, fixed her eyes upon it, and her lips moved in constant prayer. She fell back upon the pillow in unconscious slumber, and we were unable to wake her for over a day. Brother John remained at her side, constantly praying, and dribbling physic between her lips. On the third day she woke, and lifted herself up, and was as well and hearty as the day I married her, over twenty years ago. God be praised.

Be not involved in sedition, my friend. Live quietly as we do, and turn away from turbulent speakers, I implore you. We must wait until our time is come. It is in the hands of God. Heaven has no need for more martyrs.

It has happened, the worst that can be. He is taken, seized while he tended his garden and carried to London for trial. I shall smuggle myself there, that he shall see a friendly face at least when he meets the executioner. I know not what happened to the Holy Blood and pray that it is safe yet.

A fire lit in his chest. Documentary proof that a relic known as the Holy Blood of Hailes had somehow survived the Dissolution of the Monasteries and the dismantling of the shrines. It could be a fake, of course, as all the so-called relics could be fakes, but even so, here was evidence that there were rumours amongst the Catholic community that the Holy Blood still existed. And maybe the phial he'd excavated at Hailes was the one that was being smuggled in to heal the sick.

He shivered at the thought of the risks these families ran. After the Pope excommunicated Elizabeth I and declared that anyone who assassinated her was doing so with heaven's blessing, Catholics were automatically branded traitors. Being found with a rosary, hearing Catholic Mass, being visited by a priest: all were punishable by death. The risk this man from Hailes ran, carrying what was believed to be a holy relic, was enormous. He, and the families he visited, were putting themselves in mortal danger.

All that peering at tiny writing had made his head hurt. A snooze to take him up to lunchtime would sort it out, then he'd pop into the office and check that work was being done, even without him there to crack the whip.

He closed his bedroom curtains, undressed to boxer shorts and a T-shirt, and slipped into bed. The sheets were cool and crisp and he snuggled down into the middle of the bed, soothed by the chill pillow. A little nap would put him right.

When he awoke, it was early afternoon and a soft rain was falling against the windowpane. He stretched and wandered into the kitchen, groggy from sleeping too long. Someone had been in his flat while he was asleep. His keys hung on a row of hooks under the kitchen unit, a separate hook for each key. The one on the end was missing.

On his desk he found a note:

Hi Aidan, you were sleeping peacefully so I didn't wake you. I've borrowed your car and gone to get the Holy Blood. Won't be long. See you later, Eden. P.S. Please stop drinking coffee – it won't help your headache xx

He didn't like it, didn't like it one little bit. His head throbbed at the memory of being struck. Whoever had stolen the Blood was willing to kill for it, and now Eden was going to snatch it back.

He rang her mobile. It went straight to voicemail.

'Eden, it's me, Aidan. Stop whatever it is you're doing. Please. It's not safe.'

He hung up and bounced the phone against his lower lip, thinking. What was it he'd seen that morning when he tidied up Eden's flat? A pile of papers and envelopes, and tucked amongst it all, a business card. What was the name? Something about *Ulysses*. He chased the memory until he caught it, then did a quick Internet search to hunt down a phone number.

'Hello, my name's Aidan Fox,' he said, when the phone was answered the other end. 'I believe you've met my girlfriend, Eden Grey. I don't know where she is right now, but wherever it is, she's in terrible danger.'

CHAPTER
TWENTY-EIGHT

Tuesday, 3 November 2015

14:32 hours

A productive morning, Eden thought, as she sped up the motorway, moving easily between the gears and overtaking a line of cars in the middle lane. A couple of drivers glanced over at her as she passed, a spark of respect and envy at Aidan's immaculate black Audi. Her car, elderly and rather disreputable, simply wouldn't do for the mission she had in mind.

Both Bernard and Gabor had identified the same relic collector: a man called Jonathan Luker, and she'd spent the morning trawling the Internet for everything she could find about him. He certainly flashed a lot of wodge at auctions, and had he been Frankenstein, he owned enough bits of saints to make up a whole one and reanimate it.

She clicked on the indicator, changed lanes, and took the slip road off the motorway, heading towards a small village outside Wolverhampton, and to an address revealed by the electoral register as Luker's residence. The house was tucked down a narrow, potholed road and she winced each time the car bounced and the exhaust scraped on the road. She missed the signpost the first time: it was obscured by a stand of trees. Evidently if you needed a sign to show you where you were going, you didn't belong here. Doubling back, she found the road and bumped along to the village: a chocolate box arrangement of Georgian brick homes around a triangle of village green, a tiny Norman church with a graveyard that was three feet higher than the path, and a pub that charged fifteen quid for a ploughman's lunch and served game pie with a julienne of carrots.

Beyond the village was a lane that led to Jonathan Luker's house. She passed through wrought-iron gates, up a recently repaved driveway and around a carriage sweep. She parked, checked her appearance in the rear-view mirror, and stepped out of the car. Dressed in a plain black suit with black boots, a pale blue blouse and a sapphire silk scarf, she looked sober and respectable but avoided shades of undertaker. Her briefcase was impeccable black leather. She grabbed it from the back of the car and looked up at the house.

It was a Queen Anne villa with Dutch gable ends in a pleasant pinkish brick. A shrubbery stretched either side of the carriage drive, dripping disconsolately, the leaves blackened with frost. The front door was wide, pale oak, set in a stone porch. She pulled the handle to the side and heard a jangle echo deep inside the house.

The door was opened by a short Filipino man in a Nehru jacket and taupe trousers. 'Yes?'

'I'm here to see Mr Jonathan Luker,' Eden said.

'He expect you?'

'I'm here on official business,' she said, hefting her briefcase. As predicted, the man's eyes tracked the briefcase.

'What business I say him?'

'I'm from his insurers.'

The man stood aside and she stepped into a square hallway panelled in dark wood. The doors leading off the hallway were all closed, and the only light came from the glass panel above the door. It was like entering a cave.

'This way.'

She followed the man through the house to a conservatory at the back, overlooking a sloping lawn and borders crammed with the skeletons of old rose bushes. 'Mr Jonathan, person to see you,' the manservant said, and scuttled out of the room.

The back of a large leather armchair faced her, and on the arm of the chair rested a bony hand. A figure rose from the chair and stood in silence before her. He was tall and thin framed, and his skin hung in grey pouches as though it was too big for him. His hair was shorn away, leaving a plain of stubble.

'Mr Luker?' she said. 'I'm Sara White from Wisley and Brakeman, your insurers.'

He shook his head. 'They're not my insurers. I'm with one of the big firms.'

'They pass the specialist cover onto us,' Eden said. 'Antiques, artwork, high-grade jewellery.'

'And do you have any identification, Miss White?'

'Of course.' She snapped open the fasteners on the briefcase and extracted a thick, creamy envelope. Inside, on embossed letterheaded paper, was a sentence stating that Wisley and Brakeman handled specialist insurance, and requested that their employee, Sara White, be given every assistance and courtesy. Eden had designed it and had it printed that morning.

'We believe that you're underinsured,' she said. 'The gold price has rocketed in recent years, as I'm sure you know, and though it's not at the same level, we've found a number of clients haven't increased their insurance. I'm here to do a valuation and check that you have adequate cover.'

Jonathan Luker rubbed his chin. 'I doubt it's a problem. I tend to over insure.'

Eden pulled a notepad out of her briefcase and flicked through the pages. 'You bought a Russian triptych last year? At the time it was valued at one hundred thousand pounds.'

That was what Luker paid for it at auction.

She consulted the notepad again. 'Our current valuation estimates it's worth approximately one hundred and eighty thousand pounds.' She let the silence swell between them, determined she wouldn't be the first one to speak.

'Interesting,' Luker said, pulling his lower lip thoughtfully. 'You're proposing to do the valuation now?'

'Yes, if that's convenient. I can update the list of insured items and check you have the right cover.'

Luker hesitated. She glanced around the room and her eye fastened on a small chair with a shield-shaped back in the adjoining room. When she'd joined Revenue and Customs, years before, she'd shadowed each of the different teams, getting a view of the whole of the organisation's work, and had spent three months with the team that valued antiques for probate and capital gains. She dragged up some of what she'd learned and prayed she was correct.

'Nice Hepplewhite-inspired chair,' she said. 'Nineteenth century?'

'Very good,' Luker said.

'I've got a list of the items you've specified on your insurance documents,' Eden said. 'If you can show me where they are, I can do the valuations and add anything that's needed. My first item is that Russian triptych.'

'This way.'

Luker led her from the room. There was a square patch of white skin on the side of his skull, bordered with a dark line – the ghost of staples and stitches. She followed him through the house to the first floor, where Luker unlocked a door with a key he carried on a chain attached to his trousers.

'It's all in here,' he said.

The room had high ceilings and a plain wooden floor that echoed when they stepped inside. Thick blinds shrouded the windows, blotting out what little daylight there was, giving the room a subterranean feel. Around the walls were glass cabinets and glass-topped display cases stood in the centre of the room. Luker pressed a switch and tiny lights came on in each cabinet.

Eden stifled a gasp. Gold glittered in every cabinet. Dead-eyed Madonnas glared at her, clutching chubby infant Jesuses. And the jewels: sapphires, rubies, pearls, emeralds. Everywhere she looked, precious gems fired coloured arrows at her.

'It's quite a collection,' she said, fighting to keep her voice professional. 'How long have you been interested in religious material culture?'

'I started collecting icons in my twenties,' Luker said. 'And then I discovered reliquaries.'

Eden recovered herself. 'The value of the reliquaries will obviously only be on the container itself, not the relics inside.' She blessed Aidan's recent lecture on the subject.

'Of course.'

'Let's make a start,' Eden said, putting down her briefcase and taking out the notebook again. 'First item, that Russian triptych.'

Luker unlocked a cabinet, put on a pair of white cotton gloves, and removed the triptych, carrying it over to her as though handling his first-born.

'Thirteenth century,' Eden said. 'Oil on wood painting, framed in gold. These have gone up in value enormously. Russian collectors, anxious to return them home.'

She scribbled a figure on her notebook next to the description of the triptych, then called out the next item. 'Reliquary containing the toe bone of St Barbara,' she said.

Luker went to a cabinet on the far side of the room, unlocked it, and drew out a gold statue about eighteen inches high studded with rubies and pearls. At the bottom of the statue was a tiny window of rock crystal, and behind it was a fragment of bone.

Luker had paid seventy thousand pounds for it, five years before. Eden had spent the morning wrestling with gold rates, and had recalculated the scrap value of each of Luker's reliquaries. Now she took that value and bumped it up a bit.

'I think that should be insured for ninety thousand pounds,' she said, scribbling a note. She glanced at him. 'Have you been unwell lately, Mr Luker?'

His hand crept to the back of his head. 'A brain tumour,' he said.

'I'm very sorry to hear that.'

He gave a quick smile, his eye teeth flashing. 'Don't be,' he said. 'I've made a miraculous recovery.' A chill ran through Eden and she hurriedly turned the page of her notebook.

Next was another reliquary, and Luker fetched it from the same cabinet. Pretending to survey the whole collection, Eden peered into each cabinet, searching for the Holy Blood. The collection was organised according to type and location. All the Russian icons were together; and all the jewelled reliquaries were together; but there was no sign of the Holy Blood. On another circuit of the room, Eden spotted a curtain hanging across a recess in the far wall. It was tucked away in a gloomy corner, but a chair was placed in front of the curtain, as if Luker spent time sitting and contemplating what was behind it.

'Is there a painting behind here?' she asked.

'No,' Luker said. He turned with the next item in his gloved hands and she dragged her attention to it.

They worked on for an hour, Luker collecting each item in turn, Eden offering a valuation and making a note.

Part way through, the Filipino man appeared at the door, poking his face round as though afraid. 'Mr Jonathan? Phone for you. Say it important.'

Luker locked the cabinet and pocketed the key. 'I won't be long,' he said to Eden.

As soon as she heard his footsteps receding, she ran to the curtain and yanked it open. Behind was a glass case set into the wall, and in the case was the Holy Blood of Hailes. The crimson phial blazed despite the dim light, and the silver stopper gleamed. The glass case was a simple display case and the lock flimsy. Within seconds, Eden had inserted a paperclip and was jiggling it about, feeling for the resistance that would tell her she'd found the sweet spot. Desperately listening for Luker's return, she thumped the glass door, the lock suddenly gave, and the door swung open.

A footstep in the corridor outside.

She yanked the silk scarf from round her neck and swaddled the Holy Blood in it, stuffing it in the bottom of her briefcase and piling papers on top. Then she swung the door shut. It wouldn't lock, but she pressed the door to and jerked the curtain closed, then scuttled over to one of the far cabinets. When Luker came back she was gazing at one of the Madonnas.

'They always look as though they know something we don't,' she said, indicating a sleepy-eyed Madonna.

'That's because they do,' Luker said. He stared at her for a moment. 'That was your boss on the phone.'

'What?' She recovered herself. 'What did he want? Have I forgotten something?'

'He wanted to remind you to value the reliquary of St Thomas,' he said.

Eden looked down her list. Luker had bought that reliquary two years before, according to the auction reports she'd found on the Internet. A sudden unease crept over her, as though he was trying to catch her out. And who the hell was it on the phone? 'Yes, I have it on my schedule,' she said. She held his eye. 'You do still have it? You haven't sold it?'

'I have it,' Luker said. He opened a cabinet and hefted out a solid gold reliquary adorned with angels and studded with sapphires and pearls. He took a step towards her. 'What I don't understand is why your employer felt the need to call the house. Surely you have a mobile phone?'

'Probably just checking up on me,' Eden said, fighting the urge to take a step back. Luker was so close she could smell old-fashioned talc on his skin.

'He didn't say where he worked,' Luker said. 'Just said he was your boss. It was altogether rather odd.'

He suspects me, Eden thought. He knows there's something wrong here. Time to make an escape.

At that moment, the glass door behind the curtain swung open. Luker let out a cry and ran over. He wrenched back the curtain and let out a yell that was half-howl.

'What have you done with it?'

Eden picked up her briefcase and made for the door. Luker was across the room in a trice.

'Stop right there!' He swung the reliquary, aiming for her head. She ducked, and it came down hard on her arm. The blow sent her staggering backwards and she crashed into one of the cabinets.

Luker came at her again, swinging the reliquary in a huge arc. It hit the cabinet, shattering the glass and sending icons spinning across the floor. The next blow struck her shoulder. She dropped to the floor, gasping, stars sparking in her vision.

Luker was breathing heavily. He lumbered over and bent to grab her briefcase. With a surge of effort, Eden swung it up into his face. Blood spurted from his nose. She scrambled to her feet and chopped him hard on the back of his neck. Luker fell face first onto the floor and she was on him in an instant, straddling his back and dragging his hands behind him. A shard of glass poked into her knee. She yelped and released her grip, then fought again to gain control.

'Why did you kill him, Luker?' she panted, struggling to hold him. 'You didn't intend to, so what happened?'

'We had an agreement and he broke it. Demanded double what we'd agreed,' Luker said. He bucked and writhed, heaving her onto the floor, his arm against her throat in an instant. "Filthy Luker". That's what he kept calling me. Shouting it in my face and shoving liquorice into his mouth.'

Eden wrestled one arm free. Her fingers groped around in the glass.

'So you killed him?' She struggled to breathe, her windpipe crushed.

'He had thirty thousand from me. I turned up with another two hundred and he laughed in my face. Said now he saw how much I wanted it, the price had gone up.' Luker leaned harder on her throat. 'He went into the bathroom, still laughing at me, then came out clutching his face and screaming about his eyes.'

She was starting to black out. It was now or never. Her hands sifted through the shards and closed around the reliquary.

'You hit him and searched his room.' Her fingers, sticky with blood, took a firmer grip. She'd only have one chance.

'It wasn't there!'

'So you put the room to rights and left him to die,' Eden said. She swung her arm up hard and smacked Luker with the reliquary. He fell back and she hit him again.

'Jonathan Luker, this is a citizen's arrest.' Her throat was on fire and she panted with the effort of keeping him down. Luker was twisting and howling like a wounded animal. Both of them were bleeding from the glass, their blood slicking the floor. 'I'm arresting you on suspicion of the murder of Lewis Jordan.'

'He was alive when I left the room! He was groaning, for God's sake!'

The door crashed back on its hinges and the Filipino man spun into the room crying, 'Mr Jonathan!'

Close on his heels was Bernard Mulligan.

'What the hell are you doing here?' Eden croaked.

'Giving you a hand,' Bernard said. He hauled her to her feet. 'You hurt?'

'A bit. I'll live.'

Bernard dragged Luker into a chair. 'The police are on their way,' he said.

'That was quick,' Eden said.

'The butler chap had already called them when I turned up. Heard the rumpus up here.'

Eden tested herself for injuries. She could barely move her arm and shoulder, and there were cuts all over her hands and legs, but nothing seemed to be broken. Another week or so of bruises, she thought ruefully, fingering her throat. Luker himself looked terrible: his skin had turned to putty and he'd aged fifteen years. A tremor started in his hands and shuddered through his whole body.

'My tumour,' Luker said. 'They gave me six months. The Holy Blood saved me.'

A police siren wailed up the drive.

'Time's up,' Eden said.

CHAPTER
TWENTY-NINE

Monday, 9 November 2015

09:45 hours

A festive air hung over the Cheltenham Cultural Heritage Unit. A large tin of chocolates graced the table in the meeting room, an insensitive touch considering Mandy had not long been discharged from hospital, Eden thought, though Mandy herself seemed unscathed and was already digging through the tin in search of a big purple nutty one.

'Leave over, Mandy,' Trev said, barging her aside and trying to grab them for himself.

Aidan came into the room with a folder and the artefact known as the Holy Blood of Hailes. 'Don't eat all the best ones,' he said. 'Save some for me.'

His black eyes had faded and was now just the merest touch of green at his temples. Eden's bruises on her arm, throat and shoulder were still developing, and she found it hard to lift her left arm.

Aidan took a seat opposite her, then the door opened again and Bernard Mulligan and Lisa Greene came in. Lisa had her head tipped back and was laughing gaily at something Bernard had said. He held a seat out for her, and tucked her in before taking the seat next to her. Seemed she'd made another conquest.

'Right, everyone,' Aidan called over the racket. 'It's been quite an exciting time. I'm sure I'm not the only one round here who doesn't have a clue what's been going on. Eden, do you want to fill everyone in on Lewis, then we'll get to the archaeology.'

'Sure,' she said, looking round the table at everyone. 'Jonathan Luker was a relic collector who believed the Holy Blood of Hailes would cure his brain tumour, but he needed someone dodgy to get hold of it for him. He paid Bernard to do background searches on everyone even remotely connected with the Blood, looking for someone he could bribe to steal it.' She nodded at Bernard to take up the story.

'Lewis Jordan had huge debts and was the obvious weak link,' Bernard said, prodding a toffee from his back teeth with his forefinger. 'Luker approached him with a deal. Thirty thousand down payment, then an extra two hundred thousand when Lewis delivered the Blood.'

'Two hundred and thirty thousand pounds?' Mandy echoed.

'Small change to Luker. His family are the Luker sweet makers, worth millions,' Bernard said.

'So Lewis stole the Blood when you were all packing up after filming,' Eden said. 'Trouble was, Lisa was on to him, went to his hotel room, and stole it back.' Lisa pinked and primped at her role in the drama. 'Lewis didn't have the goods to hand over to Luker that evening, but typical Lewis, he thought he'd use it to try and get more money.'

Eden paused. 'Earlier that day, someone had gone into Lewis's room and put oven cleaner in his eye drops. Revenge for him being a complete shit and ruining her sister's family years ago. But when Lewis put his drops in and was blinded, Luker saw his chance. He bashed Lewis's head in and searched the room for the Blood. When he didn't find it, he worked out it must still be at the Cultural Heritage Unit, so came back to steal it.'

'I disturbed him and he hit me, too, with Andy's Roman amphora,' said Aidan.

'Which I'm now gluing back together again,' Andy said, shaking his head at the injustice of it all.

'So then you went to get the Blood back?' Mandy asked, her fingers scrabbling in the tin of chocolates.

'Bernard and the barman at the Imperial recognised a photo of Luker from a line-up of high-rolling relic hunters. And I remembered that the American couple next to Lewis's room said they heard him shouting about money. I wondered if what they'd really heard was "Luker".'

'That's what Lewis kept on saying when I was with him,' Lisa said. 'His phone was ringing and he laughed and said "filthy lucre".'

'Except it wasn't money he was talking about, it was Luker, the collector,' Eden said. 'So I went to Luker's house and stole the Blood back.'

'And I turned up in time for cake and medals,' Bernard added.

'And here's the Blood,' Eden concluded, and all eyes switched their attention to the bottle on the table. 'The thing that was worth killing for. Apparently.'

'And so to the archaeology,' Aidan said. 'Mandy?'

Mandy opened her notebook. 'The relic was supposed to have been destroyed during the reign of Henry VIII, but letters dated after that talk about the Hailes relic being taken to Catholic families,' she said. 'It seems the relic was known for miracle cures.'

'Like our friend Luker,' Bernard added. 'Believed it would cure his brain tumour.'

'When do the letters start to talk about the Holy Blood?' Eden asked.

'From the Dissolution,' Mandy said. 'There are small hints here and there from 1539 about a relic that survived the fire and was healing the sick. Then it seems the relic was a way to rally people to oppose Elizabeth I. One letter talks about seeing the relic and being asked to perform the Lord's work. By that time the Pope had excommunicated Elizabeth and said that anyone who assassinated her wouldn't be damned.'

'And how long do the letters mention the relic?'

'Nothing after 1571.' Mandy shrugged. 'Maybe the plot was uncovered and that was the end of it. They believed in it, though.'

'But how could it be the real relic?' Eden said. 'And surely that was a fake, anyway?'

'Let's see,' Aidan said. 'We've got the results on the residue in the bottom of the phial.'

The room seemed to still and the air grew close as he pulled an envelope out from between the pages of his notebook and slit open the flap. He put on his spectacles and read the results, ran his hand through his hair and read them again. Then he put down the paper and breathed, 'Well.'

'Well what?' Eden grabbed the results before any of the others could get there. She scanned the paper then glanced at the relic.

'Come on, what's it say?' Trev said.

Eden cleared her throat. 'OK, the analysis says that the substance in the artefact is human blood.' She swallowed. 'The DNA is too degraded to say more than that it is human. The residue also had traces of honey and saffron.'

'That's what was said about the original relic,' Mandy said. 'It was made up of honey and saffron.'

They all stared in silence at the artefact until Trev said, 'Come on, we're scientists. This can't possibly be the real relic, even if it does contain human blood.'

'OK, so this is what we know,' Aidan said, briskly. 'The artefact resembles the relic known as the Holy Blood of Hailes; was found at Hailes Abbey and contains human blood, and we have documentary evidence that something thought to be the relic survived the Dissolution.'

Silence again.

'The question is, what should happen to it now?' Aidan said. 'I think it, and the documentation, should go somewhere where it can be properly preserved and where lots of people can see it.'

'Agreed,' Mandy said.

'How about the British Museum?' Lisa suggested. 'They already have one of the thorns from the Crown of Thorns.'

Aidan glanced at them all in turn. One by one they nodded their agreement.

'I'll call Hailes and check it's OK with them, and make the arrangements,' he said, gathering the papers together. He paused at the door. 'Maybe a team outing to London? What do you say?'

Mandy tore the foil from another chocolate. 'One thing I don't understand,' she said. 'Did Luker send those poisoned chocolates?'

'No,' Eden said. 'That was someone else entirely, and I'm sorry you got caught up in it, Mandy.'

Unwilling to be questioned further, she slipped from the room and went to Aidan's office, where she found him with his head in his hands.

'Aidan?' She went over and rubbed his back. 'You alright?'

'I'm fine,' he said, his voice muffled. 'Just don't know what to think right now.'

She crouched down beside him and gently took his hands from his face. 'That Catholic upbringing doesn't let you go, hey?'

He shook his head. 'Those Catholic families, risking their lives for their faith. Plotting to kill the Queen because they believed it was what God wanted.' He sucked in a deep breath and visibly composed himself. 'To be honest, I wanted the DNA to prove the Blood was real.'

'Hey, God doesn't work like that,' she said. 'Doesn't lay it all out in black and white, you know that. The thing is what you believe.'

'I'm a scientist,' he said.

'One who wants to believe that relic is real,' she said, quietly. 'You certainly did your bit in the Hailes story. Getting a bash on the head trying to defend it. My hero.'

He attempted a smile; it came out crooked. 'You want to come to London, too? If it wasn't for you, we wouldn't have the Holy Blood at all.'

'Sure, I'll come along,' Eden said. 'I have some unfinished business of my own to attend to.'

CHAPTER
THIRTY

Winchcombe, September 1571

The mare stood shivering, head hanging low between her front legs. Lazarus ran his hands over the animal's hide, feeling the bones beneath her skin. Yesterday's ride had broken her. Enough was enough, Lazarus thought, he'd take her to the knackers' tomorrow. He filled up the feed trough and fetched a bucket of fresh water for the beast and slapped her side.

He wrapped his cloak tightly about him against the chill and trudged along the main street and out towards Ashford Grange. His leg was stronger today, but after five miles he was forced to stop and rest, massaging the muscles to ease the pain.

When he eventually got there, the boy Edgar was alone in the yard, rubbing beeswax onto a saddle with a rag. He stood when Lazarus entered.

'Master John isn't here,' he said, twisting the rag round and round his fingers.

'It's you I want to see,' Lazarus said. He glanced about him, checking the manor house windows in case they were over-looked. 'You met a man in the woods the other day.'

The boy flushed. 'I didn't!'

Lazarus stepped closer and spoke in a low voice, 'We work for the same master, boy.'

'I … I don't know what you mean.'

'Maybe this will refresh your memory,' Lazarus said, and pressed a coin into the boy's hand.

The boy eyed him warily, like an unbroken colt about to run. 'When do you next meet him?'

'I … I leave a sign that I wish to speak to him,' Edgar said.

'Do so. And when you meet, give him this.' Lazarus took off his glove and tipped out the folded scrap of paper he'd stolen from Brother John's house.

'What is it?'

'Read it.'

The boy glanced at the paper and shook his head.

'Better if you don't know,' Lazarus said. 'What I can tell you is that this is important, and he will pay you handsomely, but you must act fast. Do you understand, boy?'

Edgar nodded. His shoulders trembled as he pocketed the square of paper. 'I will leave the sign at once,' he said.

'Good. Tell your friend that he must get this paper to Cecil at once.'

'Cecil at once,' the boy repeated. His eyes met Lazarus's. 'Who is Cecil?'

Lazarus sighed. They'd duped the boy, told him a pack of lies to get him to do their work and likely they'd forget him when it came to dividing the guilty from the innocent. These were dangerous times, when a man needed his wits sharper than a rapier and the suspicious nature of a snake to keep his head on his shoulders.

'Make sure he gets it,' he said again, and headed back to the road for the long trudge back to Winchcombe.

The Abbey ruins loomed as darker shadows against the black sky. It was a moonless night, the stars obscured by clouds; a thin rain falling and turning the track into a slippery mire. Lazarus had borrowed a staff from the innkeeper to help him to walk. After his long journey to and from Ashford Grange that day, the wound in his leg had reopened and each step was torture, but he had to see Brother John.

A narrow slice of light knifed between the shutters of Brother John's house. Lazarus rested upon the staff for a moment, then rapped on the door with it.

'Matthew,' Brother John said, when he opened the door. 'I have been expecting you.'

'We must leave at once,' Lazarus said. 'There is no time to waste.'

'Leave? I have work to do.' Brother John waved his hand at the shelves of jars and ointments.

'You can tend the sick anywhere in the world,' Lazarus said. 'But your work isn't physic any more, is it, Brother?'

'Are you in a fever, Matthew? I can't understand what you're saying.'

'I heard you, I heard the plans you made at Ashford Grange. Treason, *Master* John.'

Brother John rubbed his lips together. 'You followed me.'

'Aye, and heard it all. And we must leave now, before it is too late.'

Brother John's eyes burned like sapphires. 'I cannot. I have made promises.'

'Forget them and save your life!' Lazarus said. 'Hurry! Grab what things you need and we'll be gone.'

'Who sent you, Matthew?'

Lazarus leaned heavily on the staff, easing the weight off his leg. 'I was taken out of Newgate to find you and kill you.'

Brother John spread his arms wide. 'I'm still alive.'

'Because it was not my wish to kill you.' Lazarus scraped his nails down his beard. 'We can make it to Bristol and get a ship there to France.'

'Neither of us has papers allowing us to leave.' Brother John's voice was cool.

'We have coin, that is enough for most men,' Lazarus said. He pulled the blanket from the bed and started to load Brother John's linen into it.

'Stop.' Brother John stilled him with his hand on his arm. 'I cannot leave.'

'But you must!' Lazarus cried. 'Don't you understand, they are coming for you. I gave them the paper, the list of people you are to visit with the Holy Blood.'

'Perhaps I should change your name,' Brother John said. 'Judas, not Lazarus.'

'I'm here to save you, God damn you!' Lazarus cried. 'By the time they come for you we can be far away. They'll take the others but they won't find us.'

'No.' Brother John shook his head. 'I'm no coward, and it is God's work I'm doing.'

'Treason? God's work?'

'I must do His will.'

'Brother! Please!'

Brother John planted himself squarely and folded his arms. 'You must go alone.'

Lazarus searched the shelves with his eyes. 'Where is it?'

'What?'

He grabbed a jar and threw it to the floor. It smashed into tiny shards and a puddle of pungent ointment leaked into the earth floor. A bottle of physic joined it. A box of dried herbs, a salve, a wash to remove lice.

'Stop it!' Brother John cried, dashing over and hanging onto Lazarus's arm as he reached up to the next shelf.

'Where's the Blood?'

Brother John wrestled him away from the shelves and the two men fell on the broken glass and pottery. When Lazarus pushed himself to his feet, a shard of glass stabbed through his palm. He roared with pain and yanked it out. His palm gushing blood, he set about clearing the rest of the shelves, grabbing at bottles and jars in a frenzy and smashing them on the floor. The smell of wormwood permeated the hut, making him choke.

'Where is it?' he bellowed. A second shelf was emptied. He started on the third, then turned to see Brother John burrowing in a box under his bed. Lazarus launched himself across the room and barged him aside. Tossing out linen and bandages, at the bottom of the box he found a dark glass phial with a carved silver stopper. For a second, the sight of the Holy Blood froze him to the spot, then he rammed it inside his shirt and headed to the door, wrenching it open and hobbling into the black night.

Brother John roared and hurtled after him, flinging himself at Lazarus's legs. The two men fell heavily to the ground. Lazarus crawled away on all fours, kicking at Brother John as he grabbed at his ankles. With a huge effort he regained his feet and lurched away through the infirmary ruins, tripping over broken stones and skidding on wet moss. He clambered over the wall, and set across the field, skirting the old Abbey fish ponds. His foot slipped and he began to fall, putting out his hand to brace himself. He righted himself and set off again, then a blow to his shoulder stopped him dead. Pain knifed through his body and his knees buckled.

He pushed his palms down hard in the mud and brought himself upright. Turning, he saw Brother John brandishing the walking staff.

'Brother!'

'It is God's work!' Brother John cried, his voice strangled.

'No.' Lazarus turned to run, his feet scraping for purchase.

Another blow, hard, on the back of his skull and he knew nothing more.

He fell face forwards into the fish pond, the greedy fronds grasping his body and sucking him into the mire at the bottom.

Brother John stood heaving for breath at the edge of the pond. 'Matthew!' he cried.

He scrabbled about at the edge of the pond, praying his hands would meet flesh, that he would pull Matthew free and take back the Holy Blood. Each time his hands swept through the water they came up tangled with slime. He prodded the water with the heavy staff, but it brought forth only a harvest of weeds.

That was how they found him the next morning, kneeling beside the old fish pond, sifting the waters with his hands, and weeping.

'John Ashford? I have a warrant for your arrest on a charge of treason.'

Brother John looked at them, unseeing. 'It is gone,' was all he said, before they carted him away.

CHAPTER
THIRTY-ONE

London

Friday, 13 November 2015

The wind off the Thames was chill as Eden leaned against the side of Vauxhall Bridge. Cyclists sped past, grimacing at the rain. To her right was Thames House, the MI5 headquarters; to her left was the green and cream monstrosity that contained MI6. The Secret Intelligence Service, SIS, she thought, remembering how touchy they all got about being called MI6. Bloody James Bonds. Awkward bastards. How many times had they got sniffy about an operation she was running.

She scanned the faces of the people heading along the footpath, searching for one face in the crowd. For a week she'd used a 'find a phone' app to establish a pattern of life for her target. She was pleased and shocked at how easy it was. Now Hammond had hold of her mobile number he could track her every move. And Hammond was the reason she was here.

Eden sucked in a deep breath and fought to calm her breathing. She'd been betrayed, she knew that. The only way Hammond could know that Jackie Black wasn't dead but resurrected as Eden Grey was if someone had told him. And there was only a handful of people who knew. Even the team who made her new passport, birth certificate, and qualifications didn't know who

Eden Grey really was. They'd meticulously created a backstory for her, but to preserve her anonymity and protect her life, they never knew the woman who was set to disappear.

But someone knew, and that someone had blabbed to Hammond.

A few days ago, with Mandy in hospital after eating the poisoned chocolates that were destined for her, Eden had phoned Nick, her ex-husband.

'Nick, it's Eden,' she'd said. 'You met me in Cheltenham.'

There was a pause while his mind made the connection between his ex-wife Sara White and Eden Grey. 'Yes, I remember,' he said, his voice bristling with caution. 'How are you?'

'I'm fine, but I nearly wasn't,' she said. 'Did you send me a box of chocolates?'

'No.' There was a pause. 'I'm sorry, I wish I had sent something, but it was so awkward ...'

She interrupted him. 'You sure you didn't send them? Only they were my favourites, and on the note it said "kiss kiss". You used to write that instead of drawing crosses.' How long ago it all seemed now; the telescope of memory.

'Yes, I do that.' Do that, present tense. Kiss kiss wasn't hers exclusively, then; his special sign-off had been recycled. And in the background she could hear a woman's voice and a child's piping answer. Holly, Nick's daughter with his new wife, Naomi, the willowy blonde. 'No, I didn't send you any chocolates. I wish I had, it would've been a nice thing to do.'

And Nick was always nice, she thought, rubbing her temple. 'Has anyone rung you and asked about me?' she said.

'No.'

'Any unusual calls? Visitors?'

'No ... there was a woman doing market research, but that wasn't ...'

'When was that?'

'I'm not sure. Look, it was just someone asking about what we bought.'

We, Eden noticed, Nick and his new wife. A wave of loss crashed over her.

'Anything in particular about what you bought?'

She heard Nick turning aside and saying, 'It's nobody, I'll just be a minute.' When he spoke into the receiver, he said, 'About holidays, special meals and treats. Actually, I said something about flowers and chocolates then.'

'Did you mention any brands?'

'Yes, of course, it was a market research survey. Though she was hardly here ten minutes.'

'She came to the house?'

'Going door-to-door, she said.'

Eden leaned against the wall, her mind whirling. 'What did she look like?'

'I don't know.' A puff of air as he breathed out. 'Smallish, dark hair, I think. Forties, but well presented, glossy, you know.'

'Anything else?'

'She had a huge ring on her finger, with a stone in it. Not a diamond or anything like that, a yellowy sort of stone.'

The world spun and she steadied herself by bracing her arm against the doorframe. She knew someone who wore such a ring; had watched it, mesmerised, in operational meetings. And when she and Nick ended the call and she thought about it, there could only be one person who had betrayed her, and was revealing her every move to Hammond.

And now that person was making her way along Vauxhall Bridge, bang on time. The pattern of life analysis had shown her attending MI5 each day at 2 p.m., leaving just after three to go to the MI6 building. There must be a big operation under-way requiring liaison between all the agencies: MI5, MI6 and the undercover branch of Revenue and Customs.

The target wore a navy pencil skirt, a black wool jacket, and low-heeled court shoes. She walked along at a clip, her phone clamped to her ear, an outsize black leather bag hooked in the crook of her elbow. It was three years since Eden had last seen her, and she hadn't changed a jot. Eden shrank against the edge of the bridge, waiting for the target to draw level, then stepped in front of her.

'Hello, Miranda,' she said.

Miranda stopped dead and gaped at her. She muttered into her phone, ended the call, and stowed the phone in her bag. The huge tiger's eye ring flashed on her middle finger.

'What are you doing here?' Miranda asked.

'Looking for you,' Eden said. 'I wanted to say thank you for the chocolates.'

'What are you talking about?'

Eden moved a step closer. 'Don't try that with me,' she said. 'OK, maybe you didn't send me the chocolates, but you told Hammond which ones to send, and what to write on the card.'

There was a long moment while Miranda stared at her, then she sagged and gave up the struggle. 'How did you know?'

'You kept on ringing me, Miranda. Warning me about Hammond. And whoever tipped him off knew exactly who I was. Seems to me you've been playing both sides.'

Miranda looked out over the Thames. The murky waters flowed past, keeping their secrets. Eden eyed her former boss, the woman who had terrified her at first, and then earned her respect and trust. The woman who now had betrayed her, and was playing Russian roulette with Eden's life. Anger surged in her, and she fought the urge to tip Miranda over the bridge into the river.

'Why?' she said.

'You won't understand.'

'Try me. What is it? Money? You need money for your mother's nursing home?'

Miranda hitched her bag on her elbow. 'He's not paying me. He found out I wasn't exactly clean, and he's threatening to expose me.' Her eyes flicked up to meet Eden's. 'I'd lose everything.'

'What has he got on you?'

'Backhanders from drugs.'

'Drugs! You hate drugs! How could you be so fucking stupid!'

Miranda made a helpless gesture. 'I know. I was stupid, and greedy. You know what the pay's like.'

'So how much is my life worth, Miranda? How much have you taken?'

Miranda licked her lips. 'About a quarter of a million.'

Eden snorted. 'I'm flattered! Quarter of a million! I never knew I was worth so much.'

'Look, I didn't want to get involved in this,' Miranda said. 'I've tried to warn you about him.'

That did it. Eden grabbed Miranda's collar and hoisted her onto the edge of the bridge, shoving her back towards the river below. 'You wouldn't have had to if you hadn't told Hammond I was alive and where to find me.'

'Please!' Miranda cried.

Passers-by drew up short and stood back to watch. One brought out his phone to film it. Eden ignored them and held Miranda there, suspended over the water, and slowly pushed her back until she was perfectly poised between safe ground and death in the river. The handbag released its contents, papers fluttering, lipsticks and keys tumbling into the Thames. Miranda struggled and kicked, her hands slipping on the rail.

'Call him off,' Eden said.

'I can't! He knows too much!'

Eden pushed her another couple of inches, held her there, then dragged her back onto the bridge. There was an ooh from the crowd. Miranda tugged her jacket into place and smoothed back her hair, fighting for composure.

'Nothing to see here,' she said, staring down the gawkers. 'Go on, piss off the lot of you!'

Miranda waited until they'd dispersed before saying, 'The genie's well and truly out of the bottle. He knows everything and he's sitting pretty in prison. Got it set up exactly how he wants it. We can't touch him.' Her chest heaved a few times, then she said, 'He's planning something big. I don't know what exactly, but watch out, OK.'

'Will you tip me off if you get a sniff?'

Miranda's face drooped. 'All along I've tried to help you, to give you the nod on Hammond.'

'You're all heart,' Eden said. She went to walk away, then turned back. 'One more thing.'

She swung her foot back and kicked Miranda, hard, on the shin. She was wearing hefty leather boots and the kick landed squarely on the bone with a dull thud. 'That's for hurting my friend,' she said, thinking of Mandy, sick and shivering after eating the chocolates meant for her.

Eden rammed her fists in her pockets and headed back along the bridge towards Westminster. Time to go home.

ACKNOWLEDGEMENTS

Writing a book is always a team effort, so huge thanks to Kelly, Sara-Jane and the RABSes, who read and commented on early drafts of the book; to my agent Jane for her help and support; and to Matilda and the team at The Mystery Press for making the publishing process so much fun.

Thank you to the people who kindly allowed me to 'borrow' their names – you know who you are.

Big love to my cheerleading gang: The Pink Panthers, Mike, Harriet, and Wimsey.

And last but not least, thank you to all my readers – I hope you enjoyed Eden's latest adventure.

www.kimfleet.com

ABOUT THE AUTHOR
KIM FLEET

KIM FLEET holds a PhD in Social Anthropology from the University of St Andrews and is a Fellow of the Royal Anthropological Institute. A freelance writer, life coach and teacher, she is the author of *Paternoster: An Eden Grey Mystery* and has had over forty short stories published in magazines in the UK and Australia, including *Woman's Weekly*, *People's Friend*, *Take a Break*, and *That's Life Fast Fiction*. She has spoken at the Cheltenham Literary Festival and at CrimeFest in Bristol. She lives in Cheltenham, Gloucestershire.

Visit our website and discover thousands of
other History Press books.

www.thehistorypress.co.uk

@thp_local